This book is dedicated to the memory of David Monaghan-Jones, ex-detective and author, 'Jay-Dee'. His enthusiasm for this story knew no bounds, and his knowledge and expertise helped me greatly. I'm more sorry than I can say that he never lived to see it finished, but even more sad that I, and many others, have lost a friend whose humour lit up our days. I know I'm not the only author he helped with his invaluable advice on police procedures. My thoughts often go out to his beautiful wife and family, because he's left a gaping hole in their lives.

Prologue

It had to be the coldest night of the winter so far. The temperature was so low, it was far too cold for snow. The grass, frozen stiff, was sharp on his naked body as they dumped him on the ground. A moment or two ago, he was wrapped up in a duvet or something, so hadn't felt the cold so much, but now, unwrapped and lying unprotected, his teeth chattered. As his limbs were being arranged, he could do nothing, he couldn't move, but he felt the pain. He knew they were somehow shackling him to the ground. He could hear the hammer banging something around his legs and arms, keeping them in certain positions, completely exposed and shamed. The drug administered by injection meant he knew what was happening but was as helpless as a rag doll. This had promised to be a night of pleasurable sensations, a satiation of his bodily needs. It turned out instead to be a nightmare, full of sensation indeed, but far from pleasurable.

He vaguely heard the voice telling him why he was going to be left to die, but now he was shaking uncontrollably from the icy air enveloping him. His gaze left the face of the person talking to him and lifted to the skies. It was a beautiful, clear night, full of twinkling stars. It would be the last beautiful thing he would see. He tried to formulate a prayer for help, then stopped, for why should a god he didn't believe in help him now? His killer was obviously determined to watch him die. It didn't take long before the searing cold gave way, and incredibly, he noticed warmth seeping in... A moment of relief - had they had rescued him? But no, the watcher was still talking, still making sure. He remembered reading once that someone dying of hypothermia would feel warm just before death. As the final darkness enveloped him, his last coherent thought was 'I'm sorry,..'

Chapter 1

Sunday, January 13th, 1991

Della groaned at the sound of her phone, insisting that she draw herself from a deep sleep. Her sister's engagement party last evening meant that she'd only been in bed for a couple of hours and there was no doubt she was still intoxicated.

Barely able to open one eye, she fumbled for the phone and then swore when the receiver fell from the bedside table to the floor. She hung out of bed and fished around for the cord. Her head thumped worse than ever as she did so, and she hastened to rectify the situation, bringing the phone up with her.

"Go away!" she snapped down the phone and banged the receiver on the cradle and laid back in her bed, trying to keep control of her swimming head. Eyeing the phone with one eye closed, she willed it to stay silent, but knew it wouldn't because of course she knew who it would have been, but, feeling bloody minded, she wasn't going to call back. She was supposed to be on her days off.

She was right, for it was only moments later the phone started again. She wrapped herself in her duvet and grabbed it.

"What?" she grunted sharply. "You do know it's stupid o'clock, don't you? And you know it's Sunday and I'm supposed to be off duty?"

"Morning Della, sorry, but we need you. We have a fatality."

"Where?"

"Off Gladioli Grove."

"Is that the Gardens area?"

"The very one."

"Things don't happen there. It's a posh place."

"Does now. I'll be round to pick you up in half an hour."

Della groaned again. "But I'm still drunk, Ben. I was at my sister's party last night, remember? I've only been in bed a couple of hours."

"I'll bring the coffee. Get in the shower."

"I hate you."

All she heard before the phone went dead was a manly chuckle. Cursing under her breath, she gingerly drew herself out of bed and staggered towards her bathroom. Standing under her shower, she felt the water performing some magic, helping to wake her up, but she still had a thumping headache. Inwardly, she cursed again. Normally, she didn't drink much, but the party last night had been a special occasion; after all, her sister didn't get engaged every day, and so she'd allowed herself several glasses of champagne, which seemed to flow freely. Now, she knew why she didn't drink much - champagne was deceptively toxic. And now, some inconsiderate person had gone and got themselves killed. Blinking typical, couldn't they have waited until she felt more herself?

Completely unable to be vigorous, she dried herself, pulled on some warm clothes, and gave her hair a quick blow with the hairdryer, grateful her short bob didn't take much drying. As she looked at herself with one eye closed in defiance, she knew she looked awful; her eyes red-rimmed and her face pasty. She shuddered, looked away, and instead made her way into the kitchen. All she could think about was orange juice, ice cold. Thank goodness she always had some in the fridge. She poured a large glass, popped two paracetamols from a blister pack and sank onto a chair at the breakfast bar to self-medicate.

The bell rang just as she swallowed the tablets and, groaning, she slid off the chair and went to answer the door. Her head thumped with every step. How was she ever going to do her job? Fumbling with the security chain, she finally opened the door and stood back.

A grinning detective constable brought his bulk inside, carrying a tray with two large coffees and a paper bag. With him, a blast of cold air came in and Della shivered. She'd need to wrap up going out, especially at this hour in the morning - the dawn chorus had barely started. Catching the smell wafting from the bag, Della wrinkled her nose.

"Take it away!"

"But I brought it for you for breakfast, lass." DC Benjamin Curran grinned at her. With a warm coat on, which made him look even more cuddly than usual, Ben was the nearest Della had found to a human teddy bear and normally she loved his twinkly blue eyes and ruddy face. "I must say, you don't look good, Sarge."

"I don't feel good. Go away and eat that, and be quick about it," she ordered, and pointed to the open front door. "Out there! And put the paper in the bin. I don't want any lingering aromas in the car, thank you, Ben."

"No probs. It'll be gone by the time you're in the car. Don't forget your coffee."

He headed out the door and Della turned to fetch her coat and boots from the cupboard under the stairs. Ben was true to his word; all evidence of whatever had been in the bag was gone as he climbed into the driving seat next to her. She clutched the tray with the two coffees. Before he started the car, Ben took his drink and knocked it back in seconds, plonked the carton back into the tray and they set off.

Della tried to relax and sipped her coffee, grimacing because it was black and she hated it like that, but knew she needed it, for when they arrived at the crime scene, she'd need all her wits in order.

It only took twenty minutes to reach the area known as The Gardens; not nearly long enough as far as Della was concerned. She barely noticed where they were going, but braced herself when the car finally stopped.

Looking around, she realised they were at the far end of Gladioli Grove, which was on the edge of The Gardens, the countryside rising from the other side of the fencing at the end of the road. Now, the area was lit with the silent flashing blue light from a police car and a uniformed constable stood by the gate that led into the field beyond the fencing. A couple of other vehicles were parked in the road, a white van and a sleek Ferrari, which Della knew belonged to the pathologist, Dr Tom Boyden.

They showed their badges to the constable.

"DS Della Downs and this is DC Ben Curran. Where are we going, Constable?"

"Through the gate and turn left. You'll see the white coats."

"No DI?" she asked, although she knew the answer. It was obvious the guv wasn't here, in fact, they'd be lucky if he turned up at all. As the constable shook his head, she hoped the guv wouldn't show. She didn't want him to see her in this state.

They could see a white incident tent in the opposite corner of the field, near to the hedge, which had a small copse of trees behind it. Della and Ben hastened towards it. They again showed their IDs to the uniformed constable; Della guessed he was the other constable's partner. She'd forgotten to ask his name - normally, she made sure she knew the names of those working with her. She blamed her present condition.

"What's your name, Constable?" she asked.

"Constable John Whitten, ma'am."

"No need to call me ma'am, John. I'm a Sergeant. So, what do we have?"

"A male, found dead at first light. White, naked and laid out in the field near the hedge."

"Hmm. Who found the body?"

"A Mrs Sarah Sutton. She was walking her dog. She lives at number five, Gladioli Grove. Because it's so cold, I took her home while my partner stood guard. As you may imagine, she was pretty shaken. Her husband assured me he'd look after her."

Della nodded. "Were you first on the scene?"

"Yes, ma'am - I mean, sergeant. I called in and the doc and forensics arrived."

"Okay, thank you. I want you to call in and ask for replacements. I expect you were on night duty?"

"Yes. I believe others are on their way."

"Good."

Right now, she hastily donned protective clothing handed to her by a member of the forensic team, and Ben did the same. She hated putting them on at the best of times and this morning her limbs felt more uncooperative than usual. Eventually, she achieved her aim.

"Ah, good morning, Della. You finally joined us then." Dr Tom Boyden choose that moment to leave the tent.

"Don't you start! I shouldn't be here at all!" she snapped, and then winced as her head thumped its protest.

"No, I agree. From what I've been hearing, you were the entertainment after we left; you do a good turn on table-top dancing!" Tom was a friend of the intended groom.

"I didn't - did I?" she groaned. Then she realised that Tom and the surrounding others were all grinning. "Oh, hilarious! If I have to do this, what do we have?"

"Male, white Caucasian, around thirty-five to forty. At first impression, I'd say he died of hypothermia."

Della frowned. "A tramp?"

"Frankly, I don't know of many tramps who would lie in a field, stark naked, arms and legs splayed out and pinned down with metal hoops; croquet hoops, I'd say. No, definitely no tramp. Certainly, foul play here. He stood no chance in this freezing cold weather. Couldn't have been a worse night for him to be so exposed."

Della sighed. "Poor guy. I suppose I have to see?"

"The team has already been over the ground around him and he's been photographed in situ. We're just about ready to take him away."

Della and Ben stepped into the tent and gazed down at the man on the ground. The body was indeed naked. His right arm was underneath him and what looked at first like blood appeared to be between his legs. At first, Della feared he might have had his tackle cut off, but it was all there.

"Paint." Tom was brief. He nodded towards the chest. "That's blood though."

"Can't quite see what it says," Ben leaned closer. "It looks like it could say 'guilty'. What's that all about?"

"Can't begin to guess," Tom shrugged. "Too much blood to see what sort of knife carved the letters."

"Done when he was alive, then."

"Afraid so."

"Time of death?" Della asked.

"Hard to be precise, but I'd say between twelve and eight."

"Poor bugger," commented Ben. "Wonder what he did to deserve that?"

"At a wild guess, someone has been judge, jury and executioner. Oh, here he comes," commented Della, looking at a figure striding towards them.

Detective Inspector Tim Masterson wore a smart wool coat over his dark grey suit, an expensive - looking scarf around his neck, and a woollen beany pulled over his dark hair. It should have looked odd, Della mused, but somehow it didn't. Even out here, his cheeks slightly reddened by the cold, there was no denying he was attractive, damn him!

"Good morning, Della, Ben. What do we have?"

Della explained briefly, and Tim glanced in the tent, nodded his head at Tom, and withdrew.

They left the tent and waited while the team carefully finished examining around the body, which was finally zipped into a body bag, the metal hoops having been pulled out carefully with gloved hands. Dr Boyden followed them.

"I'll be in touch, Tim, as soon as I can."

"Thanks, Tom, much appreciated."

"Do we know who he is?" DI Masterson turned to Della.

"Not yet, guv.'"

"Who found him?"

"A woman walking her dog. Lives at number five, apparently. We're going there now."

"Right. I'll get the team drummed up to help with the house to house.

"Thank you, guv."

"Let me know if you need a family liaison when you find out who he is."

"Yes, sir, will do."

"Right. See you later then."

"Guv."

Della watched her boss stride away and sighed. Ben looked at her. "Don't waste your time, love."

"Oh, I'm not. I just wish it was me going back to a cosy office."

"Well, these houses don't look too shabby. I bet Sarah Sutton's house is cosy. C'mon, pet, let's go see her."

Chapter 2

Sarah Sutton's house, number five, Gladioli Grove, was as imposing as its neighbours. The houses in the Grove were individual, but all were large, all attractive. Obviously, these people had money. But death was death, and murder was murder. So, rich or not, there were questions that needed answering.

Della and Ben walked up the drive of number five and knocked on the front door. It was opened by a man looking as if he'd just woken up, wearing a dressing gown over jeans and a casual shirt. His dark hair was tousled, although some effort had been made to smooth it down. His face was pale and his bespectacled eyes distressed.

The two detectives showed their IDs and asked for Sarah. The man showed them in and introduced himself as Sarah's husband, Philip Sutton.

"She's in here. She's considerably shaken, as you may guess. Please be gentle with her."

"Don't worry, Mr Sutton. I'm sure this won't take long."

They walked into a large, very modern lounge., Although expensively furnished, Della felt it was somehow soulless. A woman rested on the white sofa; a small brown dog cuddled at her side. As they entered, the dog issued a half-hearted bark, but lay down again when the woman's hand smoothed its head. It kept its head up, its ears on alert. Della's expert eye could tell the woman was petite, even though she was covered by a pink fleecy blanket. Her face, as she turned towards the detectives, was tear-stained. Philip hurried towards her and took her hand.

"These are Detective Sergeant Downes and Detective Constable Curran, darling," he said to her gently.

"Oh, Detective Sergeant, it's so awful," Sarah Sutton said, detaching her hand from her husband's, looking at Ben and somehow exuding feminine flattery, despite her tearfulness.

"This is Detective Sergeant Downs, Mrs Sutton," said Ben gently, and Della stepped forward.

"Oh." It was like something switched off. Della was well used to this reaction and frankly, couldn't care less at the moment.

"Please sit down," said Philip. "Would you care for a drink? Tea? Coffee?"

"Oh, yes, please. I could use a coffee. What about you, Ben?" Della answered gratefully, as she sat on a chair near Sarah.

"Please call me Della, and this is Ben. May we call you Sarah?" Della used her 'gentle with traumatised witness' voice.

The woman on the sofa held a tissue to her face and nodded.

"Now, can you tell us your movements this morning and how you found the body, please? In your own time."

"Oh, Della, it's so awful! That poor man. Poor Amy, she'll be so upset when she knows!"

Della sat up slightly. "You know the man?"

"Yes. It's Darren from number ten!"

"You mean he lived on this street? He's one of your neighbours?"

"Yes, yes! That's why I'm so upset. They're not only neighbours, they're our friends! We're all friends in the Grove."

"Okay. Please tell me what happened this morning."

"We were planning to go out for the day, to visit Philip's family as we weren't able to see them over Christmas, so I said I'd take Sukie for a little run early so she'd be okay in the car."

"I see, so what time would that have been?"

"Well, it was still only half-light when I went, but as there's a thick frost, it seemed quite light. Just before eight o'clock, I'd say. What do you think, Phil?" Sarah looked up as her husband entered the room with a mug in each hand.

"What's that, darling?"

"The time I went out with Sukie - was it about eight?"

"Yes, just before that, I'd say." He handed a mug each to the two detectives. Della took hers gratefully and held the mug to warm her freezing hands.

"And then?"

"Yes. Well, I often take her into the field. It's a good place where she can run around and it's reasonably safe, few holes to trap one's feet in or to get iced up to slip on. She raced off when I slipped the lead and ran straight across to the other end of the field. I didn't want to be out long, because it was so cold, so I called her but she didn't come. She was fussing around something I couldn't see. So, when she didn't come, I walked towards her, calling her to come but she didn't take any notice. Until I got close enough to see what she was fussing about. She was licking his face and nudging him. She knows him, you see. He always makes a fuss of her - made a fuss..." her voice faded and the tears welled again. Philip put his arm around her shoulders as he sat awkwardly by her side on the arm of the sofa.

"He - he was stark naked, and, and spread out, like this." She spread the one arm outwards and a dainty leg in tight jeans scissored out from under the blanket. The leg was put back, and the blanket pulled into place.

"I see. So, your dog licked him. Did you touch him at all?"

"I'm afraid I did, yes. I tried to wake him up by touching his face and chest. Then I realised he was dead, so I grabbed hold of Sukie and ran home. I made Phil come and look, which he did, and then he called the police."

Philip nodded. "That's right. Sarah was so upset, she couldn't tell me anything at first, but once I got the gist, I went to look and called the police on my mobile."

"And what time would that have been?"

"About eight-thirty, I should think, not ever so sure."

"Never mind, they will have logged the call. Will you be alright, Sarah?"

Sarah sniffed and nodded.

"I'll look after her, erm, Detective Sergeant."

"Della. My name is Della. This is my card. If you think of anything you'd like to talk to me about, just call the number on it. An officer will be here to take your statements - just a formality, you understand?"

Della and Ben stood. "Thank you for your time, Sarah and Philip. Thank you for the drink, too. It helped a lot. We'll leave you in peace now and hope you will feel better soon, Sarah. You've certainly had a nasty shock. I'm guessing you won't be visiting your relatives today, after all?"

"No. I called and told them we couldn't come today after all," replied Philip. They followed him to the door and bade him farewell.

"To the victim's home now, boss?" asked Ben as they walked down the drive.

"Unfortunately, yes. But I have to say I'm grateful that we at least know who he is, he will not be a John Doe, poor bloke, and it gives us a starting point."

Even though there were only five houses on either side of the road, Gladioli Grove was a tidy step from one end to the other, even from number five, because of the size of each house's grounds.

Silence met their knock on the door of number ten, so Ben rang the bell. Eventually, they saw through the patterned glass in the door, the figure of someone coming towards them. A woman's face peered at them through the slim opening the safety chain allowed.

"Hello?"

Della stuck her ID card in front of the woman's eyes. "Good morning. Are we speaking to Mrs Darren Holbeach? I'm Detective Sergeant Della Downes and this is my associate, Detective Constable Benjamin Curran. We'd like to speak with you, please?"

"Oh! Right. Hang on."

The door closed, and they heard the chain being removed. The door opened again, and they were invited inside. Della estimated the woman was in her mid-thirties or younger, had short, brown hair and a pleasant face, not beautiful, but there was something attractive about her, maybe it was her smile.

"Are you here to see Darren? I don't think he can be up yet. His evening out must have worn him out," she giggled, a little nervously, Della thought. "Do please come in and I'll call him. When he's been on one of his nights out, he sleeps in another room so he doesn't wake me when he comes in," she explained.

"Actually, it's you we've come to see, Mrs Holbeach," said Della, as she stepped over the threshold. Della thought she'd never get used to seeing that moment of realisation that comes over a family member's face as realisation creeps in. She saw it now; the woman's face slowly became devoid of colour and a hand flew to her mouth.

"No! Something's happened to Darren, hasn't it? Whatever could have happened? Did he get run over or something? I never heard anything –." She stopped, abruptly.

"Can we sit down?"

"Oh! Erm, yes. This way." She led them into her lounge, which was just as large as the Suttons' but felt completely different. The furniture did not match but somehow it worked and instead of the modern art pictures that complimented the decor in the Suttons' house, these walls had needlecraft pictures on the walls, probably worked by this lady herself, and the odd watercolour of countryside scenes.

The woman seated herself on the edge of the sofa, and Della sat next to her but with a distance between them, so she could face her. Ben chose a wooden armchair.

"Mrs Holbeach, I am so sorry to have to tell you that a body has been found, and we have reason to believe it is your husband, Darren," said Della gently.

"A - a body? Been - found?" A puzzled frown creased the woman's forehead as she strove to understand what she was being told. "Who found? Where? And why do you think it's Darren? I'm sure that can't be right. I'm sure he's still asleep upstairs. I'll look!" She got up, but Della put a hand on her arm. She looked at it and subsided into the seat.

"Can I call you by your name?"

"Oh, erm, yes. It's Amy. I'm Amelia really, but everyone has always called me Amy." She lapsed into silence.

"Amy, the reason we believe the body is your husband is because it was - he was - found by one of your neighbours when she was out walking her dog. She recognised him, as did her husband, when he went to check."

"Oh, my goodness! Who found him?"

"Sarah Sutton. Her husband, Philip, went to look and confirmed it."

"Oh..." the tears started to come then, and Amy fought valiantly to keep them under control. She dug up the sleeve of her jumper and pulled out a tissue. "But - but, where was he?"

"In the field up yonder."

"So that's what all the blue lights have been about? I wondered what was going on, but with the trees out front, I couldn't see much. What do you think happened to Darren? Why on earth was he in the field?"

"We can't say, as yet," replied Della, carefully. "But it seems likely he was out there all night."

"Oh no! You mean - he probably froze to death?"

"We think that's likely, yes."

"I bet he got drunk and lost his way, stupid, stupid man! I was always telling him he drank too much when he goes out. But I'm surprised he did last night. It was -" Amy stopped abruptly. "That is, he never usually drank that much when he was, I mean..." she stumbled over her words and came to a halt. "Oh, how do I know what he gets up to?"

"Does he go out a lot?"

"Not as much as he used to. But he has a regular monthly meetup, where he was last night."

"In order to get a picture of his movements, can you tell me what time he left here last evening?"

"Just a couple of minutes before seven thirty."

"And he didn't take a car?"

"No, he always leaves the car. I don't think he has far to go. Or maybe someone picks him up round the corner. I don't know. He's never told me where he goes." Amy sat and shredded the tissue, rolling it between her fingers as she spoke.

"And he does this every month, you say?"

"Yes. It's an arrangement. Every second Saturday of the month."

"I see. So, he left here at just before seven-thirty. When he goes on these regular monthly evenings out, what time would you normally expect him home?"

"He's always been home not later than midnight. But as I said, as I'm usually in bed by then, he sleeps in another room, but as far as I'm aware, he's never been later than that. I do often hear him come in, but he thinks I'll be asleep."

"So, it's likely he would have been on his way home not later than midnight?"

Amy nodded. "Yes, that's right. I can't for the life of me think how he ended up in the field, even if he was drunk. I know there's a 'kissing gate', but surely, he wasn't that drunk he didn't realise he was going into a field? I've never known him to get so drunk he couldn't find his way home before. Whatever was he up to?"

"So, presumably you spent the evening alone? What did you do?"

Amy's face turned a little pink, and she looked down. "Well, I had a visitor for a little while. My neighbours all know Darren goes out every second Saturday of the month, so one of them checks in on me to make sure I'm okay."

"Well, that's very nice of them. Very caring neighbours."

"Oh yes, they're all lovely. We're all great friends and we have picnics, barbecues and so on together in the summer and we saw in the New Year together. Darren and I were invited to have Christmas dinner with one of the couples, which was really nice, too. Last night, Liz sent her husband Bill over here to check up on me. He loves the cakes I make, so he stopped and had a cup of tea and some cake with me. Liz was busy doing something, so Bill was glad of the company, too. He's a nice man, a bit staid, and a little henpecked, I think!" Amy laughed, then obviously remembered Darren, and the laughter subsided quickly. "Oh, how could I be laughing when Darren is dead?"

Della patted the woman's arm. "It hasn't sunk in yet, I'm sure. Do you have someone who can be with you, any family we can contact?"

"I have no one. But Darren's parents will need to know - oh, how am I going to tell them?"

"We can do it, if you'd rather? Where do they live?"

"No. No, I'd better do it. I'll drive over there when you've gone."

"I don't think you should drive at the moment. We'll inform them, and no doubt they'll come over to you."

"Perhaps you're right."

"Now, although this might be difficult for you, we need you to identify the body. I'm not sure when that will be as he hasn't yet been taken to the hospital."

"Oh!" Amy put her hands to her cheeks.

"It will be hard, but it's necessary. We have to be sure, you see."

"Yes, of course."

"I'll contact you when it's been arranged. We can take you and bring you back."

"That's good of you, thank you."

After getting the relevant information for Amy's parents in law, Della and Ben went to leave the house. Just as they reached the door, someone rang the bell. Della opened it. On the doorstep was an attractive woman in her sixties, shoulder-length white hair, face expertly made up, figure still good, if a little thigh-heavier than she would have been a few years ago, Della judged.

"Ah, hello, are you the detectives?" Before Della could answer, the unknown woman spied Amy hovering behind them. "Amy, darling, I've just heard the dreadful news!"

Della and Ben had to flatten themselves against the wall as the woman pushed past them and Amy fell into her open arms.

"Oh, Liz! It's just dreadful! Poor Darren!" Amy sobbed into the woman's chest.

"So sorry, detectives. I'm Elizabeth Harrington-Smythe from number nine. Philip just called me. He thought someone should be with Amy."

"I see. Well, I'm glad she has you to be with her. We were concerned about her being alone here. I understand your husband came to check on her last evening, knowing Darren would be out?"

"That's right. I sent him across to keep her company for a while, as I was busy. He's a good sort and very fond of Amy. She's like a daughter to him."

"That's nice. Is he at home now? We'd like to just have a few words with him."

"Yes, the old bugger is always hanging around my feet!"

Della summoned a smile, nodded to them and left, followed by Ron.

"Number nine is it now?" Ron asked, concentrating on his feet.

"Of course. Did you notice how Amy coloured a bit when she said he'd been over?"

"I did. Do you think there's something funny going on between them?"

"Hard to imagine her having an affair with anyone. She didn't seem the sort."

If Della expected to see an old duffer in slippers smoking a pipe and wearing bushy whiskers down the sides of his face, when the door of number 9 was opened to them, she was severely disillusioned. What she actually saw was a very handsome man with a good head of silver hair the same colour as his wife's, his face was tanned a light golden brown and when he smiled, it was obvious it was his own teeth looking straight and clean. He must have been nearing seventy, but he was upright and sprightly. In fact, Della had to admit to herself, he was very attractive indeed. Certainly 'old duffer' and 'hen pecked' didn't seem to suit him at all. Was it possible he'd tried something on with Amy and she was embarrassed at the thought? Della knew appearances could deceive; she'd give him rope to hang himself if need be.

"Mr Harrington-Smythe? Detective Sergeant Downs and Detective Constable Curran," she said, holding up her ID yet again. "Could we possibly have a quick word with you, sir?"

"Of course, of course! Come away in, do. Let's get the door shut quickly, keep the cold out. It's such a beastly day out there. A beastly day all round for poor Amy and the Grove! Never had anything like this happen in all the years we've lived here."

They followed him down the impressive hallway; it was all shining wood panels and an antique-looking table stood at one side, with a gilded mirror above it, reflecting the artfully arranged flowers in front of it but still leaving room for a person leaving to check their hat was on straight. A classic coat stand stood next to it.

"Come into the kitchen. I was just making a cuppa. Do you fancy one?"

"Thank you, I would. What about you, Ben?"

"Yes, thank you. But I wonder if I could, um, you know...?" Ben looked embarrassed.

"Use the facilities? Of course you can. No need to be shy, it's the cold you know, we all function the same! Down the hall, second on the left."

Ben left the room and Della made herself as comfortable as she could on a high stool by the breakfast bar. The kitchen was enormous, probably larger than the entire ground floor of her house, and was full of shiny worktops, gleaming taps and kitchen equipment. Della didn't much enjoy cooking. Nevertheless, she felt a tiny tinge of envy.

Bill poured tea from a teapot into bone porcelain cups with saucers.

"Liz always insists we use a teapot, you know, and that we use bone porcelain cups. Says the tea tastes better," he said, conversationally. He also produced a packet of Jaffa Cakes and deftly arranged them on a matching porcelain plate. Obviously, he was at home in the kitchen.

He sat on another bar stool diagonally from Della across the breakfast bar. "Do help yourself, m'dear. If you don't mind me saying so, you're looking a tad delicate."

Della smirked. "Is it that obvious? I was at an engagement party last night - very late."

"Ah, and you had to drag yourself out of bed before you were ready this morning. Poor young woman! Trust Darren to die on such an inconvenient day for you, m'dear."

Della couldn't help laughing. Despite her earlier thoughts, she liked this man, and if Amy was having 'something' with him, in some ways, she couldn't blame her. Despite his handsome face and youthful figure, somehow, he reminded her of a teddy bear, and was sure he'd be a good person to cuddle, especially when distressed.

Ben returned while they were laughing. "What have I missed?" He asked.

"Nothing really, just something silly. There's your tea, Ben."

"Oh, ta. Oo, are they Jaffa Cakes?"

"Yes, lad, help yourself." Bill pushed the plate towards the detective constable.

"Now, did you want to ask me something?" asked Bill.

"Yes. Amy said you went over and spent some time with her last evening. Is that correct?"

"Indeed, it is. Liz was busy and we're always concerned about Amy, y'know. She's such a nice lass, and he's always out on a certain Saturday every month, apparently. So, someone in the Grove likes to check up on her, stop her being lonely, y'see?"

"Well, that's very caring of you all. So, can you tell me what time you went over there?"

"Hmm, not too sure. A bit after seven thirty, I think. He's always gone by then, you see."

"Yes. And how long did you stay with Amy?"

"Oh, hard to say. About three hours, maybe. She makes the most wonderful cakes, you know, and we had a cuppa and some cake and a natter. Actually, I admit I went to sleep! We were watching something on the box, something she wanted to watch. I didn't mind, but I'm afraid I nodded off. We men are a bit like that, aren't we?" Bill directed his question at Ben, who nodded ruefully. Della smiled; she knew he often fell asleep in the chair in the evenings; his wife Shona was always complaining about it.

"So, I was quite late coming home. Amy's too sweet, she wouldn't wake me up! I think I left about half-ten, eleven. Can't be precise, I'm afraid. Don't know if Liz can tell you more accurately, although she was still busy when I came in, so I didn't see her. I just went to bed."

"Right. So, you were outside around half past ten, eleven o'clock. Did you see anything? Any movement anywhere? Anyone about?"

"Not a thing. All was quiet as the grave - oh, terrible choice of words there, sorry! Do you know how Darren died? Can't think how he came to be in the field - what the heck was he playing at?"

"We really can't say. Hopefully, we'll know more after the post mortem and the forensic reports."

"Well, I hope you get to the bottom of it. Poor Amy, she's not had an easy life with him, you know, but I'm sure she wouldn't have wanted this."

"Really? Can you tell us more about them? How long have they lived in Gladioli Grove?"

"About eighteen months or so. Not sure, something like that. Immediately took to Amy, we all did, but there was something about Darren, couldn't really take to the chap."

"What sort of something?"

"Well, he was a bit - well, supercilious. He'd put her down in front of people. Eventually, we came to know he's had numerous affairs, can't help dipping his wick in, if you get my meaning? I don't really know how Amy has stuck it all these years. Anyway, I shouldn't be telling you all this, not my place. You should talk more to Amy."

"We will certainly need to talk with Amy again. Thank you, Bill, you've been very helpful."

"Always happy to help wherever I can, m'dear."

As the door closed behind them, Ben said, "Where to, now?"

"The station, Ben, quick as you can. My bladder is bursting."

Chapter 3

"Right. This is what we have." DI Tim Masterson was standing at the incident board, his team looking on. He tapped the photograph of Darren Holbeach, given by Amy, next to one of him dead. "Darren Holbeach, aged thirty-four. Found dead in a field this morning just after eight a.m. by Sarah Sutton, who also identified him, which his wife has confirmed just half an hour ago. He left his home, dressed for an evening out at just before seven-thirty. So far, we have no witnesses who saw him as from that time. So, do we assume he really left home? I think we can, as apparently a neighbour from across the road spent some time with Amy Holbeach in her home and there was no sign of Darren while he was there. William Harrington-Smythe left the Holbeach home at around ten-thirty. He saw no one during his walk from Amy's home to his, only a few minutes' walk. It's true, as they live directly opposite each other.

"So, what questions do we need to ask?"

"Could he have come home?" asked a voice from the back. "Often, in these situations, it comes back to the wife having done it."

"Good one - who was that? Ah, Mike. Yes, well done."

"Where did he go when he left home, and how can we find out?" Ben said. "Who was he going to meet?"

"Another good question. We believe Darren was a ladies' man who had many affairs. Was he seeing a woman?"

"I want to know where his clothes are," said Della. "Obviously, someone took his clothes off him. Did he get caught by an irate husband who wouldn't let him have his clothes? Or, did his wife have him followed with a plan to killing him?"

"Also, good questions. At the moment, we can't answer any of them. So, it has to be a house to house, you all know the drill. And I want the area searched for his clothes. Every moment counts in a case like this because any trails go cold. We'll meet here tomorrow morning at eight. Hopefully, we'll have some reports coming in from forensics by then. Della and Ben, I want you to attend the post mortem. Tom's doing it at four o'clock today."

"Great," muttered Della. "Just what I need to round my day off."

Ben clicked in sympathy; he knew she hated attending them. Come to that, he wasn't that keen himself.

It was almost time to attend the post mortem. Della realised she'd had barely anything to eat and her stomach was finally ready. However, she also knew how her stomach often reacted to watching post mortems.

Ben, who knew her very well, said he was going to take her to get something after their visit to the mortuary. "You know I can't cope with food before a P.M. I'll need a revival afterwards."

Della laughed and hugged his arm. "You silly. I know you're only saying that for me."

He grinned at her. "Mind you, me stomach thinks me throat's been cut. I hope it's a quick post mortem."

"Not a good choice of words there, Ben, but I agree with the sentiment. I think I could cope with a sandwich. Let's go to the canteen. Not much to get excited about, but it'll help the gap not to moan. We have time before we have to leave for the hospital."

*****

An hour later, they were with Tom as he began his preliminary examination of the body.

"White male, Caucasian. We know he is Darren Holbeach, aged thirty-four. On his body, there are no obvious signs of a struggle, but on his back and buttocks there are faint marks, consistent with being beaten, but they are old."

"Beaten? Who would beat him?" Ben frowned.

Tom looked up and grinned. "I'd say our boy had been with a lady who - um - indulged in certain practises."

"What? Oh!" Ben's face reddened, and he clamped his mouth shut.

"Continuing on, there is bruising around his neck, lower arms and his ankles, here and here, see? Consistent with the iron hoops found to hold him down. As they were found as part of the scene, there's no speculation about what was used."

"So, someone undressed him and then shackled him so he couldn't move in the field," said Della.

"Looks like it. There's also this word scratched onto his chest." Tom waited while the photographer made sure it was photographed and then cleaned the wounds. More photos were taken. "It definitely says 'guilty'. Guilty of what, I wonder? Something for you to work on, Della."

She nodded in response, gazing at the word. She wondered again what he had done that had made someone wreak such a terrible revenge on the man.

"What sort of knife was used to do that, do you think, Tom?"

"I'd say a Stanley knife. It would have been very sharp, as the cuts are thin and not deep. It's not that easy to carve a word on someone's skin, but the poor devil would have felt it all the same."

Della shuddered, glancing at Ben, who frowned back at her in sympathy. They turned back to Tom, who said, "Oh well, here goes. Are you ready, my dear?"

"As I'll ever be," replied Della, grimly, and screwed up her face as Tom made the first long cut.

*****

After she and Ben shared a pizza, he dropped Della off at her house and she thankfully fell onto her couch to watch some mindless television, in front of which she fell asleep. After a couple of hours there, she awoke feeling cold and dragged herself off to her bed, thankful for her electric blanket. As she luxuriated in the cosy warmth of her duvet, she spared a thought for Darren Holbeach who, only last night, had been spread out to die in the freezing cold. She hoped it hadn't taken long. Tom had assured them it was probably quick, given the temperature out there; he would have soon stopped shivering and would actually have begun to feel warm and then simply float away into death. "It wouldn't have been unpleasant after the first feelings of extreme cold," Tom explained. "If anything, it's probably quite a pleasant way to go."

Della shuddered at the memory of his words. Pleasant or not, the fact remained that someone had intended for him to die. It had been hinted that the Holbeach's marriage was not that good, and in that kind of case it would seem obvious it would be the wife who had the motive. But try as she might, she couldn't imagine Amy being a killer. After all, she'd been married to the man for - what - eight years? She'd meekly put up with all sorts. Had he done something that had finally been the last straw? Even if it was Amy, she'd have had to have help or how would she have got him in that field, stark naked at that? So, who would have helped her? By his own admission, Bill Harrington-Smythe was at her house all evening. Would he have helped? Della shook her head; she couldn't imagine that either.

Hopefully, tomorrow they'd have more to go on. Forensics would give their report, and Tom had promised the toxicology report would be theirs as soon as possible. Also tomorrow, the interviews from the surrounding residents would be available to be read up on. Maybe someone had seen something without realising what they'd seen.

She made herself stop thinking about it; she had ways of training herself to think of something mundane while trying to fall asleep. But actually, after last night's party and the too little sleep before her rude awakening, took its toll, and she was in dreamland before she realised.

Chapter 4

Monday

The following morning differed vastly from the previous one. She was up early, showered, and had a hearty breakfast. She always tried to have a substantial breakfast, never knowing when she'd get to eat again when on a pressing case such as this one, and was in the office well in time for the day's briefing.

Tim Masterson was in his office when she arrived, and he called her in.

"Della, I know you're supposed to be on your days off, so I appreciate you giving up your time to help us with this case."

"To be fair, guv, I wasn't given a lot of choice! Ben almost literally dragged me out of bed and I wasn't at my best yesterday. I shouldn't have been working, really."

"I know, I know. It's my fault. In my opinion, you're the best man for the job - sorry, woman. When this case is done, you can have some extended leave, if you wish. Hopefully, it won't take long, but I have a feeling about it, that it's going to need your expertise in sniffing out what happened to this guy. We don't have much to go on just now; hard to know where to start. But I wanted you in from the beginning, as it's hard to pick up from the middle sometimes."

"Well, I appreciate you saying so, guv. I'll do my best, as you're aware. I'm bright-eyed and bushy tailed this morning. Yesterday I wasn't firing on all cylinders. I'm going to read all the interview reports to see what comes of them."

"That's exactly what I've been doing. They strike me as being - well - odd, somehow. But I can't quite put my finger on it. See what you think."

"I will indeed."

"Thank you, Della." Tim kept his gaze on her face for a few moments. Della felt like a rabbit caught in headlights, not knowing quite what to do. Then she cleared her throat and rose from her chair. That broke the moment. He nodded briefly, and she made her escape, hoping she didn't appear as flustered as she felt. Damn the man! She wished she didn't find him so attractive. Where was Ben? She needed his down-to-earth attitude right now. She glanced at the clock on the wall; the others were gathering for the morning brief. She saw Ben enter the room, carrying a cardboard tray with two coffees. Thank goodness for that! She needed both him and the coffee to help calm her wobbly insides.

"So, despite all we did yesterday, we don't have much to go on." DI Masterson began. "I want to know where Darren Holbeach went that evening. He didn't take his car, so it had to be somewhere not far away, or he was meeting someone picking him up. I want the house to house taken further. I want any pubs or clubs or any kind of venue nearby, he may have gone to investigate. See if there are any CCTV cameras around that may have picked him up. I want to know everything there is to know about Darren - his upbringing, where he went to school, who his friends are then and who they are now. This wasn't a chance mugging; this was a meticulously planned murder, deeply personal, if that word on his chest is anything to go by, which is why we need to find who might have had a motive to kill him. Della and Ben, I want you to see the widow again, glean as much information about his life as you can, and also re-interview the residents of Gladioli Grove. Have you had a chance to look at the statements given to the team from them?

"We both have, guv, and we agree there is something odd about them, don't we?" replied Della. Ben nodded.

"Right. You and Ben know what you're doing, Della, so I'll leave you to it. I'll delegate the others."

"Thank you, guv."

Della and Ben left the room. She looked at her watch.

"Hm, bit early to be calling on the widow. Let's just go somewhere quiet and discuss those statements from the Gladioli people."

"The Gladioli People! Sounds like a race of people, sort of like the Amazons or the Incas only with flowers," grinned Ben.

Della giggled. "Does rather! But the ones I've seen so far aren't very flower-like. For a matter of interest, what did you think of Sarah, who found the body?"

"Um, tricky one, that. She put on a good appearance of being totally devastated, and yet I found myself not being impressed, but can't say why. Certainly, Philip, her husband, came across as a nice guy."

"He did, yes. But there was something about Sarah Sutton that I didn't quite trust. Can't work out why, though, nothing she said seemed wrong, did it?"

"No, not at all. Perhaps she wasn't as devastated as she seemed. Maybe she didn't like Darren."

"Well, we're going to ask her. As to the other neighbours; the couple at number seven, next door to Bill and Elizabeth, who are called, um, Louise and Richard Newton, had visitors who could vouch for them, which seems straightforward. We know Bill Harrington-Smythe was at Amy's while his wife was 'busy', although busy at what, we don't know. We have the time of death as between twelve and eight in the morning. Normally, we'd look for alibis for the time of death, but, unless the killer stayed to watch him die - and I agree that's a possibility - we don't have a precise time frame. And if he never got to where he was going, the time frame could be several hours. It's frustrating. I think we'll return to the Suttons' first under the pretext of checking that she's got over her shock. I'd like to know what she did that evening."

"You can't think Sarah did it? I can't see her slinging him over her shoulder and carrying him up the field. She's only a bit of a thing."

"I'm not sure what I think at the moment. But I want to see her again. Was there a follow up statement from her and Philip?"

"Never saw one."

"Well, that's a good enough reason to go back. We'll see them, then visit Amy. Let's go."

The door to number five, Gladioli Grove, was opened by Sarah herself. She was dressed in a pink fluffy jumper, jeans, and a pair of slippers that could have been bought as a 'set' with the jumper, as the pink fluff was exactly the same shade. Her blond hair was immaculately styled and her make-up flawless. On seeing them, her eyes momentarily narrowed, then her face changed in a flash.

"Oh, hello, detectives. So nice to see you again. Do come in. Shush, now," she said to the little dog yapping and running around the feet of the visitors.

Della stepped over the threshold, followed by Ben. Sarah shut the door behind them and hooked her arm through Ben's, eyeing him in a flirty way. "I was just about to have a cup of tea. Would you like one?"

"Yes, please," Della said, inwardly smiling at Ben's panicked face. Sarah guided them into her kitchen and kept hold of Ben's arm all the way until they arrived there. To his profound relief, she let him go and went over to pour hot water into mugs. She brought two mugs over and gave them to Della and Ben, then collected a third.

"Come through, detectives," she said, and led the way to a conservatory, comfortably heated and furnished with wicker chairs. Tall leafy plants in pots were strategically placed for the best advantage to create a green and relaxing atmosphere. Sarah sat in one chair, expertly picked up her dog with her free hand and crossed her legs casually. "Do sit down." She waved her free hand at the other chairs. Della and Ben obliged; Della placed herself opposite Sarah, Ben to one side.

"I hope you are feeling better today, Sarah. Got over your shock?"

"Oh, it was terrible, you know. Poor Darren, poor Amy. They have only lived here for about eighteen months."

"Is that so?"

"Yes. Amy told me it was her dream to live in a house in this area. Looks like the dream has turned into a nightmare."

"Indeed. Do you think she'll stay?"

Sarah shrugged her shoulders. "Who knows? It's one thing, she won't have any problem selling the house if that's what she decides to do. There are always people wanting these houses."

"Oh? I'd have thought they were rather expensive for the average family."

Sarah waved her mug. "I suppose so."

"Last time we met, you told me about what happened when you found Darren yesterday morning. We are asking everyone in the street about their movements the evening before. Can you tell us what you did, as from about seven thirty?"

"Oh! Well, let me see. I was expecting a friend who was coming to spend the evening with me. Phil went out so that me and my mate could have a good chinwag - he's good like that. But my friend never came. Migraine, apparently. So, I spent the evening watching a dvd and consoling myself with a bottle of wine until Phil came home."

"What time did he arrive home?"

"About just after ten, I think. He's never that late."

"You didn't think to send him a message to say your friend hadn't come after all?"

"Oh no, I didn't want to mess his evening up as well. It really didn't matter."

"And what did you do when Phil came home?"

"We went to bed. I think I was a bit sozzled by then. Frankly, I'm surprised I could get up early enough to walk Sukie in the morning. But I've always been able to hold my drink quite well."

"Is Phil here?"

"No, he's had to go into work. He was going to stay with me today, but I assured him I was okay. He got a call, some crisis he needed to sort out."

"I see. Do you know where he went that evening?"

Sarah shrugged. "Not a clue. I expect he went down the pub with some of his friends."

"Okay, thank you. I think that's all for now. Would you mind popping into the station to make a statement about both times, the evening before and when you found the body in the morning?"

"Yes, that's no bother. I'm going into town soon, anyway."

Della stood, and they all left the conservatory.

"Thank you for the tea. That was most welcome," said Della, putting her mug in Sarah's hand and Ben followed suit with a smile and a nod. "We can see ourselves out."

Once the door closed and they were walking down the drive, Della said, "There's something about that woman I don't trust."

"I agree, Del," said Ben. "But at the moment I can't say why."

"Nor me, but you can be sure I'll sus it out, believe me."

"I know you will." He had seen Della in action before. They'd been partners for some years, and he knew she was gritty and determined. He also knew she was the reason their guv, Tim Masterson, was so successful as a DI. Because of Della's doggedness, Tim had an impressive record of solved cases. No one was fooled. Even though they took their orders from Masterson, they knew who was the real brains behind the team.

As they walked up the road, there were several police vehicles, including dog handling vans, parked near the entrance to the field. There was a police constable on guard, preventing anyone from going through the gate. But they weren't going as far as that.

Amy didn't look much better when she opened her door. She invited them in.

"Would you like something to drink?" she asked.

"No, thank you. We've just come to see how you are."

The young woman sighed. "I've been better. But the day is going to go downhill. Darren's parents are coming over and they insist they want to stay with me." She shuddered. "Don't get me wrong," she continued, as she waved her arm at the chairs, "but my mother-in-law is hard to get on with - she's so snooty! His dad's alright, if a bit starchy. He is kind, but she's not. She never liked me and it's got no easier as the years have gone on. In her eyes, no one was good enough for her darling boy. He played up to it like mad, you know. Had her wrapped around his little finger, but his dad could see through him. I often saw him grimacing behind their backs and he'd give me the hint of a wink to let me know he knew."

"Was he an only child?" inquired Della, as she seated herself in a chair.

"Oh no, he has a brother and a sister. His sister, Louisa, she's quite nice; she's rather like her father. She always stuck up for me - said we girls should look after each other. Simon, the brother, is much older and a cross between his parents. He's a bit stiff and proper, but he's okay. Darren was the baby of the family and could do no wrong in his mother's eyes. She's devastated, of course, and she as good as blamed me for his death! I didn't have anything to do with it, I didn't, honestly."

"There now, don't get upset again," soothed Ben. Della smiled; he couldn't help doing his 'daddy bear' thing. It seemed to comfort Amy anyway, as she sniffed into another tissue and put her head on his chest for a moment. Then she straightened up and gave a watery smile.

"Sorry, it comes over me now and then, and the thought of having his parents here is making it feel worse."

"We can understand that, can't we, Ben?" smiled Della gently. "When are you expecting them?"

"Any time now. When Dad retired, they moved to Burton-on-Trent to be nearer to Louisa."

They heard the doorbell ring. Amy jumped up, nervously. "Oh goodness, they're here already."

She left the room and Della heard voices. A few moments later, Amy reappeared with a man and woman. Della and Ben stood.

"Dad, Mother, this is Detective Sergeant Downs and Detective Constable Curran."

The woman strode over to Ben. "Well, what are you doing about finding out what happened to my son, Detective Sergeant? And why isn't a detective inspector on the case?"

"Now then, my dear. Give them a chance," Mr Holbeach gently admonished his wife. He was a tall man and Della noticed the similarities with his dead son, only this man was almost bald.

"But our son is dead, Douglas! My baby is dead and I want to know why!" The woman pulled off her gloves and loosened her scarf. Her husband helped her off with her coat and Amy took it and went out of the room with it.

Della eyed Brenda Holbeach, knowing exactly the kind of woman she was up against here. But she also understood the woman was distressed; after all, she'd lost a beloved child.

"Why don't you sit down, Mrs Holbeach? My partner will make you a nice warm drink, as I'm sure you're ready for one." She held up her ID. "I'm Detective Sergeant Della Downs. I'm very glad you're here because Amy has had to face this terrible thing alone and I know she'll appreciate having you and Mr Holbeach with her for a while so you can console each other. I would like to hear everything about your son, his life, where he went to school, who his friends are, what he enjoyed doing. I'm sure you're the best person to tell us all that, with your husband's help, of course."

"I'll help make the tea," said Amy, hastily, and hurried to follow Ben to the kitchen.

Della eyed Darren's parents, who sat uncomfortably, obviously on edge. Mrs Holbeach quietly dabbed at her eyes and cheeks, while her husband held onto her hand as he sat next to her on the sofa.

"What do you need to know about our Darren, Detective Sergeant?" he asked. "It's hard for us to think straight; it's been such a shock. And we only know our son is dead, we don't know how. All Amy could tell us is that he was out all night and froze to death. How could that happen, Sergeant?"

"Call me Della, Mr Holbeach," said Della gently. "I think we need to wait until Amy comes back with Ben. So, where were you living when you had your family?"

"We lived in Mickleover. All our children grew up there. We only moved to near Burton-on-Trent when I retired." It was Douglas Holbeach who replied.

At that moment, Ben and Amy reappeared with a tray of drinks and a plate of biscuits, which they placed on a coffee table.

"Amy, come and sit down. We have something serious to say to you and Darren's parents."

"What? What is it?" Amy stumbled towards a chair, and Ben put his hand under her elbow to steady her.

"I'm afraid there's no easy way to say this, so I'm just having to come out with it. We believe Darren was murdered."

There was an audible gasp from both women and Mrs Holbeach sobbed, "No! Who'd want to kill my lovely boy?"

"That's what we are going to find out."

"How?"

"We're not able to say, I'm afraid, but the evidence we have strongly shows someone intended for him to die."

"Oh!" Mrs Holbeach's sobs became more evident. Her husband went to put his arm around her. She left it there for a moment and then shrugged it off. Resigned, he moved away slightly. For the first time, Della began to see the dynamics of the marriage and her sympathies edged towards Darren's father. He looked at her for a moment and they gazed into each other's eyes. Della felt he was trying silently to communicate with her. Then the moment was gone. Della resolved to talk with these two separately. She turned to Amy.

"I'm sorry to be the bearer of further bad news, Amy, but it's important that you know. We will need you to tell us everyone you know who he associates with, his friends, who he goes out with, any pubs or clubs he frequents and so on. In particular, anyone you know of who might have a reason to want him out of the way."

"I'll have a think," replied Amy.

"I'm going to arrange a family liaison officer for you. They will help you. It will be someone to talk with and also, we can let you know what is happening through them."

"We don't need anyone."

"Just for a couple of days. We will be very busy investigating, so we can't be popping back frequently."

"I see. Yes, that makes sense, I suppose."

Della stood. "We're going to leave you now; we need to talk with your neighbours. I will return with the liaison officer when they arrive."

Amy saw them to the door. "Thank you," she said.

"Good luck," replied Della, nodding towards the lounge. "I'll be back soon."

Amy grimaced and nodded.

They gave a discreet sigh of relief once they were on their way and Amy's door was closed. They walked past the sleek Audi on the drive, which Della assumed must belong to the Holbeach parents.

"I don't think Amy is going to have an easy time with mother-in-law," commented Ben.

"That's why I decided to have an FLO put in there, if possible. They will act as a buffer between ma-in-law and Amy. I got the impression that Mr Holbeach doesn't wear the trousers in that relationship. I'm just going to call in about the liaison officer. Then we'll go next door."

******

The woman who answered the door to number eight examined the IDs presented to her by Della and Ben. There was something about her that reminded Della of the Queen; she had that kind of bearing. She was about five feet eight inches, with her brown hair arranged in a short, neat bob. Della guessed she was nearing her mid-forties.

"Do come in. Can I get you a drink or anything?"

"No, we're fine, thank you. We'd just like to ask you a few questions, if we may?"

"Anything I can do to help. That poor girl, as if she didn't have enough to cope with already without this." As she spoke, Celia Davenport led them into a small room to one side of the hallway. It was a cosy room with two red matching Chesterfield armchairs placed either side of a fireplace with a coal-look gas fire. A small, round table stood beside each of them. The room had one wall lined with bookshelves, full of books, all looking immaculate. Another, much smaller bookshelf by the side of an arched window held a pile of magazines and papers.

Celia obviously noticed Della's interest, for she said, "We call it the snug. I like to be in here when Neville is out as it's more friendly and cosy - gets warm quickly and stays warm. Our lounge is lovely, but it takes a lot of heating - something we don't always take into consideration when selecting a home!"

Della liked this woman. Despite her almost royal bearing, she was warm and friendly.

"Do sit down and get warm. I have another chair here I can sit on." She drew a small, armless, upholstered red chair nearer to the other chairs. "No, detective constable, I'm quite alright here - you sit near the fire."

Ben reluctantly did as he was told.

"Now, what can I help you with?"

"I have your statement here that you and your husband spent the evening in question across the road at Mr and Mrs Newton's house. Is that correct?"

"Yes. They had visitors, and invited us to join them. It was the couple who used to live in number ten and we were quite close friends with them, had lived next door to them a good few years, you know, so it was pleasant to see them again."

Della nodded. "Quite so. How long did you stay over there?"

"Until about eleven, I think. Can't be exact, I'm afraid. But it couldn't have been any later, because Angela and Peter needed to drive back to Chesterfield and didn't want to leave it too late, knowing how black ice can form in these low temperatures."

"Did you see or hear anything as you were leaving there?"

"Not a thing. It was silent and still; not a breath of air stirring. I was glad we didn't have far to go. It would have been worse if the wind had been blowing."

"I don't suppose you saw Darren when he left home that evening?"

"I'm sorry, I certainly never saw him; obviously I can't speak for Neville. But it's pretty hard to see anything out there once it gets dark and the hedge does rather impede the view as well."

"Yes, I noticed the hedge is quite tall at the front. Can you tell us anything about Darren and Amy? Did you get on well with them?"

"Oh, Amy is such a nice girl. I'm not so keen on Darren, but we all put up with him for her sake, you know. We're all friends in the Grove. We get together a lot in our gardens in the warmer months and have each other around when it's not so warm - we've all got these huge lounges - hard to heat but great for get-togethers! We can all easily get twenty people in any of our houses and we have such a good time because we all get on so well. Oh dear, we're going to be an odd number now, aren't we? How sad. How is poor Amy? I went round to spend some time with her yesterday. Elizabeth did too, and so did Ruth next door to me."

"Well, she has her in-laws with her now. It seems they've come to stay with her," offered Della.

"Oh no! Not Darren's mother! I met her before - can't stand the woman! Thinks her Darren is an angel - how disillusioned can a woman get? His dad's alright though, quite a nice man really. Surprised he's stuck with her all these years - she's definitely the boss!" Celia laughed a little. "Poor man! Poor Amy. Let's hope they don't stay long."

"I think they intend to stay until we find some answers," replied Della drily.

"In that case, I hope you find them quickly, for poor Amy's sake."

"We'll certainly do our best. But anything you can tell us about Darren's movements, not only the night of his death, would be helpful. Do you know where he went on his nights out? Did he go out regularly?"

"I don't know, I'm afraid. Amy did once tell me he'd had other women over the years, but she didn't seem to think he had one currently. In fact, I think she hoped being here would be a new start for them. She is desperate for a baby before her body clock runs out, but he always refused to allow it. He didn't want his life spoiled by a child!"

"Hm. Well, thank you, Mrs Davenport. We're grateful for your help. I think that's all we need for now, but if you think of anything, here's my card, please call me.

Reluctant as we are to leave the warmth of your lovely snug, we have to make ourselves face the cold."

*****

Ruth Cuthbertson, next door to Celia, was only about five feet tall, with a wide smile that lit her entire face. Her long brown hair was tied back in a sleek ponytail and she looked about fifteen. However, Della knew she was in her early thirties and her husband was the headteacher of a local comprehensive school. Della wondered how they could afford a house like this because other head teachers she'd come across didn't live in such an expensive place. Perhaps having no children had something to do with it.

They were led into a gorgeous kitchen.

"Sorry, but you caught me in the middle of a baking session, so I need to finish what I'm doing and keep an eye on the oven. Hope you don't mind. I'll make a brew for you; I'm just about ready for one myself."

She drew out a couple of chairs that were clear moulded plastic from the table that had a snowy white tablecloth on it. In the middle of the table stood a small vase holding an interesting twig of holly. Next to it stood a salt and pepper pot set that looked like snowmen. Before they could draw breath, Ruth had put before them a plate of cookies, obviously homemade and not long from the oven. They smelt delicious.

"Do help yourselves," she sang, as she poured water from the just-boiled kettle into a pretty teapot, decorated festively with a robin on a holly branch. The cups and saucers put before them also had the same pattern. Della couldn't help being charmed. This woman's kitchen was a mixture of ultra-modern and old-fashionedness. She picked up the salt pot to look at it closer.

Ruth giggled. "I know! Tony thinks I'm nuts! He's all for the chrome shiny stuff, but I love cute ceramic things and tablecloths! I think they add character, don't you? I saw these chaps in a catalogue and couldn't resist. I've got a whole collection of cruet sets and teapots with matching porcelain. Today, I'm using the robin ones, but tomorrow I might use my Royal Doulton! Well, it keeps me amused anyway. And what else am I going to fill my cupboards with? A house this size is full of cupboards! Quite honestly, in some ways, I'd rather have a much smaller house. This one is a full-time job - when I've finished cleaning throughout, it's time to start again - rather like the Forth Bridge!" She giggled again.

Della couldn't quite work out if the other woman was always that talkative or if she was nervous. But what could she have to be nervous about? According to the statements, Ruth and her husband had joined another four households at Emily and George Taunton's house for the evening.

"These cookies are delicious," Della ventured.

"Thank you. I love cooking. I'm always trying things out because I enjoy giving cookies and cakes to my friends." She jumped up again and hurried over to fetch a tray from the oven. She set it on the worktop and switched off the oven.

"Sorry about that. I'm all yours now." She pulled out a chair for herself and sat down. She poured out a cup of tea and sat with her arms on the table. "What can I help you with?"

"Can we just verify what time you and your husband went next door on the night in question?"

"Next door? Oh! Yes, next door. I think it was around half past seven."

"Did you see Darren at all?"

"No, but Tony said he spotted him walking down the road."

"Was he alone?"

"Yes."

"Did he see where he went?"

"No, I'm sorry, I don't think so. We only went as far as next door, as you're aware, so we - he - only saw him for a moment."

"And you saw no one else that doesn't live in the Grove?"

"No, not at all. We arrived next door at the same time as Chris and Brian from number one. They may have seen where Darren went."

"We'll certainly ask them. So, what time did you leave next door?"

"Around half past ten, I think. Tony didn't want to be late because he's had a lot of late nights lately. Pressure of work, you know."

Della did know. "So, did you see anything when you were coming home?"

"Not a thing. We hurried home because it was so cold. I didn't think of looking around. I just wanted to get home."

"I can understand that."

"To think of poor Darren lying out there in that field. Although he may not have been there yet when we went home. Probably wasn't, come to think of it. Didn't like him, but I would never have wished that on him."

"Why didn't you like him?"

"He was smarmy, thought he was God's gift to women. And he treated Amy badly. He'd put her down in front of us. I didn't like that."

"Have you met his parents?"

"Oh...yes. They came here in the summer. Nothing was ever right for her. He wouldn't say boo to a goose. No wonder Darren was like he was. With a mother who worshipped the ground he walked on, no wonder he turned out to be so obnoxious. Thought the world should revolve around him. The woman ran poor Amy ragged, trying to please her. We were all relieved when they went home, I can tell you."

"Well," said Della, standing up. "They're here again. Amy's going to need her friends because I don't think her in-laws are going to be much comfort to her."

"Oh gosh, poor Amy. She doesn't need that. I'll see what I can do."

"Thank you for your time. If you think of anything you feel we need to know, please call me."

Della handed Ruth a card.

Once outside, she took a deep breath.

"Don't know about you, Benjamin, but I've a feeling we're going to get nowhere with any of these people. We'll go to the next house but..." her phone ringing interrupted her.

Once she'd answered it, she turned to Ben. "The FLO is here. Thankfully, it's Anna Hargreaves; she'll cope with Ma Holbeach just fine. She's waiting outside their house - ah yes, there she is. We'd better just brief her."

Anna Hargreaves was a smart-looking officer in her forties. She smiled grimly as Della told her about the Holbeach parents.

"Don't worry, Della, I'll cope."

"I know you will. I let the guv know exactly what an FLO would be dealing with so that's no doubt why he asked for you. You always do a great job. Come on, let's beard the lioness in her den."

*****

A couple of hours later, back at headquarters, Della felt exhausted. Her earlier comment to Ben had proven to be true. They'd got precisely nowhere.

"They all said the same thing. Four couples gathered at one house for the evening. No, none of them saw where Darren was going, although some saw him walking down the road. Elizabeth was 'busy', William was with Amy. Sarah was waiting for a friend who had never come and

Philip was 'out'. Where was he? Where did he go? We'll have to return to see him, Ben, and the other husbands, the ones we didn't see. The Davenports were visiting with the Newtons because of their visitors, who used to live in the Holbeachs' house."

"It all looks too neat to me, Del. Why did the remaining four couples gather on that particular night? It was so cold, I didn't want to go anywhere, even next door! And my next door is much closer than theirs. It was slippery underfoot in places too. Why would they want to go out? Is it something they did every Saturday night?"

Della frowned. "Good point. I wonder if there was something particular about that night. They were all pretty unanimous in their opinions of Darren, weren't they? What if they decided collectively to rid Amy of her burden?"

"It's certainly worth a thought, Del. But we'd need proof, because all we have just now are a bunch of people giving each other alibis."

"And what about those visitors of the Newtons? What a night to visit; you'd have thought they'd have postponed. We didn't manage to see Mr or Mrs Newton today; we're going to have to call on them at some point to get more details. If their visitors were leaving around ten-thirty to eleven, they may have seen or heard something."

"That's true. We'll need a statement from them. Did the initial statements give their details?"

"Yes, they did. We'll follow that up tomorrow. I wonder what information the others have. Let's find out."

Chapter 5

Tuesday

"We have made a search of the woods and surrounding area of the field where Darren Holbeach was found. There was o trace of his clothing. Officers will have search warrants tomorrow for all the gardens and houses of Gladioli Grove. From there, if they find nothing, the search will be extended to properties nearby." Tim Masterson paused as he looked around the room at the team. His gaze landed on Della for a moment.

She tried not to react, but she felt a strange, mild, 'pins and needles' sensation seep upward through her chest before it subsided in her lower jaw. Yet again, for the umpteenth time, she wished he didn't have an effect on her. However much she tried to ignore it, her body always betrayed her. And even though she made an effort to give no sign, it was as if he knew, somehow. She felt a slight nudge at her side and knew it was Ben bringing her back to earth. Again, as if he knew, Tim's gaze moved on.

"Uniform has been to every pub and club within walking distance of Gladioli Grove; there are only two pubs and the Conservative Club and we are pretty certain Darren Holbeach wasn't at any of them on the night in question. Only The Derbyshire pub landlord reckoned he'd seen Darren before and always in the company of other men from Gladioli Grove. They're known there, and they're also known at the Conservative Club. The other pub, The Red Lion, did not recognise him at all. So, where did he go that night? We need to know if there are any CCTV cameras in the area at the opening of Gladioli Grove. Perhaps someone picked him up in a car?

A voice came from the back. "Guv, there aren't any CCTV in the area. Apart from the two pubs and the Conservative Club, which have cameras, and a trio of small shops a few streets away, there are no cameras in the vicinity, except any personal ones on individual houses. But by law, homes may not have their cameras pointing at the street, only at their own property."

"Right. Thank you. I'm well aware of the law, Mike," a few titters sounded as the group turned to look at Mike, whose ears turned a fiery red as he looked at his lap in embarrassment. "But well done for having the initiative to look; it saves us a job. I want you to take Ros and ask to see footage for the night in question from those establishments; it's possible our man may have met someone outside one of them - try the Derbyshire first, it's the nearest. Actually, on second thoughts, only try the Derbyshire, as I'm sure if he was meeting someone, he wouldn't have gone further away than that on such a night."

"Yes Guv." Mike glanced at his partner, Rosalind Parry, who nodded at him at then looked to the front at Tim as he spoke again.

"Did anything occur as a result of the house to house?"

"No guv. The houses in the next street are still pretty much set back from the road. It would have been difficult for most to see anything, even someone walking past their property, especially in the dark, although there is the usual street lighting. But all the residents have been interviewed and not one of them saw anyone walking out of Gladioli Grove that night. And one man said he was walking his dog at around seven thirty and never saw a soul, although he admits he never stayed out long. He said he would have seen if someone had walked out of the Grove because he was walking towards it and he was sure his dog would have heard if there was someone behind them on the way back to his house."

"Right." Shane, I want you and Carol to pick up the parents to come here to headquarters. Tell them your DI would like to talk with them and as I am so very busy making sure the investigation is going the right way for them, ask them if they'd mind coming here to talk with me, please? Carol, you're good at persuading people - you know, grovel a bit, lay on the flattery - you know how to do it. Della and Ben, I want you to have another go at talking with Amy Holbeach, and I want you to search the house. It would be better if you did it than sending in the heavy mob. I heard from Anna Hargreaves earlier and they're giving Amy a hard time. I thought it would be prudent to get them out of the way for a while - to give her a break and also to give you a free hand without interruption and interference from her mother-in-law."

"Good thinking, Guv."

"Okay, do we all know what we're doing this morning? Right, off you go. Good luck, everyone."

*****

This time, Anna Hargreaves answered their knock. She smiled widely and welcomed them in.

"I suppose you know the dreaded mother-in-law is out of the building!" she laughed as she led them into the kitchen. "Amy and I are in here. While the cat's away, the mice are playing! In other words, we're having scones and cream with coffee. You're just in time to join us."

Amy looked up as they entered the room, which smelt gorgeous and was also cosy and warm. She had just put plates and a plate of scones on a tray and was busy filling mugs with creamy coffee from the machine.

"Hello, Amy, how are you getting on?"

"Hello, Della, Ben. At the moment, I'm okay. When Darren's parents return, I won't be so okay. Anna's been wonderful; I can't thank her enough. I wish I could say I'd forgotten how awful Darren's mother is, but I hadn't. Now he's dead, she's twice as bad. Anna's been a buffer between us. She really blames me for his death, but I can't work out why, or how she thinks I did it. I never could get Darren to do anything he didn't want to do, and I'm sure he would never have wanted to go into a field at night."

They made themselves comfortable in Amy's lounge. Della helped herself to a scone already decked in jam and cream and bit into it, taking a moment to savour the deliciousness. She licked her lips and dabbed them with a paper napkin. "Perhaps they think you drove him away?"

Amy frowned. "But I've stood by him through thick and thin. I've put up with all his affairs, all his put-downs and the times he's embarrassed me. I really thought - hoped coming here would help him change. I've never been enough for him. I would never have been enough for him. Frankly, I don't think any woman would have been enough for him. He thought he had the right to play around the way he did. He's always had loads of women. To think, I thought he'd changed when he asked me to marry him. He was so sweet and ardent over me, I thought he'd put his past behind him. But he never did. Until we came here. The past six months at least, he's not had anyone else, I'm sure of it. The friendships offered by our neighbours seems to have helped that change. He's still inclined to put me down in public, but he's been more content to stay at home or go out with me. I really thought things were getting much better. I'm shocked and upset that this has happened just when I thought we were finally making a go of things."

Anna put out a hand to pat Amy on the arm. She touched the policewoman's hand for a moment. "I can't thank Anna enough for being here with me. It's helped me no end."

"Drink your coffee, Amy. Now, I'm sorry to do this, but we have to search your house. Our boss sent us to do it because he wanted to spare you the heavy mob."

Amy waved her hand. "Search away. I've got nothing to hide. What are you looking for?"

"Anything that might help give us a clue where Darren may have gone that night, who he may have seen. Did he have a mobile phone?"

"Yes, he did. I assume he had it with him."

"Have you tried calling it?"

"Yes, several times, but he must have switched it off."

Della and Ben finished their coffee and scones and begun their search of the house.

Darren had a dressing room, and Amy had a walk-in wardrobe.

"How the other half lives!" laughed Ben when he saw Darren's dressing room. Then, "Ops, my bad."

"They might be rich, but it hasn't brought happiness, has it? Amy's had a tough life, by all accounts. You and your Shona are richer by far."

"Oh, I know that, lass. Well, I suppose I'd better get on with it."

It took some considerable time for the pair to search the house, but they found nothing helpful. It was as if any former life Darren might have had had been completely wiped from his life and his home.

"Well, I don't think we need to keep you any longer, Amy. I'm afraid your parents-in-law may well be here again soon. I think you need to get brave and tell them to go home."

"Oh my! I'd have to be brave indeed. It's a miracle I'm still alive, the looks she gives me! It's bad enough that I have nightmares about what happened to Darren at night, then during the day I live more nightmares with her. Now he's not here to keep her in line. She's awful. Dad is no good. He lets her have her way all the time. I'm just amazed he's put up with her all these years."

"Well, good luck, Amy. Look after her, Anna. I'm going to see if they've had any leads from elsewhere. We'll be in touch."

*****

"Nothing! We have nothing! All that time, all that searching and we come up with zero! I hope the chaps at headquarters have got something for us. This investigation is not giving us anything at all. I knew I should have gone away for my days off," grumbled Della once they were in the car.

Ben chuckled. "Something will come up, Del. We just need to be patient. Maybe the guv will have worked everything out while we've been gone. It'll make a change for him to find the answers instead of you. Maybe the parents will have given him something."

"Frankly, it's my opinion that he'll be lucky to get anything out of that woman. She saw no wrong in her son at all. I'm sure he would never have let her know what he was really like and if she knew, she wouldn't believe it."

Ben started the car.

"Actually, Ben, before we go back, I want to just have a quick word with the Newtons. We haven't yet caught them in. I'd like to try now."

"Right you are." Ben killed the engine, and they climbed out and walked to number seven. Della never failed to be impressed as they walked up to each house. Each was different but all attractive. What money could do!

A man answered their ring on the doorbell. The old romantic description skipped through Della's mind - 'tall, dark and handsome'. It was this man to a 'T', although the hair was shot through with silver. The penetrating look he gave her through deep brown eyes sent an involuntary shiver, which she suppressed as she held out her ID.

"Mr Newton? I'm Detective Sergeant Downs, and this is Detective Constable Curran. I wondered if we could have a quick word with you and your wife, sir? Just to clarify a couple of things in your statement."

"Why, yes, of course. Come in. My wife's in the patio room." He shut the door. "Follow me."

The patio room turned out to be an attractive room, something like a conservatory, but was an actual room, not an addition. Most of one wall, facing out towards the back, comprised of a very large pair of patio doors, and either side of it were large picture windows, giving the occupants a panoramic view of the garden, which was spectacular, even in the winter. Della's sharp eyes spied large clumps of snowdrops about to burst into flower and bright cyclamen interspersed them.

"Louise, my dear, these detectives wish to talk with us for a few moments. Do sit down, detectives. Would you like a drink or anything?"

"No, thank you, Mr Newton. We won't be with you for long," replied Della. She walked towards the woman seated in an armchair. She was also dark-haired, like her husband, although Della was certain the colour came from a bottle. Her face was immaculately made-up and blue eyes looked through a pair of glasses, which were removed and the book she was reading was placed on the arm of the chair along with the spectacles. "I'm pleased to meet you both. No, please don't get up, Mrs Newton. I was just admiring your garden; how beautiful it is."

"Thank you, er..." Mrs Newton spoke.

"Della. Please call me Della, and this is Ben."

"Della," continued the woman. "Gardening is my passion. I designed it."

"Very impressive. Now, I believe the night in question you had a couple of visitors, a Mr and Mrs Peter Moorcroft. Is that correct?"

"Yes, that's right. They used to live at number ten."

"So I believe. Obviously, you were expecting them?"

"Yes, it had been arranged for a couple of days."

"But the weather was awful, wouldn't you have expected them to cancel?"

"Ordinarily, yes, but they were already in town visiting some other friends. I believe they'd been in Derby a few days. In fact, I met up with Angela - that's Mrs Moorcroft, in town on the Wednesday before. They said they'd spend the evening with us and then go home. We invited Celia and Neville to join us as they'd become friends, same as us."

"But not your other neighbours? I thought you were all friends in the Grove?"

"That's right, we are. But the others said they had something already planned. We thought we'd meet up again in the summer, have a barbeque as we often do, but invite Angela and Pete over to join us."

"Right. Fair enough. Can you tell us around what time the Davenports left here?"

"They didn't want to be too late, so I think it was around ten-thirtyish. What do you think, Richard?"

"Umm, I'm not sure, but I think it must have been about then."

"And what time did the Moorcrofts leave? Surely, they were worried about the roads by then?"

"Actually, they ended up staying the night. They heard on the local news there was an accident on the motorway and so they decided it would be better to stay until the morning and hope the road would be cleared by then."

"I see. You didn't mention that in your statement."

"We weren't asked. They only asked us about the evening. We didn't think we needed to say they stayed overnight."

"So, when did they leave?"

"Around eight, half-past eight. Not entirely sure, really. Can't quite remember, can you remember, darling?"

"I think it was around eight-fifteen."

"Why does it matter about what time they left?"

"I'm sure it doesn't matter at all, Mrs Newton. I just like to have the facts straight in my mind."

Della stood, and Ben followed her example.

"Well, thank you for your time. I believe we have Mr and Mrs Moorcroft's contact number and address?"

"I gave it to the other officers. Why would you need to speak with them?"

"We just need to confirm what you've told us, that's all."

"I'll see you out," said Richard, and he led the way.

In the car again, Della said, "What I don't get is, why would the others say they all had plans and got together at another house when they'd been invited to meet their old neighbours again? Except for Elizabeth and Bill and Sarah and Philip - and Amy and Darren? Well, I suppose we can understand Amy and Darren because they didn't really know the Moorcrofts, they only bought the house from them. And Sarah was expecting a friend - and I've no doubt Sarah always does exactly what she wants and Philip has to do whatever she wants. Actually, Ben, slide the car towards number five. I want to ask Philip where he went that evening."

Ben followed instructions and stopped near the assigned house. To Della's relief, Philip himself answered the door, looking somewhat pale behind his horn-rims.

"Hello again, detectives. If you want to see my wife, I'm afraid she's out."

"Actually, it's you we wanted to see. Can we come in for a moment? It won't take long but it is rather cold out here."

"Oh! Of course, sorry! Come through to my office. It's nice and warm in there."

Philip's office was a curious mix of ancient and modern. Modern, as he had a couple of computers on a specially fitted desk along one wall and there were other electronic things that Della didn't recognise. Turn your back on the electronic wall and the room reminded her of the Davenports' snug because the fireplace held an electric fire with glowing coals; the fireplace was an old style with a mantlepiece. In the middle of the mantle was a beautiful clock, which ticked away steadily. On either side of the clock were porcelain ornaments, looking somewhat out of place in a man's study. The window overlooked flower beds, looking a bit sorry in January, and next to the window was a single glass door. The remaining wall had rows of shelves on which there were files, books and all sorts of other things. Above the clock there was a big painting of a country scene with a lake and hills. It was beautiful.

Philip noticed Della's gaze. "My mother painted it; she was a talented artist. The clock and the ornaments were hers, too. I like to have them near me while I work. It makes me feel as if she's still here. Does that sound silly?"

"Not at all, lad." It was Ben who answered. Della nodded in agreement. Philip continued with a small laugh that contained no humour, "Sarah won't have them in the house, apart from in here anyway. You've seen the lounge. I hate it, all those horrible, meaningless paintings and white furniture that look like a load of boxes! But I spend most of my time in here anyway. This is where I work. Do have a seat. Would you like a drink?"

They sat in a pair of brown leather armchairs and Philip sat in his computer chair. "How can I help you?"

"Sarah said she was expecting someone that evening. Do you know who she was expecting?"

"No, sorry, I don't."

"So, you don't know who your wife was expecting to visit her, but you accommodate her by going out?"

"I know it looks strange, but that was our usual arrangement. It's no big deal. I've got used to it."

"And you don't worry about who might visit your wife?"

"To quote a famous film, 'frankly, my dear, I don't give a damn.'"

"Like that, is it?"

"Yes. I'm afraid so. It's been going downhill for a while."

"I'm sorry to hear that. So, can you tell us where you went that evening?"

"Yes, of course. I went to see Elizabeth. I often go there. She and Bill have been like second parents to me. I had to go out, and I needed someone to talk to, so I went to talk to them. Bill had gone across to see Amy, so I didn't actually see him. I think he came in and went to bed while I was still with Liz. We like to play chess."

"I see. Well, that clears that little mystery up. And you didn't happen to see anything suspicious when on your way home? What time was that?"

"It was about eleven, I think, and no, I didn't see anything."

"Oh well, thank you. We'll leave you in peace now."

On their way back to headquarters, Della and Ben discussed things. "As far as I can see, the only thing I've picked on so far is the time discrepancy between Sarah saying Philip got home at ten and him saying it was eleven."

"Hmm, well, if she'd gone to sleep, it would be a simple mistake to make," remarked Ben. "Let's hope there's more information found by the others. This thing is really getting to me now."

"Me too. I'm hungry. Let's go find some lunch."

Chapter 6

"Della, can you come in for a briefing? Ben too." Tim called her as soon as they arrived at headquarters. They joined him in his office.

"How did you get on with the parents?" asked Della.

"What an appalling woman! It was impossible to talk with them together. She kept interrupting, shouting at me why haven't we found her son's killer. In the end, I sent her with a WPC to get a drink and we talked to her husband. He was very helpful, at least, he tried to be. He gave us names of his son's childhood friends, teenage friends, where he went to school and so on. According to the father, Darren was something of a ruffian as a teenager, but whenever the father tried to talk with his wife about their son, she always refused to listen. Apparently, he is quite a few years younger than their older son and daughter and was always his mother's favourite. Consequently, the boy used to get away with murder, so to speak. So, we have the team following up on all the background info the father has given us. He's a nice man; can't think how he's put up with her for so long." Tim echoed Della's own earlier thoughts. "So, what information have you gleaned?"

"A big, fat zero, guv. We searched the house, there was nothing we could use. We spoke to the Newtons and discovered their visitors stayed overnight. That means it's even more necessary for someone to see them. Philip Sutton spent the evening with Elizabeth at number nine in order to leave the way clear for Sarah's visitor, whoever that should have been. The only discrepancy we found was Sarah said

Phil came home about ten and he said it was eleven. I guess it doesn't matter much, though. Unless someone comes up with something in the searches, we've hit a wall."

"No luck with CCTV or the Derbyshire?" asked Ben.

"Not a thing. We really need something. We have to keep digging. I know that's something you're good at, Della."

"Thank you, guv. I keep thinking that Amy knows more than she's saying. I don't think she's guilty of his murder, but I do think she may actually know where Darren went that night, but for some reason, didn't want to say."

"And we're not likely to get any information out of her while the abominable mother-in-law is still there. If Amy was left alone with Anna, I think we'd stand a chance. Anna's very good at gently winkling information out of witnesses."

"She is that. Maybe Providence will be kind to us. So, I want you to go see the couple who visited the Newtons. You have the address?"

"Yes guv. Right, Ben, let's go."

The trip was straightforward and pleasant. The weak winter sun had melted the thick frost that had coated the fields and caused black ice on the roads. The Moorcrofts lived in a leafy suburb of the picturesque town of Chesterfield. The house was smaller than the one they'd left in Gladioli Grove, but it was still obviously expensive. A woman answered the doorbell. She was in her fifties, Della judged, probably nearer sixty, with short hair in a severe style that suited her bespectacled face that was devoid of makeup. She wasn't very tall and her jumper showed she had something of a 'spare tyre' around her middle.

"Mrs Angela Moorcroft? I'm DS Della Downs and this is DC Ben Curran. We've come to speak with you about Saturday night. May we come in?"

"Yes. Yes, of course." The woman opened the door further, and they followed her in.

"Is your husband here too? We'd like to see you both."

"Yes, he's in the lounge watching television. Would you like some tea? I was about to make some."

"That would be lovely, thank you."

"I'll take you through, then make the tea. I've just boiled the kettle, so it won't take long."

Angela took them into the lounge. "These are two detectives from Derby, Pete. They want to talk to us about Saturday night."

The man lounging in a recliner chair straightened up and switched off the television. He stood up to meet them and they shook hands. Della introduced them and said, "We're grateful to you both for being so willing to see us. I'm assuming you know what happened on Saturday night?"

Pete reminded Della of a slightly older Sean Bean in a way. He was grey-haired, but his skin was leathery, as if he spent a lot of time outdoors. His face was serious as he answered her.

"You mean young Darren? Yes. Richard called us. Terrible news. That poor young woman, his wife, whatever must she be feeling?"

Angela came in at that point, bringing a tray of mugs of tea which she handed round. "We liked them when they came to view the house, didn't we, Pete?"

"We did, love." Pete took his tea and sipped cautiously, then held onto it.

"Well, at least, I liked the young woman a lot," said Angela, sitting in another armchair.

"Did you have many people who wanted to buy the house?" asked Della.

"Three couples, I think."

"What made you decide to sell to the Holbeaches? Just curious, you know."

"A few things, really. They had no chain. They had no house to sell, and we'd already bought this one, so we wanted a quick sale; they were offering cash. Apparently, they'd come into money, an inheritance or something, I believe. But the clincher was young Amy really, she whispered to me it has always been her dream to live in The Gardens and I found I wanted her to have it, didn't I, Pete?"

"You did, love."

"I feel bad now, though. Her dream has turned into a nightmare."

"Indeed, it has, Mrs Moorcroft."

"Call me Angela, dear. Is your tea alright?"

"Yes, it's great, thank you. So, can you just run us through Saturday evening? I understand you stayed the night after all?"

"That's right, dear. The night was so awful and we heard there'd been an accident on the motorway, so we felt it was best to stay. Louise and Richard have plenty of room. We decided it would be safer to travel in the morning - there's always the threat of black ice."

"What time did you arrive at the Newtons'?"

"Oh, about six, I think, wasn't it, Pete?"

"Yes, love."

"And what time did you leave in the morning?"

"Not sure. It was about eight fifteenish, I think. Is that right, Pete?"

"Yes, it was about that. I didn't really take special note."

"And you saw nothing that morning? Did you see Sarah at all?"

"As a matter of fact, we saw Sarah running down the road with her little dog, but we just waved at her. She didn't wave back, so I think she didn't see us."

"I see. And that was about eight fifteen, you said?"

"Well, it must have been just after. We'd obviously pulled out of the drive and started down the road."

"Right. Yes, of course. And you didn't see or hear anything strange during the evening or night?"

Angela slowly shook her head. "No – no, not a thing. Did you, Pete?"

"Nope. Can't say that I did."

Della stood. "Well, thank you very much and thank you for the tea. It was just what we needed. We'll leave you to enjoy what's left of your programme."

Pete nodded. "Any time, Detective. Don't hesitate to call if there's anything else we can help you with." He turned his attention to the television, switching it on again as they were leaving the room.

"Here's my card," Della said to Angela. "If you remember anything you think may be helpful, call us. Sometimes, when you're not thinking about it, you recall a noise or something that may be just what we need to crack the case. You can call me anytime."

The drive home was slower as they were caught up in tea-time traffic. However, it didn't bother them too much, for they felt they'd be able to finish for the day when they finally arrived.

"Fancy a quick drink before we go home, Ben?" Della asked as they neared Derby.

"Sure. Got anywhere in mind?"

"I thought we could try the Derbyshire," she said, casually. Ben grinned; he understood his partner very well.

"That sounds like a plan. We won't have to go into Derby, it being on the outskirts and conveniently on our side of the city."

"Just what I thought, mate."

In the pub, they sat at a small table quite near a window. Della looked around at the pleasant room which had beams across the ceiling and the bar had matching dark wood tops. Horse brasses decorated the walls, along with pictures. Despite the dark wood, it wasn't depressing. The low wattage lighting enhanced the cosiness of what was actually quite a large room. There were few people in, it being early. Della let herself relax. In some ways, right at this minute, she didn't really care if they picked up any information that night. She didn't mind if they needed to return here.

And indeed, nothing of interest happened, and they conceded defeat, drank up and left.

They both lived in Chaddesden, so Ben dropped Della off at her house and promised to collect her in the morning.

She was thankful to have time for a leisurely bath. Later, Anna was going to come over, and they'd decided to have a meal out. The two women had been friends for quite some time and got together whenever they could.

Anna arrived at eight o'clock, and the pair walked to the local Toby Carvery, as it was only about a ten-minute walk from Della's house.

Having enjoyed their meal, they sat back to chat and relax over their coffee.

"I know we try not to talk shop when we're out, but I can't help wondering how you're getting on with the ghastly mother-in-law?"

"Oh, Del, she really is dreadful! To be frank, I hate leaving Amy in the evenings. I've come straight here from work as I stay with her as long as I can. I know that woman hates me being there, so I take pleasure in making sure I can string it out as long as possible! I'm sure she launches into an attack as soon as I've gone. I can see Amy becoming more and more withdrawn and nervous as the time goes on."

"I think I need to drop by and tell them to go home," commented Della grimly. "I have no authority to do it, but I don't think they'll know that. I'm of the mind that Amy may open up to you if they're not there."

"I agree. She definitely has something on her mind, but she's being forced into silence by that woman. Flip, if I ever get married, I'll make sure I get a man without a mother!"

Della snorted into her coffee. "Now look what you've done!" She hastily mopped up the drops from the table, thankful it hadn't gone onto her clothes. "I – " she stopped, and put her hand up to stop Anna speaking, and put her hand behind her ear to show she was listening to something.

Behind Della was a group of four young men who were joking and laughing as they enjoyed their meal. As they listened, they heard: "I'm surprised nothing has happened there before! Poor bloke. I bet the loving neighbours found someone they couldn't love and decided to bump him off. Old Jim couldn't wait to get away. He said they were a bunch of perverts and he should know, growing up there."

Della's eyes met Anna's. Della turned around and cleared her throat. "Excuse me, but are you talking about the incident in Gladioli Grove, by any chance?"

The speaker, who was sitting diagonally to her, turned. "So, what if I am?" he asked with narrowed eyes. "What business is it of yours?"

Della held up her ID. "I happen to be one of the officers investigating the case. Would you mind telling me what you meant by 'loving neighbours' and who is Jim?"

The young man's face coloured. He cleared his throat; aware his companions had fallen silent and were watching with interest. "Can we talk privately? It's a bit embarrassing, you know."

"Well, it's obvious by what you said that your friends here understood what you meant, so why worry?"

"Um, alright then. Jim was a friend of mine. We went to school together and were mates. His parents live in Gladioli Grove, Mr and Mrs Boothe. I used to know all the kids who lived in the Grove, in fact. There were a few of them, some older, some younger than us. None of them are around now. They couldn't wait to leave; said they were embarrassed about the way their parents behaved."

"Oh? How did they behave? They all seem like pleasant, friendly people."

"Erm, well, they were always pleasant and friendly. But they were even more friendly than usual neighbours, if you get my drift? Privately, their kids called it Groping Grove..." his voice tailed off. Della looked around at the other three pairs of eyes that were looking anywhere but at her or their friend, who was speaking.

"What is your name?"

"Oh! Erm, Jon Matthews."

"Well, Jon, I'd like to thank you. You may have just given us some valuable information. Can you give me your contact details, please? We may need to talk to you again. I'm off duty now and would like to continue enjoying my evening with my friend, as I'm sure you do. But this is my card, in case you think of anything else you feel we need to know."

Della looked around at the group. "I'm asking all of you to please not speak of this to anyone else. It's a serious case and I don't want anyone - and I mean anyone – to hear that there's been any rumours that might warn any possibly guilty party that we may be onto something. If I discover there's been any careless talk from any of you, there may well be serious consequences. Do you understand?" She cast her sternest look around the table and eyed each one until they'd all agreed. Then she took down their names and phone numbers. "Thank you, all. Especially thank you, Jon. Now, please enjoy the rest of your evening and kindly stay off the subject of Gladioli Grove."

She turned around to face her own table and Anna. "Have you finished, Anna? Let's leave these young men to their meal."

Once outside, the two hurried away from the pub until they were some distance from it. Then Anna finally gasped, "Oh my! Groping Grove!" The pair of them laughed and giggled the rest of the way back to Della's house.

Chapter 7

Wednesday

Amy rose tiredly from another disturbed night. She slouched wearily to her bathroom for a shower in the hope it would help. She stood longer than usual, allowing the warmth of the water to soothe her aching body. Her muscles screamed because she was so tense all the time. She was dreading yet another day of having her in-laws around. The woman did nothing all day, expecting to be waited on hand and foot while throwing abuse at Amy, at the police, at Anna and at her unfortunate husband. He largely ignored her, it had to be said. If the situation wasn't so awful, Amy might have found watching the pair of them amusing. But she found it far from amusing, and she just wanted them to go away and leave her alone to get over the shock of Darren's sudden death. She knew she should be relieved she was now free of him, but it was still a shock. Any love she'd had for him had been killed off a while ago and the move here had been the last-ditch attempt to reclaim the marriage. It was a gift from the aunt who had raised her after her mother had died of cancer that had enabled Amy to fulfil her dream of living in The Gardens.

But it seemed the dream had not been within her reach after all. Having to continue living with Darren and his abusive ways had definitely taken the shine off her hopes for the future. As she stood in the shower, she allowed her thoughts to drift to a day when she had an unexpected visitor…

Darren was out yet again, playing golf with Tony, Neville and Brian. A ring came at the door and when she opened it, to her surprise, there stood Philip. He had an expression on his face that gave her the idea he knew he shouldn't be there, but was grimly determined.

"Oh! Hello, Phil. This is unexpected. What can I do for you?" She was a little worried, as she remembered the old saying about having to watch the quiet ones. She hoped he wasn't going to take advantage of her or anything.

"Amy, I haven't come to stop. I just wanted to say…" he hesitated. "I'm sorry, I shouldn't have come." He turned to go.

"Don't go! Please, why don't you come in? I've just made tea. Would you like some?"

He grinned then, which changed his entire face. He reminded her of a little boy. "Yes, if you're sure? Do you have time?"

"All the time in the world," she grimaced. "It'll be nice to have some company for a while. Come through to the kitchen."

He followed her through and watched her as she went to the kettle. "I hope you don't mind a tea bag in a mug?"

"No, of course not. Can I help you?"

Amy put a tray on the worktop and put the mugs of tea on it, then she took a packet of biscuits out of the cupboard and put them on the tray.

"Thank you. Could you bring the tray for me, please?"

He picked it up and followed her into a pleasant room that overlooked the garden. It had a squashy sofa with a brightly coloured throw in all colours draped on it, and a couple of armchairs that didn't match but looked comfortable. A coffee table sat in the middle of the room and next to one chair there was a big, round wicker basket with a lid.

"Please put it on the coffee table and sit where you like," Amy said and watched while he did as he was told, setting the tray down carefully. He sat gingerly on the sofa near to where he'd put the tray. She sat in the chair nearest to the end where he sat. He looked around at the room.

"I like this room," he said. "It's…homely."

"It's my favourite room in the house," Amy replied. "It's where I do my embroidery and other things and where I like to read. Sometimes, if I feel like it, I paint in here too, although my studio is upstairs."

"You're an artist?"

Amy gave a small laugh. "Well, I try! I'm not much of one, as Darren will tell you, but I enjoy it and it's something to keep me busy when I'm here alone."

"Are those yours?" Phil nodded at some watercolours on the wall.

"Yes."

Phil stood and went over to look at them more closely. Amy watched nervously. "They're not very good, I know, but I like them and I think they make the room more cheerful."

He turned to look at her. "Well, I think they're excellent. I know a bit about art. My mother was an artist, and I have a friend who runs a gallery. She would be impressed with these. I don't know why Darren says they're no good. He obviously knows nothing about art."

"Really?" Amy felt the colour rise up her neck and into her cheeks. "Oh!"

Phil returned to his seat and picked up his mug. "Actually, that brings me to why I'm here." He took a sip of his tea and then set the mug down. "Although I now don't think I have the right to say what I'd come to say."

Amy was curious now. "Please, go on."

"It's just that I can't stand the way Darren puts you down in front of everyone. I know you've seen Sarah laughing, and I'm sorry about that. I wanted you to know that I don't feel it's anything to laugh at. I'm sorry if you don't like me criticising your husband, but I want you to know how I feel about it."

Amy felt the colour rising to her face again, and to her embarrassment, tears welled. Phil noticed and reached out to her. "I'm sorry." At the touch of his fingers on her hand, she felt tingles in her arm and her eyes widened. 'Act normally,' she told herself. 'He won't notice'.

"I'm alright, don't worry. I agree with you, he shouldn't do it. But I'm used to it. It's nice of you to tell me what you feel. We're still so new here and we don't know everyone as well as you obviously know them, even though it's been nine months since we came. It's nice to feel we're wanted by you all and it's good of the other men to take Darren golfing and things. It's really helped."

She waved her hand at the biscuits. "Help yourself, please."

He took one and sat back.

"He's always been like that? Even when you were first married?"

"It didn't take long," she said sadly. "I hoped moving here would help make things better."

"And has it?"

"Seems to. He doesn't hit me now. I think he doesn't want all of you to see it."

"He hit you?" Amy looked at his shocked expression and smiled slightly.

"Oh yes, after he'd been with one of his women, he'd tell me I'd never measure up and would punish me for it."

"One of his women?"

"He's always had affairs."

"Why haven't you left him?"

"I - I don't know. He's always sorry afterwards and is nice to me for a while, and does everything to convince me he'd changed. So, I stay. But I don't know why I'm still with him. I don't like him anymore. I wish he'd go away, but he won't."

"Why won't he?"

"He calls me his 'safety net'. And for another thing, I own everything. He lives on my money. If he left, he'd have no money, no income, no home."

"I see. I dislike the man even more! Why does he call you his safety net?"

"Oh, it's so he can have fun with women, but he can't have a permanent relationship because of me. His poor little wife that he has to take care of because I depend on him for everything," she said bitterly. "If I left him now, I wouldn't be able to sell the house because he'd claim sitting tenancy and sue me for at least half the money. I'm not going to give him the satisfaction. Why should he have it? Isn't it enough that he lives off me? I always dreamed of living here, in a house in this area, and I've finally achieved it. I'm not leaving a house I love to get away from him."

Phil nodded slowly. "I suppose I can understand that," he said. "But it still seems like a high price to pay."

"In some ways, it is. But coming here, I've found good friends in Ruth and Liz and I love Bill too. The others are nice to me, except –." Amy suddenly realised she was going to say Sarah and stopped.

"Except Sarah," finished Phil. He stood. "Don't worry, I'm well aware of it. But you're not the only one, believe me. Sarah loves the men," he said, bitterly, "but she's not so nice to the women. If I were you, Amy, I'd think seriously about things. Do you really want to live the rest of your life with Darren? Is a house, even a beautiful house like this one, really worth it?"

He'd touched her arm lightly as he went to leave and she felt again the frisson of electricity inside.

"Just remember, Amy, you're not alone. If you need any of us, just call." He'd given her a last smile and was gone.

She'd watched him walk down the drive, and berated herself. 'He's just a nice man who is concerned about you because your husband is a bully. He doesn't fancy you.'

In some of her lonely hours, she allowed herself to think of him, his gentle eyes and his kind smile, and wished with all her heart she'd met him years ago when they were both free. But of course, he didn't want her! Why would he, when he had a beautiful wife like Sarah? She mustn't let him know how she felt about him; she had to make sure no one ever knew.

Amy didn't allow herself to dream about Philip often. She kept her resolve to stay away from him, making nothing obvious. It was easy; when they had all-neighbour gatherings, she stayed around Ruth or Liz and Bill. But occasionally, she'd catch him looking at her. She'd smile and drop her eyes, or look elsewhere. She always knew when he was in the room. It was as if there was some kind of telepathy that told her when he came in or was nearby. But only surface conversation passed between them and he never touched her again. She couldn't help her heart yearning, just a bit. But she reasoned it was because of her situation, because she really didn't know him, did she? It was obvious Sarah ruled the roost; she ordered, and he jumped to it. In fact, all the men would do her bidding, fetching her drinks or food, or partnering her in games of cards or whatever she wanted. Except Bill, who would smile gently at her, pat her arm, and return to Liz.

Now, thinking back over the last few months, she had a light-bulb moment. This was *her* house; it was her aunt's money that had bought it and it had been a condition it should be entirely in her name. Darren had had the choice to take it or go. He couldn't resist the chance to live in such a grand place and so he'd went with it.

It was *her* house - and her husband was gone. She didn't have to put up with his mother anymore! She owed them nothing at all. They had no right to come to her house and throw their weight around. Stepping from the shower, Amy dried herself vigorously, and she put on her favourite jeans, a bit tatty but comfortable, and her most baggy jumper over her t-shirt. She dried her hair and tied it back in a messy knot, securing it with a large slide. Then, she stood in front of her full-length mirror and gave herself a pep-talk. "You can do this, my girl! This is your house and they have no right to be here. You didn't invite them. You are free of their cheating son. I don't know who killed him, but whoever it was, they've done you a favour. Go do it."

She ran lightly down the stairs and in the kitchen switched on the kettle. She made herself an omelette with cheese and ham, poured herself a mug of tea, and sat at her kitchen table with her book propped in front of her. She was still reading when Darren's parents came into the kitchen.

"Where's our breakfast?" demanded Brenda. Amy looked up from her book.

"The cooker is there. Help yourself. If you want toast, you can see the toaster there near the cooker. The kettle needs filling." Amy's eyes returned to her book.

"Well! The least you can do is make breakfast."

"Why? I've had mine, as you can see. You've spent two days here being waited on hand and foot. Well, no more. If you want to eat, get it yourself. The bread's in the bread bin, and there's fresh food in the fridge, jams and spreads are in the cupboard. Help yourself."

While his wife stood with her hands on her hips, Douglas went towards the kettle and filled it at the tap.

"Douglas! What do you think you're doing?"

"Making tea, Brenda. I'd like one, even if you don't. It's very easy to make. You boil the kettle and pour the hot water over a tea bag."

"I know how to make tea, you stupid man! But she should do it. We are her guests, after all."

Amy looked up from her book. "That's where you are wrong, Brenda."

"What?"

"I said, that's where you're wrong. You are not my guests. I didn't invite you here. You brought yourselves."

"But this is our son's house, and we have lost our son."

"And I have lost my husband. Not that he was much of a husband."

"What do you mean? He was a good man."

"No! He was not a good man! He mistreated me, he often put me down in front of others. But worse than that, he was a controller and an abuser and now I've finally realised where he got it from - he's just like you, his mother!

He was a serial adulterer, too. He had no respect for marriage at all, no respect for the promises he made to me. And I put up with it. All these years, I stuck by him because I believed in the sanctity of marriage! I was a fool; I should have looked more closely at you and Doug - look what you've done to him. I don't know how he has stuck with you for so many years. Eight years with Darren and I'd had enough!"

Brenda stared at Amy; her mouth open. Then, "You killed him! You killed my son!"

"No! I did not kill him! I don't know who killed him, but whoever it was, I'm grateful to them. Because I've been set free. I never once betrayed my husband, but he betrayed me repeatedly. And you're to blame for that. You are entirely to blame for everything your darling son did, because you would never hear a word against him. You created a monster - and I was unfortunate enough not to see it until after I'd married him."

Brenda sat down with a thump, still staring at Amy as she carried on talking.

"So, as I've said already, you invited yourself here and I've waited on you hand and foot for two days and put up with your constant bullying. But no more. I don't owe you anything. I'm sorry for you that your son is dead, but now I'd like you to leave."

"Leave?" whispered Brenda.

Amy stood and gathered her breakfast crocks. She walked over to the sink and put them down on the draining board.

"Yes, that's what I said. You are not welcome in this house - which, incidentally, is *my* house, completely in my name, because it was a gift from my aunt, so you will have no claim on it at all. So, you can get yourselves some breakfast, have what you want, I don't care, but then you are to pack your things and leave. And I don't want to see you again until the funeral and after that, as far as I'm concerned, I'll be happy never to see you again." Amy turned to Doug, who was quietly standing where he was, sipping his tea. "I'm sorry, Doug, I've nothing against you. You've always treated me with kindness, and if you're ever in need of my help for anything, you only have to ask. But not with her."

"Well done, lass," Doug said, quietly.

Amy gave him a small smile. "I'll leave you to it then."

"Where are you going?" asked Brenda.

"Somewhere you're not. And when I return, you'd better be ready to go."

Amy went to leave the kitchen and stopped momentarily when she finally noticed Anna watching in the doorway, grinning at her. She mimed clapping. Amy grinned back, happily. The pair turned around and headed for Amy's bedroom, where they could talk in private.

"Well done, girl! I'm proud of you!" Anna exclaimed once the door was firmly shut. "How did that happen?"

"I had another awful night, dreading more days with her, and as I stood in the shower, I realised I no longer had to be polite to his mother because Darren was gone. I'd got so in the habit of putting up with all the rubbish thrown at me from Darren and his mother I completely forgot about the fact I don't have to do that anymore, especially as this house is mine and I didn't invite them here. I'm sorry about Doug, because he's a nice man really and I'm fond of Darren's sister. But I can't stand Brenda. So, I found the bottle to tell them. Heck, I've been treated like a skivvy in my own house by that woman and I suddenly thought 'why should I?' I owe her nothing at all, except maybe my sympathy because she's lost her son, but she's never shown me an ounce of consideration."

"Well, I'm proud of you. And I'm glad you've done it because Della and I were plotting how we could get them to leave."

"Seems I've saved you a job, then. I feel lighter already and they haven't gone yet! Phew! Perhaps if I'd taken a stronger line with Darren, he wouldn't have walked all over me. But it's too late now."

"Yes. But it's good that you've had that realisation. Now, I'd better call Della and let her know there's no need to put our plan into action."

Amy went through to Darren's dressing room and picked up a box which had his bits of jewellery in. Then she went to his study and took Darren's golfing cups he'd won and some framed photos of him from a glass cabinet, selected some of his books and put them all in a box and carried them to the hall.

Then she went to sit in her lounge with Anna and they chatted quietly. They knew the Holbeach parents were upstairs gathering their things. Soon, they heard the pair in the hallway and went out to see them. She picked up the box and held it out to Douglas.

"I thought you'd like some of Darren's things, his trophies and so on," she said.

"Thank you, lass," he replied and smiled sadly at her. At that moment, she almost weakened, then noticed him shake his head slightly. She kissed him on his cheek. "Goodbye, Dad," she whispered.

"Come, Douglas!" Brenda held her head high and marched out without another word. He followed, laden with the box and their case. Not long after, Amy and Anna watched while the car crept down the drive. As it disappeared onto the road, the two hugged each other in relief.

"Let's celebrate!" laughed Amy.

"What do you have in mind?"

"Let's go to Ruth's. She's bound to have baked something nice, and we'll invite Liz and Bill to celebrate with us."

Amy was right; when they arrived, they were met by enticing smells and Ruth was putting the finishing touches to a cream sponge. When she heard Amy's news, she screamed, hugged Amy and the two jumped up and down together, while Anna looked on, smiling. Not long later, Liz and Bill arrived to hear the news, and it was a happy little group of people who sat down around Ruth's kitchen table to demolish that cream sponge.

*****

"I'm so glad Brenda and Douglas have gone, Anna. I've been thinking about this a lot since Darren was killed."

Anna and Amy were back in Amy's house after the cake celebration. They were relaxing together in the garden room, which overlooked the garden at the rear of the house. Amy loved this room; it was her favourite of the downstairs rooms. It was cosy but also very light. It enabled her to do her handicrafts in mostly natural light, so essential to match colours in her embroidery. She painted also, and over this room she had her studio. She fluctuated between her needlework and the painting.

"What's that?"

Amy was silent for a while. "You know, I was desperate for a house here in this area. I hoped it would make things right with Darren and deep down inside I also hoped that, having a house with lots of room, he'd let me have a family. But it didn't work out the way I wanted; he dug his heels in about me having children and he spent most of his time either in his study, out on the golf course or out with some of our neighbours. Now I'm alone, and after what happened, I don't think I want to stay here. I'm going to look for somewhere else to live, somewhere smaller and friendlier. Although I've done my best with this house, I feel like a marble rattling around in a tin. And I'll probably have to look for some work. I don't need to work. My Aunt Jane has left me well off, but I can't just waste my life away, can I?"

She looked at Anna, who smiled at her. "There's always plenty of volunteer work you could do if you don't need to work, you know. This is a lovely house; give yourself time to get over the shock."

Amy nodded. "It takes time to sell a house and find another anyway, but I shall start looking. It will give me purpose and help take my mind off things."

"Won't you be sorry to leave your neighbours? They're all so friendly. I'm sure they'll look after you."

"Frankly, they're another reason I need to get away from here. I don't fit in with - erm, well, now I'm single, I don't fit in and it won't be the way they want it..." Amy let her voice fade, realising she'd probably said too much.

"I'm not following you...?"

"Oh heck! I've gone and put my foot in it, haven't I?"

Anna shook her head slightly, as if in confusion. "Is there something you need to talk with Della about?"

Amy sat, her head bowed, thinking. She was aware that Anna was watching her carefully. Should she tell them? She'd never liked it, but was it relevant? What if it was? Should she really hold back?"

All at once, she decided. She drew in a breath.

"As a matter of fact, there is something I haven't told Della, but I want to tell you now. I should have said something before, but Brenda and Douglas arrived and, well, I didn't want to say anything in front of them."

"What is it?"

"I don't like letting my neighbours down, as they've been very kind to me. But I've been thinking about something over and over and feel it may be important."

"Tell you what, I'll call Della and get her to come over, then you can tell us both together. That suit you?"

Amy nodded. "Yes, I suppose that would be best. I'll wait until Della comes."

Chapter 8

Della and Ben arrived at Amy's in answer to Anna's call. After their discovery of the previous night, Della had intended to push Amy for more information, but hadn't wanted to ask with the in-laws there. Now, however, it was a different matter. Frankly, she hadn't expected it to come so promptly, but obviously the great relief Amy experienced at ejecting her in-laws had snowballed rapidly into a desire to hasten the investigation along if she could.

Anna greeted them at the door and brought them into the garden room where Amy sat nervously waiting. She stood up when they entered the room and looked at them with a worried expression.

"I'm sorry. I know I should have told you before, but I was upset and shocked. I was worried about getting others into trouble. I - I know I asked to see you, but now I'm not sure I want to tell you..." her voice faded away, and she sat abruptly and covered her face with her hands.

Della put her hand on the young woman's shoulder. "Don't worry, Amy, take your time. I know things were difficult with Darren, but we need to find out who killed him. Surely no one deserves to die like that?"

Amy nodded slowly. "You're right. It was a horrible thing to do to him. I don't know where to start."

"How about if we get Ben to make us all some tea? Then we can relax and hear what you have to tell us."

"Kettle's already boiled," said Anna. "Shall I help you, Ben?"

The pair left the room and Della chatted quietly to Amy, helping her to relax. "Amy, the best place to start is at the beginning. Start wherever you feel comfortable."

"Well, I think the beginning is when we moved here. As I've said before, I had always wanted to live in The Gardens somewhere. I was thrilled when I heard this house was up for sale. People move in on this estate and simply stay, so they don't come on the market all that often. My Aunt Jane, who raised me when my mother died, was very rich, and she gave me the money to buy this house, provided it was solely my name on the deeds. I think she must have known what Darren was really like. Anyway, things were not good between me and Darren, and I gave him the choice of coming with me, or making the break. He couldn't resist the chance of living in such an elite area, giving him the chance to mix with some well-off people on the golf course and to join The Gardens' Golf Club. I think the couple selling the house took to me, especially the lady, and wanted me to have it, despite there being others after it. I was thrilled."

At that point, Anna and Ben returned to the room with four mugs of tea, and Amy took hers and sat nursing it while she talked. Ben quietly sat to one side out of Amy's direct gaze, took out his notebook and poised, ready to write.

Amy's Story

Amy's heart lifted as she opened the door to number ten, Gladioli Grove. She had fallen in love with the house as soon as she saw it.

Now, as she stepped over the threshold into the empty house, it seemed as though the house was welcoming her.

"I hope the removals will be here soon. I'm dying for a coffee."

The sound of Darren's voice behind her broke Amy's communion with the house. She turned for a moment, looked at him and turned back, walking further into the house and down the hall into the kitchen. As she thought, there was a coffee machine there, and the previous owners had left them all they needed to make a drink. Amy smiled and whispered a 'thank you' to Angela Moorcroft, for she knew it would have been her. She set about putting the beans into the machine and turned it on. Darren went straight upstairs, and she heard his footsteps as he walked around up there.

"Amy! Come up here, will you?" She heard Darren's voice calling her. She went up to see what he wanted.

"I've chosen where my space is going to be," he told her. "I'm going to have this room as my changing room, with the ensuite bathroom.

"Well, I had thought of that being mine," replied Amy, her nerves prickling.

"What do you need a dressing room for?" he laughed. "Look at you! Is it any wonder I find other women more attractive?"

Amy narrowed her eyes. "Have the dressing room. As you say, what do I need it for? I'll have the bedroom with the walk-in wardrobe instead."

They heard the doorbell ring. "Hopefully, that'll be the removal van," commented Amy, and ran lightly down the stairs to open the door.

"About bloody time!" growled Darren when he saw the man at the door.

"Sorry, mate, we got held up on the A-52. It's crazy time out there."

"Yes, well, you'd better get on with it!" snapped Darren and walked away. The man looked at Amy, who shrugged and smiled in sympathy.

The men were great. They unloaded their household supplies, putting them in the right rooms for Amy, who directed proceedings. Darren didn't help at all, but took his coffee out to the back garden, where he found a bench to sit on, and eventually he turned sideways so he could put his feet up.

Amy wasn't sure if she was cross or relieved. It annoyed her he never lifted a finger, but she was sure it all went smoothly because he wasn't there.

Halfway through the proceedings, a woman arrived at the door, bearing a large cake.

"To welcome you and to keep the men going," she laughed. "I'm Ruth from two doors down. I know you're really busy now, but I'm looking forward to getting to know you."

"Thank you. I'm Amy."

"Hi, Amy. I'll let you get on now, but I'll see you soon. Have fun! Let me know if you need a hand with anything once the men have gone."

Amy smiled widely. "I will. Thank you so much."

She watched Ruth hurry back down the drive, then turned to the men. "Coffee and cake in the kitchen, lads."

They sat round the table and Amy dished out drinks and put slices of cake on paper napkins supplied by Ruth. The men were friendly and chatted easily with Amy.

"Where's your man, Mrs Holbeach?" asked one of them.

Amy shrugged. "Not a clue. He's gone off somewhere. Easier for us, eh?"

They grinned at each other and got on with the business of eating the cake and drinking. Amy saved a slice of cake for Darren, although really, she didn't see why she should, but she didn't want to have a row today.

When the men had gone and Amy toured the house, she had to admit their pieces of furniture didn't do the house justice; she needed to do some shopping. Not long after the men left, Darren wondered in from the garden, complaining he was hungry.

"Haven't you cooked dinner yet?"

"Of course, I haven't cooked dinner! The removal men have only just left, and I have all the unpacking to do. There's a piece of cake there you can have and then you can order in a takeaway for us. I won't be cooking anything today."

"Oh, I suppose you're right. You'd better get on then." He took the plate with the piece of cake and drifted back into the garden. Amy gritted her teeth and opened the nearest box, marked 'kitchen'.

*****

Over the next few weeks, Amy and Darren came to know all their neighbours in Gladioli Grove. It seemed they were all great friends and gathered together regularly. And they were determined that Amy and Darren should be part of their happy band. They were invited to barbecues, croquet matches, swim parties, wine and cheese evenings and many things that Amy never dreamed she'd ever be part of. Darren, of course, loved it and lapped up all the attention he received. The men invited him to play golf, and the women made a fuss of him.

Amy immediately took to Elizabeth and William - or Liz and Bill, as everyone called them. They were a couple in their late sixties and seemed to be the 'parents' of the Grove. Bill gently instructed Amy in the techniques of playing croquet, holding her hands on the mallet and demonstrating how to give it a good hard slam to make it go through the hoop and hopefully knock her opponent's ball out of the way, amid much laughter and good-natured teasing from the others when things didn't go the way it should. The lawn at number nine was perfect for the game. Bill nurtured the lawn, which was mowed to perfection and rollered to keep it flat. Liz tended the flower beds.

The Davenports at number eight had a swimming pool in their garden and so did the Hornbys at number three and the Cuthbertsons at number six. Amy and Ruth Cuthbertson became good friends and spent quite a lot of time together in Ruth's kitchen, baking and chatting. Anthony often took Darren out to his golf club, together with Neville and Brian, from number one.

Chris and Brian, at number one, were a quiet couple. He was a solicitor and was tall and thin, but was pleasant to talk to. She was chattier, with a pleasant smile. She spent a lot of time knitting for her grandchildren, but they also often entertained Brian's partners.

Sarah and Philip Sutton were younger, in their early thirties, and were childless. She was petite and blonde and seemed to spend her days not doing much at all. When the neighbours were all together, Sarah fluttered around, flirting with the men. Philip was pleasant, not shy exactly, but was inclined to be reserved. He would stand and talk with someone while eyeing his wife being over-friendly with one or more of the men.

Next to the Suttons, at number three, Amanda and Matthew Hornby lived. Amy didn't see so much of them as they both worked. Amanda was the receptionist in a high-quality beauty salon and Matthew owned several car sales outlets. He was inclined to be a little full of himself and the way he flirted around with Sarah made Amy feel he thought of himself as a kind of stud, while Amanda remained aloof and didn't appear to notice. Still, they were friendly enough when the neighbours had their gatherings.

Louise and Richard Newton, a couple in their late forties, at number seven, seemed to be just a normal couple. She had dark hair and wore glasses and her garden was her great passion. Richard was into cricket and played for a club not far away.

On the same side of the road as Amy's house, at number two, were Veronica and David Boothe. Veronica reminded Amy somewhat of an Amazon; she was sturdy and muscular, because of her many hours spent every week in a gym and her flaming red hair which curled down her back added to the effect. David was equally muscular with fair features, but had a shaved head and a blonde beard.

Last, there were Emily and George Taunton in number four. Emily was an attractive woman in her thirties, with long brown hair carefully styled and a trim figure. George owned a jewellery shop and was also a goldsmith. Emily sometimes helped in the shop, but otherwise she didn't work. Amy got on well with them and always showed an interest when they talked about the business and the intricacies of making the pieces they sold.

Amy particularly like Ruth's husband, Anthony. Like Ruth, he was down-to-earth and friendly and was always happy to let Ruth invite Amy over for company.

The ten couples in the Grove were all different, even though they had money, just as their houses were all different. But somehow, as a group, they gelled well.

That first summer as newbies in The Grove was a delight to Amy as the other nine couples drew the newcomers into their warm embrace. However, much as she liked all of them and especially Ruth, Liz and Bill, sometimes Amy had a strange feeling that things were not as they appeared. Maybe it was embarrassment when Darren belittled her in front of them, which he did often, and she'd catch various expressions on their faces, which would range from total disgust on Liz, Bill's, Tony's and Ruth's faces to amusement on Sarah's and other reactions in between. It seemed some of the men upheld Darren's remarks. Others, such as Philip, George, and Richard, carefully tried to remain neutral.

Chapter 9

Life carried on pretty much the same. Amy had to admit that the one good thing about having such a large house was she and Darren could both live there, but more or less live separately. If she wanted, she'd lock her bedroom door, and he'd have to sleep in his own room. She didn't see why she should allow him near her when she knew he was having sex with someone else.

Although she loved the house, she wasn't happy. Often, she would dream of living in a tiny cottage in the country, far away from Darren. She'd have a dog, perhaps, and maybe a studio in the garden where she could paint to her heart's content and she'd have lots of friends in the village where she would take her dog for long walks.

Amy found being with all her neighbours was quite entertaining in a people-watching sort of way. She came to know their characteristics and noticed how they reacted to each other.

She had eventually confided in Liz about Darren, who was not at all shocked. She nodded her head.

"I could see it, my dear. But I couldn't help you until you felt you could confide in me."

"How can you help me?" asked Amy. "I'm not sure there's anything that can be done. I know he's had several women over the winter. He's only stopped hitting me about since we've been here. I've had my cheeks bruised and my eyes blackened a few times over the years. He delights in hurting me, but he doesn't want you or anyone here to see what he does. So, he's had to hold it in sometimes, although he's hurt me in ways I can't talk about."

"What a bloody awful man! Whatever did you see in him, my dear?"

"He can be charming, as you've seen for yourself. He made me feel as though I was the most important thing in the world to him. Once I'd married him, I realised it was my money that was the most important thing to him. He could be a kept man, and I was too soft. I let him for a quiet life, but I wish I'd put my foot down as soon as I'd twigged. But I've put up with this for over eight years. I'm trapped, Liz, for the reasons I explained. I love this house of mine; it's something I always wanted. Why should I let him have it?"

"Too right, my dear. I'll try to think of something."

But Amy was sure there was nothing Liz or anyone could do to help her. Summer was here again and living in the Grove made life bearable, at least, outside her home. The garden parties had resumed, the barbeques and croquet games, tennis and other gatherings meant Amy and Darren were kept entertained but separate. She noted Darren hung around Sarah much of the time and she played up to him, even sometimes wrapping herself around him. Amy could see he enjoyed it and found she didn't care all that much. It only bothered her about Philip and how he might feel to see his wife cavorting so openly with another man. However, if he was concerned, he hid it well and would join the men who would be dealing with the barbeque or would casually chat with some of the other women.

It was towards the end of August when Liz came to see Amy with a proposal.

"The other members of The Grove have all agreed to this, Amy. I know it's an unusual proposition, but we're hoping if we carry it out, it will encourage Darren to stop straying."

Amy was gobsmacked; she shook her head and wondered if she'd misheard. "You have to be kidding me, Liz! Surely, that's not something Ruth, or Celia or Chris, or, or - you would be willing to do? With Darren?"

"Well, I wouldn't, but some of the other women would. It's something we always used to do and did for a good number of years; it relieved the boredom. And it's why we're all such close friends."

"It certainly explains the closeness." Amy's head reeled. Did Philip take part in this crazy behaviour?

"We had stopped, but the girls will do it again if it will help you. There would be conditions, of course."

"What conditions?"

"He would have to promise he wouldn't go with anyone outside The Grove; we don't want any of the girls getting anything nasty. It can only be at certain times. He can't do it whenever he wanted."

"And what about their husbands? Do they go out or something? How is it arranged? Will Darren choose who he goes to?"

"Goodness me, no! We have a certain system and he'll be told where he is to go on a particular night. We'll all take part, but when the men come to me, they know they'll be playing chess. And Bill is happy to sit and watch television."

"Are you telling me I'm supposed to entertain someone else's husband while my husband is playing with one of the other women?" Amy's voice went high as she stood up abruptly. "Liz, you're out of your mind! I can't do that! I've kept my marriage vows even if he hasn't kept his! How can I have sex with - with Richard, or George, or Brian or…?" Her voice faded away, and she descended quickly onto her chair again, and she sat, stupefied by the thought. She looked wild-eyed at Liz, and her heart thumped.

Liz laughed. "Don't worry, my dear! I'm sure the men will understand completely that you're not into it. They'll be happy to be given a drink and watch a film or something. They're good blokes, every one of them, and I think it's good of them to have agreed to do this to help you. None of them will expect anything from you. They all know you're a good girl and respect you for it. They don't respect Darren, though; they don't like the way he treats you and they want to help you. Their wives will have ways of making Darren see what he's doing to you is wrong." Liz stood. "I'll go now, but please think about it. This may be the way to stop Darren in his tracks. He'll get the excitement he craves, but he'll be kept under control."

Amy remained where she was and Liz quietly put her mug in the sink and let herself out of the house.

When Darren returned later that evening, after being out with some of the other men, he could hardly contain himself.

"There's you with all your prissy ways and you only went and bought a house in a street full of swingers!" he crowed. He could barely stand for laughing, especially when he saw her horrified expression.

"They've told you?" she said. "I thought they'd wait for me to decide."

"Well, they didn't. And I've already agreed. I can't wait to get my hands on some of those other women - Roni and Sarah are seriously hot. And the men assured me they all have their 'specialities'. What a lark! Who would have imagined Liz and Celia getting up to such things? Ooo, Celia and Louise - they're such stuck-up bitches, I can't wait to give them a good going over - they'll find out what a real man can do! And some of the lads can teach you a thing or two - it'll make life more interesting. Having sex with you is like doing it with a corpse for all the effort you put in. Perhaps that pale nerd of a husband of Sarah's has some interesting tricks to show you. There must be something about him that keeps her happily with him."

His description of Philip angered her, but she held it in, as she always did with Darren, knowing it would cost her if she didn't.

"But I can't have sex with any of them. I can't do it, Darren! Oh!" she exclaimed, as he dealt her a backhander around the face, and shrank back. He put his hand to her throat, and she staggered back until she was against the hall table.

He put his face close to hers and spoke through gritted teeth. "You will do as I say! We're going to do this, do you understand? And if any of the blokes complain to me you're not playing the game, you'll regret you were ever born. Get it?" He shoved her harder. She managed a hint of a nod, and he gave her a last shove and let her go. But before she could get away, he grabbed her, tore her clothes off, brutally raped her and walked off, leaving her bruised and shivering on the hall floor.

Eventually, she pulled the remains of her clothes around her and staggered upstairs to her bedroom. She was afraid he'd be in there, in her bed, but thankfully, he wasn't. She locked the door, and it wasn't long before she sank her poor body into a warm bath, where she lay, the tears rolling down her cheeks. Sometimes she'd thought she couldn't hate him more, but now she knew she could. She wished she were dead, or he was.

*****

Amy's narration faltered and stopped. There was silence in the room for a couple of minutes.

"So, what are you telling us, Amy?" asked Della, eventually. "Are you saying you killed Darren?"

"No! I might have wished him dead, but I didn't kill him. How could I? He's much stronger than me. How could I overpower him? Or get him into that field?"

"Perhaps you had help?"

"No, I didn't. Who would help me do such a thing?"

"So, you wanted me to know about the wife-swapping?"

Amy lowered her head and nodded. "I feel awful telling on Liz and the others, but I thought you should know. It's probably why no one saw what happened that night. They were all - busy."

"So, you think it likely they weren't where they said they were that evening?"

"No, they probably weren't. Although I don't really know how it will help the investigation."

"So, Bill didn't really come round to check on you because Liz had sent him? It was his turn to come here?"

"Yes." The reply was barely a whisper.

"You had to join in because Darren made it clear you must?"

Amy didn't speak that time, just nodded, still looking at her lap.

"So, you'd had previous visits from some of the other men? Was it a regular night each month?"

"Yes. It was always the second Saturday of the month. It began in September, so before Bill, I had four others come. But I didn't do anything. I baked cakes and gave them a special hot chocolate, piled with cream and marshmallows and we watched a film. I told them I couldn't have sex with them and I was very lucky because they were all very understanding and seemed quite happy just to sit and chat, eat cake and watch a film. In fact, most of them were relieved, I think."

Della nodded. "Right, I think we're done here for now. You've done the right thing, Amy. Although you've admitted you wanted him to go away, we still have to discover who killed him. We can't let folks get away with murder, no matter how despicable the victim was. I wish you'd told us about this before. It might have saved us a bit of time. Pity your neighbours may have lied about where they were. It means we have to see them all again. Still, better late than never."

She patted the young woman on the shoulder and turned to leave, with the ever-faithful Ben following. Once outside, she and Ben looked at each other and shrugged. "Right. Round the neighbours we go again, Ben, and they'd better tell us the truth this time, or I'll be throwing the book at them for wasting police time."

*****

When the detectives had left, Amy allowed her thoughts to return to that time after Darren had attacked her.

Amy hadn't gone out of the house for the next few days. She'd stayed indoors, nursing her hurt body. She didn't want anyone to see the livid bruising on her face where he'd hit her. She felt like running away, but where would she go? She had nowhere and no family or friends to run to. She also struggled to come to terms with the fact that all her neighbours, including Ruth, were swingers. She just couldn't believe it. Still, what did she know? She'd led a sheltered life until she met Darren. Her Aunt Lucy was a single lady and much older than Amy's mother had been.

On the third day after Darren had hit her, the doorbell rang. Amy's head shot up from the book she was reading in the garden room. She hadn't been able to paint since that day and could barely concentrate on the book, either. She wasn't going to answer it, but whoever was there rang the bell over and over. Her visitor was determined. She sighed; it was obvious she wouldn't get any peace until she opened the door. She opened it just a crack and peered around. It was Liz and Ruth together.

"Let us in, my dear."

"I'm busy, sorry."

"No, you're not. We were worried because we haven't seen you for a couple of days and you didn't come over for croquet yesterday. Bill is missing you. Come on, open the door."

"We've brought cake," sang Ruth's voice. Although it hurt, Amy smiled. Cake was Ruth's cure-all for every ailment. She opened the door so they could come in and walked away quickly. They shut the door behind them and followed her into the kitchen. By the time they walked into the room, Amy was filling the kettle. She kept her back to them as she said, "Sit down, girls. Would you like tea or coffee?"

Still with her back to them, Amy tried to pull her hair forward to cover her bruised cheek. Then she busied herself making the tea. The other two were trying to make conversation, but she kept her answers to a minimum. She didn't want to talk, didn't really want them there. She wished they'd go away.

She stiffened when an arm came around her waist, and she was pulled into a gentle sideways hug.

"Come on, love," Liz said, and guided her to a chair. She softly pushed Amy's hair back and ran a finger lightly down the bruised cheek as Amy flinched. "Don't tell us you walked into a door," she said. "He did it, didn't he?"

Amy nodded.

"I'm sorry, pet. It's my fault, isn't it? This is about the proposal I made to you, isn't it?"

Amy nodded again, and the tears ran down her cheeks. "I told him I couldn't do it. I - I'm sure all your men are lovely, but I just can't have sex with them."

"We understand, don't we, Ruth?"

"Yes, we do. You don't have to do anything you don't want, Amy. They won't expect it, honestly."

"And how can you think of having to have sex with Darren?"

"I'd do it for you, because you're my friend." Ruth reached out to clasp Amy's hand. "We wanted to do something for you, to stop Darren having affairs. And he only gets to be with each of us once a year."

"Quite honestly, I'd rather him have affairs than know he's having sex with my friends. It seems worse, somehow."

"I never thought of it that way. I have always felt that it made things safer, knowing we were keeping it between us in The Grove. I'd rather know my Tony was associating with someone here and it would never be serious than if he went with someone else. It's only sex, it's exciting to have a bit of variety and it's improved our marriage. We all feel like that."

Amy was astonished.

"And none of our husbands have ever treated us the way Darren treats you." Liz took up the conversation. "Did he do anything else? Has he hurt you anywhere else?"

Amy looked down, suddenly ashamed and feeling dirty. "He - he tore my clothes and raped me in the hallway. He doesn't love me at all, he just uses violence to make me do what he wants."

The other two women looked at each other and they both put their arms around Amy as she cried.

"Honestly, I could kill that man," said Liz.

"And I'd help you," agreed Ruth.

Amy's thoughts centred around those two statements. Was Darren's death anything to do with Liz and Ruth? No. One thing was for sure. There was no way she was going to tell the police what they'd said. Amy couldn't believe that at all. However much they wanted to help her, they wouldn't go that far – would they?

She allowed her thoughts to go to the first night she had her first male visitor. Darren had gone out, whistling happily. She was so nervous - who would come? She'd busied herself that afternoon making muffins in an effort to keep her fear under control. She'd had a shower and made sure she was wearing clean underwear, just in case. But she sincerely hoped it wouldn't come to that.

To her great relief, her first male visitor was Tony, who came in cheerfully assuring her he'd be happy to sample her muffins, drink her special hot chocolate and watch a film with her.

"Don't you worry, my dear. I wouldn't dream of forcing myself onto you. Tell you the truth, I'm not very into this anymore, and nor is Ruth. Half of us aren't. We've grown up, you see. Ruth and I are happy together and we don't need anyone else."

"Why do it then?"

He shrugged. "It was something we all did when we were young and silly. Me and Ruth, we realise it's not what we want now. We want children, but we don't want to bring them up in this kind of environment. We've seen what's happened with the older couples' children. They've left home and don't come back if they can help it. We don't want that for our kids. We want to be a proper family with our children bringing our grandchildren to see us. We're actually thinking of moving out of The Grove."

"Don't go yet, please. If I lost Ruth, I don't know what I'd do."

"Don't worry. We won't go yet. We'll see how things go. Now, what have you got that we can watch?"

In October, Amy's male visitor was Brian, and he also was happy to eat cake and chat. Amy began to relax about the arrangement. Sometimes, she couldn't help wondering who Darren was with, but knew better than to ask him.

Although she thought she could relax about it, she still worried every month about who was going to turn up on her doorstep. November was tricky, as it was Dave, and it was obvious he wanted to play. "Just a little, Amy. I won't hurt you, honest. We won't do anything you're not comfortable with. You have such nice boobs, and my wife is such a fitness freak. She hardly has any. Would you let me touch your chest? Come here, let's just have a cuddle. I promise I won't hurt you, okay? Do you trust me?"

Amy nodded wordlessly, but she found it hard to relax next to him on the sofa. He murmured to her as the television played to the room. She found it impossible to concentrate on the programme, aware of the man beside her who was someone she liked as a friend but had never imagined she'd have to indulge in any sexual acts with him. He'd brought a bottle of prosecco, and as she drank it with him, she gradually felt herself relaxing. Eventually, he slipped his hand inside her blouse and gently caressed her breast. She found she liked it; Darren was never as gentle, and it was pleasant to have a man really appreciate her. He turned to kiss her and eventually she found herself being divested of her blouse and bra and enjoying his caresses and kisses, his soft beard soothing her skin as his lips moved around her breasts. She couldn't help sighing a little, and when he raised his head to question her, she said, "I never knew a man could be so gentle. Darren is always rough and hurts me so much. He takes delight in causing me pain."

Dave's face creased with concern. "I can't believe anyone can hurt such an attractive woman as you, Amy. You not only have a beautiful body, but you are a lovely person too. Why do you let him hurt you? Why do you stay with him?"

She shrugged. "I thought it was important to keep my marriage vows. I thought he loved me, but he only loves my money. If I tried to run away, he'd find me, because he wants to have my money to live on."

"That's appalling. My Roni wouldn't put up with that." He bent his head to give a few more tender kisses, and she relaxed again in his soft gentleness.

Later, though, she was grateful he'd controlled himself and hadn't taken things further. He'd stopped and helped her put her blouse back on and they sat together to watch the television. He seemed content to recline with his arm around her and she took comfort from him, realising this was another of her neighbours she was safe with.

As she laid in her bed that night, recalling it, she burned with embarrassment and thought she'd find it hard to look at him the next time she saw him. Whatever must he have thought of her? Then she remembered what all her neighbours had been up to for the last several years and realised she'd been lucky to get away with what she had. Although her body had enjoyed it - she had to admit that, and it was an unfamiliar experience for her - there was no love involved and therefore it was not something she wished to repeat.

So, when the doorbell rang in December, she could barely quell the butterflies in her stomach. What if this was someone who wanted to go further than Dave did? When she saw who it was, her heart somersaulted; it was Philip. As she looked at him standing there, she felt the colour rise and her hand went up to her cheek. As she didn't move, he took it upon himself to step inside and shut the door. They stood looking at each other; she could barely stop herself from shaking, but couldn't pull her gaze away from his. His eyes searched her as if in question, then he stepped forward and kissed her softly on the lips. She felt as if her limbs had melted and she'd become boneless, but at the same time her whole body fizzed and spat as if she had a live wire going through her. As he raised his eyes to hers, he smiled.

"Hello," he said, softly.

"Hello," she replied, gazing into his beautiful brown eyes behind his glasses. Just the sight of him and having him so close to her made her heart do a crazy dance. What was happening to her? Last month, she'd had a new experience with Dave's gentle caresses and obvious appreciation, but this was something different altogether. Making herself step back, she smiled a tremulous smile at him. "Would you like one of my special hot chocolates with cream, marshmallows, and grated chocolate?"

"I would. It sounds delicious."

She walked to the kitchen on legs that felt like jelly, aware of him following closely behind her. Continually aware of his presence in the room, she made the drinks, and they sat at the table opposite each other. He smiled at her as he spooned the small mallows into his mouth. She watched him in fascination. She wondered what his and Sarah's marriage was like. She was sure he wouldn't treat his wife the way Darren treated her. But did Sarah treat him badly? He never looked terribly happy.

As if he could read her thoughts, he said: "Somehow, when I'm with you, I feel a peace I never feel when I'm with Sarah. When I met her, I thought she was beautiful, and I was lucky she seemed to prefer me to the other men who were always around her. I couldn't believe my luck when she said she'd marry me. But it didn't take me long to realise she wasn't what I thought she was. I try very hard to please her, but she doesn't seem to want me. I have no idea why she married me."

"Have you asked her?"

"Whenever I try to talk to her, she avoids it. She'll pick up the dog, or make some remark completely unconnected with the subject, or she says she has to do something."

"I can't talk to Darren at all. He either ignores me or hits me about. As long as I keep providing the money, that's all he wants."

"Same with Sarah. She spends my money like water, but we rarely do anything together. I don't know why I'm telling you this. It wasn't my intention to lay my problems on you."

Greatly daring, Amy replied, "I think we're kindred spirits."

He nodded, and they fell silent, sipping their drinks and shyly looking at each other. When they'd finished, Amy said, "Would you like to see my studio? You've already seen the garden room. I have more paintings up there."

"I'd love to."

They spent some time in the studio; Amy watched Phil as he carefully studied each painting. Some were water-colours, others were oils. Also, there were charcoal sketches. He saw sketches of all their neighbours. She'd captured their likenesses so accurately; he knew immediately who they all were. There was also a drawing of Sarah's little dog. The watercolours and oils were landscapes and amongst them, he recognised Dovedale, Matlock and Mark Eaton Park.

"I'm even more in awe of your talent," he said quietly. "These are all excellent. What will you do with them?"

She shrugged. "I have just done them as a hobby. I expect they'll get thrown out at some point."

"You can't throw them out!" She smiled at his horrified expression. "You could at least give them as gifts to the people in them. You have one of all of our neighbours, except me."

She dropped her eyes from his. "Oh, erm, yes, I was going to do you next." She murmured. As she spoke, he walked to her easel which had a canvas covered in a cloth.

"May I see what you're doing?" he asked, and as she stepped forward to stop him, he lifted the cover. Defeated, she dropped her shoulders.

Before him, there was a portrait of him in full colour, not quite finished. He drew in a gasp at the same time she did. She panicked as she wondered if he could see how much love she'd poured into her work. Striding quickly over, she went to take the cover from his hands to cover it again. As she did so, he held onto it so she couldn't cover it. He put his hand out to stroke her hair.

"You've done all the others in charcoal sketches, but you're doing me in colour? Why is that, Amy?" He let the cover fall over the painting so he could put both hands on her shoulders. "Look at me, please?"

He put his hand gently under her chin so she had no option but to raise her head. He searched her face as if he was trying to see into her soul. It seems he did see, for eventually, he lowered his lips to hers to kiss her and she responded to his kiss, even going so far as to putting her hands behind his head, stroking his hair and losing herself in the moment. Every nerve in her body tingled, and she felt she might fall, so weak her knees felt. His kiss was the sweetest thing she ever experienced, and she wanted it to never end.

It did end, but he held her close, murmuring into her hair. "Oh Amy, I love you so! I've kept away from you because it was safer that way, but I've loved you since the first time I set eyes on you. I hate Darren for what he does to you."

Her heart danced. He loved her! Even as the realisation took hold, he kissed her again, and she wanted him with her whole being. But it was too soon.

"Let's go back down." She took his hand and together they went to the lounge. "Would you like to watch something, a film or television?"

"I don't mind what we do. Pick a film you like."

She picked 'The Sound of Music.' "I know it's old, but it's so romantic, I just love it."

"I'm happy if you are." When he smiled, her stomach gave a delicious jump. He was so gorgeous she just wanted to look at him all the time. She wanted to put her hands through his hair again, wanted to feel his arms around her. Pulling herself together, she set the film going and allowed him to draw her towards him and sat with him on the sofa.

The evening passed in a haze. Often, they kissed, long deep kisses and at other times they cuddled together, his hand stroking her hair or her arm. She knew she wanted more, but told herself, 'Not now, not yet, it's wrong.' But she couldn't help but give up to his kisses.

The evening passed far too quickly for them both, for at last, reluctantly, he had to leave, for the deadline for all the men to be back was midnight. "Or we turn into pumpkins," he joked. "But I don't want to leave you. Now I know you love me, I want to be with you all the time. I want to have you as my wife. I want to have babies with you. I want to grow old with you."

"I want that too. I just don't know how it can happen."

"Maybe something will work out. Maybe we'll get a miracle. I think we're meant to be together. We were meant to find each other. Don't give up, my dearest love. And while I can't be with you, remember I love you with all my heart."

He slipped out into the darkness through the garden room door, as they knew Darren would probably come in through the front. The moment Phil had gone, Amy returned to her bedroom and locked her door. There was no way she was going to risk being interfered with that night.

Now, as she thought back to their conversation, she wondered if Phil had somehow brought about that 'miracle'. She didn't want to believe Phil was capable of murder, but although she loved him, how much did she really know about him?

Chapter 10

Della was not in a good mood. She and Ben had finished re-interviewing the residents of Gladioli Grove. She made it plain she expected truthful answers this time and truthful answers they got. They now had a list of who was where on that night.

"I'm going to have to make a chart to get my head around it all. Let's get in the office so I can do it."

As they walked into their room, she asked Ben to arrange for someone to go fetch some decent coffee and some pastries. "I need something to help the brain get into gear again. Those swingers in G Grove have really done my head in. Do you think they really did it to help Amy?"

Ben shrugged. "Who knows?"

Della grabbed a large piece of paper and drew two lines to represent the Grove. Then she drew five squares on one side of the road and numbered them 1, 3, 5, 7, 9 and the five squares on the other side of the road and numbered them 2, 4, 6, 8, 10. Then she wrote the names of each couple that lived in the houses and circled number 10, as that was where Amy lived with Darren.

By the time she'd done that, Ros Parry arrived with the coffee and pastries.

"Oh, thanks, Ros. Much appreciated. I'll settle up with you later. Now, Ben, let's see. First, we know that Celia and Neville Davenport from number 8 really did visit at number 7 with Louise and Richard Newton and Angela and Peter Moorcroft, who were staying with them. So,

Christine Moreton at number 1 had Tony Cuthbertson there, Veronica Boothe at number 2 had George Taunton, Emily Taunton at number 4 had Matthew Hornby there, David Boothe was with Amanda Hornby at number 5 and at number 6, Brian Moreton was with Ruth Cuthbertson. We already knew William Harrington-Smythe was visiting Amy and his wife Liz was playing chess with Philip Sutton. So, it looks like the victim, Darren Holbeach, was supposed to be visiting - "

"Sarah Sutton," finished Ben.

The two looked at each other.

"Well, that explains why she was expecting a 'friend' and her husband didn't know who she was expecting. As has been explained to us, the wives never knew who would come, and the husbands didn't know who would visit their wives. What a carry on! What a way to live."

"So, where does this leave us? The man didn't turn up. I can't imagine Sarah would have been happy about that. She likes the men. I can imagine her having a real tantrum about being let down. I pity that husband of hers. I bet she gives him hell sometimes. I suppose it couldn't be him, could it?"

"What's his motive, though? As far as I can see, he has none. And frankly, I can't see how he would carry the dead weight of a man heavier than him from their house to the field."

"What if he was jumped as soon as he left his house? It's close to the field. Apart from number nine, their house is the closest."

"It's a thought. We should keep it in mind. But if you remember, Tony Cuthbertson said he saw him walking down the road."

"Yes, you're right, he did."

"Hmm..."

"Oh, I can hear the cog wheels turning," Ben commented. Della stuck out her tongue, and he laughed. "What are you thinking, Dell?"

"What if Sarah lied? What if he did turn up? Think about what those couples get up to on that particular night of the month. He was naked, remember? And we didn't find anyone else's DNA on him, only Sarah's and that was because she admitted to touching him when she found him. What if he took his own clothes off? That would explain there being no other's DNA on him if he undressed himself. They found other fibres on him that were identified as cotton that could have come from the cover of a duvet. What if he was naked and then wrapped in the duvet to transport him to the field? And what if Sarah, having touched him already, pretending they were going to have sex, intended to 'find' him in the morning and touch him to disguise the fact she'd been with him? And she effectively annihilated tracks and any footprints already in the field by dragging Philip up there to see the body, along with the dog, to complicate any evidence further?"

"That's a theory. But I don't know what motive she'd have. Do you think Philip helped her, if it was her? That the pair of them did it together? If that was the case, we're still lacking a motive."

"I think it's worth bringing her in and having a search done of the house. We need to run this by Tim. Let's go see him."

Having obtained a warrant, forensics was called, and a team dispatched to join them at the house. Della and Ben took John, Don, Mike and Ros and were soon at the Sutton household. They waited on the road until the forensic team arrived and they all approached the house together.

"Hello again, officers, what can I do for you this time? Do you want to see Sarah? I don't think she's here."

"We have a warrant to search your house, Mr Sutton."

He looked startled. "You do? Why?"

"Just in the course of our enquiries. Nothing to worry about. We'll be as unobtrusive as possible. Can you show us the room Sarah uses when she's entertaining your neighbours?"

"Oh, erm, yes. It's this way."

"Just a moment." Della spoke to the constables. "Mike, John, Don and Ros, I'd like you to search the grounds. If you see anything suspicious, don't touch it, just show it to one of the forensic members here. Check the garage, shed, anything out there."

"Very good. What are we looking for?"

"I can't say really, but if you find something, you'll know. Copper's nose and all that." Della grinned at them and they headed off. Della turned her attention to Philip. "Okay, Mr Sutton, we're with you now."

The main bedroom was very large and, just like the Holbeachs' house, it had an adjoining room that was obviously a dressing room. The two forensic officers immediately began their search of the room, going over everything with their equipment. They stripped the bed and bagged up everything. They went over the carpet and everything else in the room. Eventually, they moved into the dressing room.

There were fitted wardrobes on three walls and the fourth wall had a dressing bar full of bottles and jars, hairbrushes and combs, a hair dryer and styling tongs. The whole place was lined with full-length mirrors.

"Hmm, someone likes themselves," Ben grunted. "Wish I'd brought my shades."

Wearing protective clothes and gloves, Della opened the nearest sliding door. It was full of women's clothes. Rifling through them, she found nothing suspicious. Ben looked through the drawers that went along the dressing worktop.

"I can't believe the number of cosmetics this woman has. Does she think of anything except her appearance?"

"Dunno, but look at these!" Della held up two hangers to show Ben. On one looked like a school uniform with a very short skirt. The other had a black classic waitress's dress, also with a short skirt and with a white frilly apron. She also dug out an old-fashioned nurse's uniform but with the usual short skirt.

"Oh my," Ben grinned. "Lucky husband."

"I think it's more like lucky neighbours."

"Cynical."

"There are more in there, too. She has an imagination, that one. No wonder she has a room such as this. I wonder if Philip is aware of it."

"There certainly doesn't seem to be much sign of him here. Wonder if they sleep together."

Also adjoining the dressing room was a lush bathroom, also surrounded by mirrors.

"This place is giving me a headache. I can't stand having to look at myself so much," complained Ben.

"Now you know how we all feel. We have to look at you all the time," joked Della.

"Funny," he growled.

"Well, there's nothing to find here anyway, although we'll get forensics to check it over too. Let's go down and we'll leave them to get on with it."

They descended the stairs. As they did so, Sarah Sutton burst in through the front door.

"What are they doing here? Philip!" she screamed. "What's going on?"

"It's alright, Sarah," said Philip, appearing at the door of the lounge. "They're just searching the house. Come in here."

"Searching the house? What for?"

"Not sure really."

"I want to know what they think they're doing! Well, Detective Sergeant? Why are you searching our house?"

"We have a warrant. Sarah Sutton, I arrest you on suspicion of the murder of Darren Holbeach. You are not obliged to say anything, but anything you do say may be taken down and used in evidence."

"Philip?" Sarah looked confused and scared.

"Sergeant? You can't think my wife had anything to do with this murder?"

"We'll see. Come along, Sarah."

"Philip! Get me a solicitor!" Sarah shouted as they led her out.

"Right. Philip, I want you to come to the station for an interview as well."

"Am I under arrest?"

"No. This is a voluntary interview. You may leave if we have no reason to charge you."

"I see. I'll get my coat."

*****

Later, in Interview Room two, Della sat with Ben next to her, with Philip on the other side of the table.

"We are going to record this interview, Philip. I hope you're okay with that?"

"Yes, that's fine. Do I need a solicitor?"

"No, you're not under arrest. You are free to leave at any point."

He nodded, so Ben switched on the machine, gave the date, Time and their names.

"You are Philip Sutton, of number five, Gladioli Grove, Derby?"

"Yes."

"How long have you lived in that house?"

"Just over five years."

"You are married to Sarah Sutton?"

"Yes."

"How long have you been married?"

"Six years."

"What do you do for a living?"

"I'm an IT specialist, working freelance."

"Okay. Thank you. Now, please tell us your movements on the evening and night of the 12th January, 1994."

"I left my house at seven-twenty and made my way to Elizabeth's house, number nine."

"Did you see Darren Holbeach coming out of his house?"

"No. It's all carefully timed so we don't see each other."

"Okay. Carry on."

"I was relieved to go to Elizabeth because she doesn't expect me - in fact, doesn't want me - to do anything, um, sexual. We enjoy each other's company. She's been like a second mother to me. I can talk to her and she doesn't judge, you know? And we both enjoy playing chess, so we drink something nice, eat chocolates and play chess."

"So, what time did you leave there?"

"About ten forty-five. We're all supposed to be home by midnight."

"So, when you came home, did you see your wife?"

"No, she was already asleep in her own room."

"So, you never saw her until the morning?"

"That's right."

"How do you know she was asleep?"

"Well, there was no sound from her room and her lights were all out."

"You didn't look in on her then?"

"No. I never do after - on those Saturday nights."

"But you knew her 'friend' hadn't come?"

"No, I didn't know, because I had already gone out as per the arrangements."

"Ah. Of course. I see. So, you thought she'd be tired after her - um - exertions."

Philip's face reddened. "She often is. In any case, whoever came to her might still be there, so I just leave her and sleep in my room."

"I see. So, when did you know her visitor hadn't come?"

"She told me in the morning, before she took the dog out."

"So, she took the dog out. Then what happened?"

"I was packing food ready for our journey, when Sarah came rushing back, crying. She could barely tell me what was wrong, so she pulled me up to the field and across to the poor chap. I made her come away and called the police. We heard the police car come, and we went out to see them."

"Okay. One thing I would like to ask you. Amy Holbeach told us you and your neighbours had stopped your swingers' habit but started up again to help her with Darren."

"That's not right. It's what she was told, but it had never stopped. To be frank, Sergeant, I hated it, but Sarah loved it. I have never been enough for her," he continued gloomily.

Della looked at him with sympathy. "And this is something you've had to do for five years?"

"No, four. They always wait until a new neighbour has been in the Grove for a year before they draw them in. I'm fortunate, because some of the women are happy to just chat or watch a film or whatever."

"Have you been to Amy?"

"I - erm, yes. Last month. She was very sweet. We watched a DVD and drank hot chocolate. She's not at all comfortable with the arrangement, but she told me Darren made her do it."

"And you and your wife didn't take it into your hands to relieve her of an arrangement she hated?"

His head jerked up. "No! Absolutely not! Neither of us had any idea Darren was to go to Sarah that night. How could we? None of us men knows where we're supposed to go until late in the day."

Della looked at him for a moment. Then, "Right. Thank you, Mr Sutton. I think that will be all for now. We may call you in again if we feel we have reason to do so. Ben?"

"Interview terminated at three, fifty-four." Ben switched the machine off.

"One last thing. Would you mind giving us a DNA sample?"

"Not at all."

"Right. If you go with Ben, he'll get someone to take your sample. It's just a matter of a couple of swab wipes on the inside of your mouth, then we'll have someone take you home. Thank you for your time."

Philip nodded. "What about my wife?"

"We need to keep her for a while. If you would arrange for your solicitor to come here so we can interview her, it would be very good. Or she can have our duty solicitor."

"I'll arrange it."

Ben took Philip out and asked Don and Ros to take him home. Then he joined Della and the DI, who had observed the interview.

"What did you think, guv?"

"He seemed straightforward enough. At least, until I mentioned Amy Holbeach. That caused a reaction, although he did his best to hide it."

"Yes. I got the idea he might rather like her. But that doesn't necessarily make him a murderer, although it might give him a motive. But would Sarah have helped him for that reason?"

"Can't see it myself. I get the feeling that woman is all out for herself. She'd be more likely to want to top Amy, rather than Darren, I'd have thought, if it was her. And frankly, I can't see Philip Sutton being able to manage a dead weight. Darren was much bigger and heavier than him. If he'd done it, he'd have needed help."

"We'll have to see if forensics has come up with anything from the search in their house. Also, if we get anything out of her. It's hard to see what motive she'd have," Della said, frowning. "Somehow, though, I have a strong feeling about her. My gut tells me she's involved, but if we can't find any evidence, the only hope we have is if she confesses. And, if I'm any judge of character, I think underneath that pink fluffiness, Sarah Sutton is hard as nails and just as immovable."

Chapter 11

Della's prediction turned out to be spot on. Sarah was outraged at the intimate examination she was subjected to and protested constantly and loudly with profanity. That didn't endear Della to think kindlier of her.

"You're holding me for no reason. When are you going to let me go home?" Sarah demanded once they were in the interview room.

"When we get the results back from your examination and the search of your house, we may let you go. But until then, you're staying. Ben."

Ben put a new tape in the machine, switched on and told it the date and time and he, Della, Mr Charles Adams, solicitor, were present.

"You are Mrs Sarah Sutton of number five, Gladioli Grove, Derby?"

"You know I bloody am."

"A simple 'yes' would have sufficed. We'd like to ask you again what your movements were on the night of January 12th, 1994."

"Okay. I was expecting someone, wasn't I? It was our swap night."

"For the sake of the recorder, there was a regular Saturday each month when the husbands who live in Gladioli Grove go to visit someone else's wife. Is that so?"

"Yes," came the sulky reply.

"How long have you lived at Gladioli Grove?"

"Five years."

"And what's your opinion of the second Saturday adventures?"

"I love it! The guys are all great and it makes up for - certain things..."

"What things?"

Sarah folded her arms. "No comment."

"Did you know Darren Holbeach before he came to live in the Grove?"

"No."

"What did you think of him?"

She shrugged. "He was okay, I suppose."

"Care to qualify that? Was there something wrong with him, something you didn't like?"

"Not really, no. He wasn't nice to his wife, but he was okay with the rest of us."

"What's your opinion of Amy Holbeach?"

Again, the shrug. "She's okay. Don't have that much to do with her really. She mostly hangs out with Ruth and Liz."

"But you're not friendly with her yourself?"

"Nah. I'm more interested in the men. I get on with them better than the women."

"I see. So, on the night in question, you were expecting someone. So, what happened?"

"Nothing. No one came. I was all dressed up and ready and no one came."

"You were dressed up - how?"

"Oh, erm, I have certain costumes I wear on those nights. The guys like it, it makes it more exciting for them."

The solicitor, who had been sitting poker-faced until that point, raised an eyebrow, although he said nothing. The corner of Della's lips quirked as she suppressed a grin.

"Can you describe what you were wearing?"

"If you must know, I was wearing a short, blue, frilly dress like a little girl would wear and my hair was in plaits tied with matching blue ribbons. Some of the guys like feeling they're with someone young and innocent."

Della felt slightly sick and the solicitor's face had turned pale.

"Okay, so you were dressed and ready for your visitor. What did you do when no one came?"

"Nothing. What could I do? I drank a bottle of prosecco, watched some telly, and went to bed around ten o'clock. It depressed me as I'd been deprived of my fun for the night. Philip and I had decided to visit his father the next day so in the morning I got up and while he made food, I walked our dog and the rest you know."

"Thank you, I think that's enough for now."

"Can I go now?"

"Not until we have the forensic results on the search of your house."

"You won't find anything."

"In that case, you'll have nothing to worry about, will you?"

The following day, they had to let Sarah go. Forensics had found no evidence of Darren's presence in the house. They also never found the garments described by Sarah that she wore that evening. When asked about it, Sarah shrugged her shoulders and said she'd got rid of it. "I put it in a charity bag. I've got plenty of other things I can wear."

When asked what charity it was, she'd shrugged again and said she had no idea. Della sighed. She had a feeling they'd be chasing a red herring with that one. Still, she supposed it had to be done.

Philip came to fetch her and Della and Ben watched them exit.

"Damn!" Della exclaimed crossly.

"C'mon, let's get a cuppa, then we can think about our next move." Ben took her elbow and pointed her towards the canteen.

Later, in the incident room, the team were gathered while a run-down of results so far were discussed. A photo of Darren, surrounded by photos of all the couples who lived in Gladioli Grove, were on the board, sticky notes showing where each man had been that evening.

"So far, we have established the whereabouts of all the neighbours, exactly when they left their homes and entered the houses where they were spending the evening and what times they each went home," Tim Masterson gave a rundown. "All the women have corroborated the men's statements. Sarah Sutton stands by her statement that Holbeach never arrived at her house, and indeed, there is no evidence to say he was ever there. The doc initially said death occurred between midnight and eight a.m., but now says it's likely to have been nearer midnight than eight, because rigor mortis was well set in long before he was found at just eight. So, if we say he died between, say, midnight and about, five, - and we know he couldn't have been lying naked out there for long before he died - where was he all that time in between leaving home and being laid out in the field?

"I know it doesn't take long for someone to die of hypothermia. Were our killers still there when he died? Did they put him there and leave him, or did they watch him die?

"We lack motivation for the killing, although I have to say, the method of killing him was interesting and should raise questions. Was it someone who wanted him dead but didn't want to actually do anything like shoot him or stab him? Why leave him in the open like that, to be found so easily? Surely, it's normal to hide a murder. There were trees not far away. Why not hide him in the undergrowth?"

"They wanted him to be found," a voice said hesitantly.

"Yes, Ros, exactly. Which poses the question - why?"

"Was someone trying to make a point, bring it to someone's notice?" DC Mike Smith contributed.

Tim nodded. "That's a possibility."

"I can't help wondering about the red paint in his groin area," mused Ben.

"It looked like blood at first," said Della. "It has to be significant, although I'm not sure what of right now. There's also the word 'guilty' that was on his chest."

"We'll need to bear that in mind," responded Tim. "And while we've been establishing where everyone was before midnight, no one has an alibi for after then - apart from spouses, and as I understood it, most of them sleep in a different room on the - erm - appointed swap nights, the reasoning behind it being that no husband should see who has been with his wife that night. I know, I know." Della put her hands up as if to ward off others. "But that's what they do - or did, because I've a feeling this will probably put a stop to their interesting activities. Apart from the Newtons and their guests and the Davenports, who presumably went to bed together as normal once the visiting was over, as they said they did in their statements."

"So, as I understand it, we have seven couples who may not have alibis, which includes the Suttons."

"Right, in the light of that, I want all those people bringing in - except for the Suttons. So, we're talking about the Moretons, the Hornbys, the Harrington-Smythes, the Boothes, Tauntons and Cuthbertsons. I've asked our civilian helpers to look into the lives of Darren Holbeach and Sarah and Philip Sutton. We'll see what happens. Della, will you give out the assignments, please?"

"Yes, Guv." Della watched as Tim, immaculate as always, walked away.

It was a massive operation for the small force; seven couples to bring in, and possibly several houses for the search teams. Della braced herself to see all of them again. She was glad their headquarters was a modern building with quite a few rooms. Each man and woman were in different places, each with an officer to watch over them. Della knew it was imperative to get through as swiftly as possible in order to relieve the officers, but was determined to cut no corners. She saw Ruth first, knowing she and Amy were close. Was it possible Ruth had decided to help her friend out?

After a gruelling half an hour, during which Ruth emotionally admitted she wished she'd had a hand in Darren's murder 'because he was a horrible, horrible man, and Amy needed to be free of him, but insisted she could never do such a thing. She also told Della and Ben that her husband, Tony, came to bed with her when he returned from being with Christine, because neither of them had actually had sex with anyone that night. Christine's husband Brian had been with Ruth, and both couples didn't want to indulge; they no longer wanted to do the wife-swapping thing.

"Did Darren visit you at all during the previous four months?"

"No, thank goodness. I couldn't have done it. I hated him for Amy."

"But you didn't hate him enough to kill him? Maybe with your husband's help?"

"No, absolutely not. Tony hasn't got a violent bone in his body, and nor have I. I cook cakes, Detective Sergeant. The most violent thing I ever do is beat cake mix with my electric mixer. I've no idea how Darren died, but I couldn't stab anyone and I don't have a gun."

"If we search your house, will we find evidence of Darren Holbeach there?"

"You'll certainly find it downstairs, but not in the bedrooms. He came around our house, just as all the neighbours do. And he played golf with Tony sometimes, so would come in if Tony wasn't quite ready."

"I see. Well, thank you. You are free to go as yet, but please be prepared to make yourself available should we need to talk with you again."

"May I wait for my husband?"

"I don't see why not. The constable will show you where you can get a drink while you wait."

Ruth's husband Tony was brought in next and his answers caused no rise for concern. He told them he played golf with Darren and said it was fine when the blokes were together, away from the women.

"But I like Amy. She's a friendly person and nice with it. I saw the way he treated her. My Ruth wouldn't let me get away with it, although of course I'd never try to do it. I can certainly understand why Ruth didn't like him, but I had no reason to do anything to the guy."

And so the interviews went on. Some of the couples, who lived further down the Grove seemed even less likely to have done anything. Christine and Brian were a couple who obviously were less than enthusiastic about the 'swinging' arrangements and had substantiated Ruth and Tony's claims they'd done a straight swap and had bedded after midnight with their own spouses.

Elizabeth and William Harrington-Smythe were another couple obviously very fond of Amy and held the same opinion of Darren Holbeach that Ruth had, but again, Della couldn't see them committing the murder, although she wasn't going to cross them off the list of suspects just yet.

"The thing is, we have no evidence against any of them, and no real motive either," grumbled Della to Ben after all the interviews were done and the place once again emptied of suspects. "I'm bushed, I need my bed."

Chapter 12

Thursday

"Excuse me, Della!" a voice called, and she turned to see civilian assistant Jessie Hawthorne hurrying towards her.

Della's sleep had been spasmodic, tired as she was after all yesterday's interviews. She'd been turning everything over in her mind - over and over and coming to no conclusions that would make her feel good about the investigations. They were up against a brick wall.

"What is it, Jess? Steady on, calm down, take a seat. Deep breaths now."

"Sorry, not as fit as I should be," wheezed Jess, and she plonked herself on the proffered chair, waving a hand as if to cool her rosy cheeks.

Della looked sympathetically at the middle-aged assistant, whose figure might have been described as 'motherly' in earlier decades, although mothers these days tended to be slim and trendy, clad in jeans and skinny tops.

"What's got you into a tizz, Jess?"

"I was looking at the position of the body on the board as I walked by earlier, and something about it triggered a memory. As you know, I used to live and work in Newark, for the police over there, and I remembered an incident a few years ago, 1986, in fact, where a young woman was found dead after a brutal rape and the picture of her lying there, practically naked with arms and legs splayed in certain ways. I was almost sure that our dead guy's body had been arranged to lie in exactly the same way as that girl's. So, I looked it up. Her name was Cindy Smith, and her boyfriend, a John Latham, was convicted for it. I wondered if this was anything to do with it - with his arms and legs being put in those positions, duck."

She held a photo out to Della, who took it, looked, and glanced towards the incident board. Silently, she handed it to Ben, who did the same, and then whistled. "My goodness, Jessie," he said, "I think you may be onto something here."

Jessie nodded. "And so, I looked into it further and it seems John Latham had a flat-mate at the time - and guess who that was?"

Della and Ben looked at Jess and frowned, each shaking their heads. "Not - Darren Holbeach?" Della ventured.

"The very one!" Jess was practically bouncing with excitement.

"Jess, I could kiss you!" Della hugged her. "You've given us a great kick-start now, what a clever girl you are - and what a splendid memory you have. Can you tell us anything more about the case, although we can look it up?"

"Oh yes, of course - I don't do things by halves, you know! John Latham always insisted he was innocent - but we know they always do, don't they? But the evidence was circumstantial. Blood identified as Cindy's was on a jacket he owned and they found a pendant on leather ties known to be his at the scene, actually clutched in the girl's hand."

"As if she pulled it off during the struggle," stated Ben.

"Exactly. John said his necklace went missing about a week before the girl died and he also reckoned he hadn't worn the jacket for a few months."

"Are you thinking what I'm thinking, Ben?"

"That John Latham is innocent?"

"Something like that, yes. And, knowing how Darren Holbeach treated Amy, his wife, he is the one who could well have been the guilty party."

"Indeed. If that's so, this death," Ben nodded towards the photo on the board, "Could be a revenge killing."

"Got it in one, my old mate! Thank you, Jess, my angel. Keep looking, will you? See what else you can find? Perhaps more about the dead girl."

"I certainly will, Della!" Jess beamed at them both and turned to hasten back to her desk.

"So, someone found out where Darren was living now and decided it was time for revenge. Could it be someone related to the victim, or a friend of the prisoner? And I wonder how they found him."

"Could be almost anyone he came across - at the golf course, or down the local. Should we talk again to his golfing buddies, do you think?" Ben frowned at her. "Never thought to ask about anyone else he's met since he came here."

"No. I was so sure it would involve someone in Gladioli Grove. Who was looking into Darren's life?"

"Mike, I believe."

Della paced towards the DC at his desk. "Mike, have you found out much about Darren Holbeach?"

"Not a great deal, boss. Before he married Amy, he lived in various places. He lived with various women, some for only a few weeks. Our boy really got around. His parents are loaded, and he never appeared to work. He went home to stay with them in between women. He went to a posh boys' school but was expelled because he got a girl from a nearby girls' school pregnant, but it appears mother and father paid the girl and her parents off. To get him out of the way for a while, they sent him to live with an aunt who lives in Lincoln. However, it also appears he didn't stay there long but lived with a mate in Newark until that mate got banged up for something and he returned to his parents. He was a rich layabout who loved to sponge off his parents and others."

"Did you find the name of the friend he shared with in Newark?"

"Yes. His name was John Latham."

"So, it was definitely him who was living with Latham."

"With a name like Holbeach, it was highly likely. It's not exactly a common name, Ben. But we had to be sure."

"So, where does that lead us?"

"Well, we can suppose someone is convinced he was the guilty party for the death of the girl, Cindy. Mike, can you check that John Latham is still in the clink?"

"Right away, boss." Mike turned back to his computer.

Della looked up to see Jess waving madly at her and hastened towards her, wanting to save the woman another breathless run. "What have you got, Jess?"

"I was looking for more information about Cindy Smith's family. She had a sister, several years younger than her. Called Sarah."

"Indeed. Very interesting. Sarah is a common name. Can you find out if Sarah Sutton was Sarah Smith?"

"No problem. Wait there, it'll take me only a few moments." Jess tapped away quickly. "Hmm, certainly it was a Sarah Smith who married Philip Sutton, and the age is right."

"I knew she had to be involved somehow. Take Mike and bring her in, Ben, please. I'm going to look further into the Cindy Smith case."

"Okay, will do." Ben paced down the room. "Come on, Mike, we have a job to do. We have to see the lovely Mrs Sutton."

*****

It took less than fifteen minutes to reach the Suttons' house. Philip Sutton opened the door to them.

"Hello, officers. Can I help you?"

"We'd like to see your wife, sir. Is she in?"

"No, she's not."

"Do you have any idea when she'll be back?"

"Come in, detectives."

Philip turned and went into the house and they followed him. In the lounge, he sat down suddenly. "I'm sorry, officers, but I think my wife has gone."

"What do you mean?"

"I mean, I think she's left. She's taken a case of clothes and some of her jewellery."

"How long?"

"I'm not sure. I had to go into work early this morning to sort something out and when I came back, she'd gone."

"Has she taken her car?"

"No, it's still there. She must have taken a taxi."

"Excuse me, sir." Ben stepped out of the room and called Della. He quickly explained. Then he held the phone away from his ear while she emitted a string of expletives.

He closed the call and returned to the lounge. "Does Sarah have a phone?"

"Yes, she does and I've called it several times but got no answer." Philip stood and paced the room. "Where could she have gone? And why didn't she take her car, for goodness' sake? She goes nowhere on public transport. I'm sure she wouldn't even begin to know how to get on a bus or a train."

"We'll find her, don't worry. But I'm also sorry to have to tell you we have good reason to believe she was involved in the murder of Darren Holbeach, so when she's found, she will be arrested."

"What? You can't be serious?" Philip sank into another chair. "How do you know?"

"I'm afraid we can't reveal that at this stage in the investigation, but it's likely she has done a runner because she knew we would come for her."

"I can't take this in." Philip put his head in his hands.

Ben looked on in sympathy. He liked this young man and could imagine how difficult it would be for him to get his head around the idea that his beautiful and petite wife could be involved in murder. And now he had another shock for him.

"Get your coat, sir. I've been told to bring you in."

Philip's head shot up. "What? Why?"

"Just get your coat, sir."

"What about the dog? I can't leave her on her own for I don't know how long."

"Would one of your neighbours look after it for you?"

"Is it okay if I make a call to one of them?"

"Go ahead."

Philip pulled out his phone from his pocket. "Hello, is that Bill? Is Liz in? No? Oh, well, I wanted to ask a favour. I have to go to the police station again. Would you mind looking after the dog, please? I've no idea how long I'll be. Sarah's not here. I don't know. You've got a key, haven't you? Thanks very much. Liz knows where everything is. I'll be in touch when I know. Thanks, Bill."

He put the phone away, collected his coat, and followed the two detectives out, locking the door behind him.

Chapter 13

On receiving Ben's phone call, Della issued orders. "Sarah Sutton has done a runner! She's not taken her car, so she probably used a taxi. I want all taxi companies contacted and the train and bus stations contacted for sightings. Ben is bringing Philip Sutton in again for further questioning."

Her colleagues hurried away to their assignments and Della arranged for an interview room to be available for her to speak with Philip. The police headquarters was only a ten minutes' drive from Gladioli Grove, so Ben arrived shortly after his phone call, a pale-looking Philip Sutton with him.

"Ah, Mr Sutton, so glad you could come," Della smiled at him.

"I didn't exactly have much choice really, Sergeant. I don't quite know how I can help you."

"Well, let's have a go, shall we?"

She led him into the interview room, where they sat in the allotted chairs. Ben sat next to Della. A young PC stood at the door.

"Am I under arrest?" Philip asked.

"Not as yet," Della replied, and noted how his pale face seemed to get more so.

"Do I need a solicitor?"

"Entirely up to you, Mr Sutton. If you feel you have the need, call one, or we can provide you with our duty solicitor."

Philip folded his arms in an uncharacteristically defiant pose. "I've done nothing. I have no need of a solicitor right now."

Della nodded. "At the moment, you're here voluntarily to help us with our enquiries. Technically, you're free to go at any time."

He raised his eyebrows. "But...?"

"But I don't recommend it."

The raised eyebrows turned into a frown. "I see."

"I'd like to record this interview, if that's alright with you?"

"Fine."

Ben switched on the machine, gave the date and Time and his name. Della added her name and, when indicated, Philip gave his.

"Right, Mr Sutton. Can you tell me when you last saw your wife?"

"This morning. They needed me at the office, so I took her a cup of tea and told her I was going in."

"And what time would that be?"

"Around 7.45, I think."

"She's not an early riser?"

"No. She usually gets up much later."

"And yet, the morning when she discovered the body, she was out walking her dog at eight?"

"Well, we were setting off to visit family, as we told you."

"Yes. So, back to this morning. Did your wife say anything to you when you told her you were going into work?"

"She said she might go shopping later. That was fairly usual; she did a lot of shopping. It was her second-favourite occupation, spending my money," said Philip, a bitter tone creeping into his voice.

"What time did you leave the house?"

"Just before eight. The bus leaves at five past."

"You catch a bus?" Della was surprised.

Philip smiled slightly. "My office is right in the middle of the city. Using a bus is more convenient than taking my car and there is no parking to worry about. In the summer, I often cycle, but this time of year it has to be the bus."

Della nodded; she could certainly see the sense in that and it could be easily checked.

"What time did you arrive home?"

"Just before two. I thought Sarah was at home, because her car was on the drive. But there was no sign of her and when I went into her dressing-room, I saw a load of clothes had gone and then I noticed she'd taken her small jewellery box from her bedroom. I called her mobile several times, but there was no answer. I couldn't understand why she'd gone and taken a load of clothes but not her car."

"And did you stay in the house all afternoon until our officers came for you?"

"I did, yes. Um, no, I didn't. I went up to see Liz, but she wasn't there, so I chatted with Bill for a while; asked him to tell Liz that Sarah had gone and that I didn't know how long I should wait until I told the police she was missing. I know it's supposed to be about twenty-four hours before they take a missing person as missing. Especially when it's obvious she meant to leave."

"Because she packed a case?"

"Yes."

"Didn't it occur to you that, as part of an ongoing murder investigation, that we should know right away?"

"Frankly, it didn't occur to me. I don't see how she could have been involved in that. I just thought she'd left me, probably found another rich and gullible guy ready to let her spend his money."

"You don't seem that upset, Mr Sutton."

"Frankly, I'm not. She was a man-eating nymphomaniac who loved to spend my money. She didn't love me, she loved what she could get out of me. She's always seen pound signs behind her eyelids."

Della changed tack.

"Did you know Sarah had a sister who was brutally raped and killed years ago?"

Philip sat up straighter. "No. At least, I knew she had a sister who'd died, but I was never aware of the circumstances."

"I can't believe Sarah never talked about it."

"Well, I can assure you she didn't. Whenever her sister was mentioned, she'd just cry, so I never pressed the subject. She was quite a lot younger than the sister. She did once tell me that her sister, Cindy, was excited because she had found a really nice guy and was hoping he'd ask her to marry him, but then she'd died."

He hesitated then. "If she died like that, was it the boyfriend who did it to her?"

Della said carefully, "They imprisoned him for it."

"What a truly dreadful thing. And Cindy thought he'd marry her. How awful. Sarah told me that Cindy was a lovely person who was always kind to her, even though the two of them were so different in age. Sarah adored her big sister and I believe she was devastated over losing her, which is why she could never talk about it."

"What about Sarah's family? Did they never talk about it?"

"She has no family; apparently, she was brought up by an aunt and uncle but she said they fell out and so she didn't have anything to do with them. When I heard about her sister, I didn't like to ask too much. Didn't want to rake up painful memories, you know."

"Yes, I can understand that. Returning to today. Did anyone see you when you were at work this morning?"

"Yes, of course. I worked with one of our new technicians. Then my manager and I went to a cafe for lunch before I caught my bus home."

"Interview terminated at," Della looked at her watch. "Five eleven p.m."

Ben switched off the machine.

"Thank you, Mr Sutton. I don't think we need to detain you any longer. I'll get someone to take you home. If you should hear from your wife, please let us know."

She noticed the relief on Philip's face and sympathised with him. She nodded to Ben, who knew what to do. He escorted Philip out.

When Ben returned to the incident room, Della said. "Right. I want someone to check out the two people Philip Sutton mentioned and get their statements. Looks like we've had no joy from either taxis or the stations' CCTV. I'm going to get Tim to put out an APB for Sarah Sutton; I'm going up there now. I want to know as soon as anything comes up on any of our investigations. I'll be back again shortly after I've seen the guv."

Although she tried to avoid being in the office alone with Masterson, sometimes she had to do it, and she marched away, grimly determined. She wasn't there long and was soon with the others in the main room and at her own computer. She needed to know more about the case of the rape and murder of Cindy Sutton. She wondered if the guv would give permission for her and Ben to go over to Newark to see what they could find.

It wasn't long before Tim Masterson came to announce to the room that the APB for Sarah Sutton had been put out and John Latham was indeed still in prison. They had recently moved him to Whatton.

"I don't suppose there's any chance we could see him?" asked Della. "I'd like a chance to speak with him."

"I'll see if it can be arranged."

"I'd also like to speak with someone over in Newark who might remember the case, guv."

"I'm not sure if there'll be anyone still there who dealt with it. They've had a major shuffle within Nottingham force over the last few years. I'm not even sure if their station is still manned."

Later, as she luxuriated in her hot bath, with soft music playing from the radio at the far side of the bathroom and watching the flickering lights of the scented candles in various strategic places in the room, Della tried to switch her mind off the case but found it near impossible. Had Sarah Sutton watched Darren Holbeach die naked in that field? And where the heck had she disappeared to?

Chapter 14

Sarah Sutton was feeling well pleased with herself. She could hardly believe how easy it had been to get away. Philip having to go into work was perfect; it played into her hands. She thought back to that morning.

The minute she heard the front door close behind her husband, she threw the duvet back, slipped her feet into her fluffy slippers and drew on her robe in one swift movement, making Sukie leap off the bed, barking excitedly. She scooped up the little dog hastily. Her bedroom faced the rear garden, so she flung open her door, and scurried as fast as she dared in the stupid slippers to a window at the end of the landing which looked out towards the front drive. She was just in time to see Philip walk out through the gateway and turn right, heading towards the end of the road.

"Yes!" Sukie yipped and wriggled at the sudden hug and tried hard to lick her mistress's face. Sarah held her away so she couldn't quite reach. "We have to get moving, Sukes."

In the bedroom, she picked up her phone and tapped rapidly. The call was brief, and she cut the call and dialled again. After her conversation, she headed for the shower. Usually, she lingered in the shower, revelling in the water, but today she hastily washed her hair and body. Then, wrapped in a towelling robe, she entered her dressing room, sat before the mirror and hacked off her long blond hair. She popped the long bits into a plastic bag, smiling ruefully at the locks. Still, it would grow back. It took only a short time to dry her remaining hair. From a deep drawer, she selected a shoulder-length auburn wig and set it on the worktop. She hastily dressed in jeans, a t-shirt, and a thick jumper, all new that Philip had never seen, then sat again to put on the wig and do her makeup. She allowed herself a few minutes before the mirror, well satisfied with the results. From the wardrobe, she drew a small suitcase, smiling to herself as she hurriedly packed underwear and clothes. A new handbag was also drawn from its recesses, and she filled it with everything she would need. Despite her haste, the whole procedure took a couple of hours until she was satisfied she had everything ready.

Downstairs, she brewed coffee and ate a piece of toast. While she waited for the coffee, she packed some food essentials, some sandwiches, apples, and a flask of her favourite hot chocolate. She intended to make another flask with coffee, but had to wait until it had percolated. Knowing she was going to be leaving Suki, she took her outside to the back garden so she could do her business and have a run around. As she did so, she heard a voice hail her and looked up to see the owner of the voice coming through the adjoining gate to next door.

"Hello there, my dear. The wife sent me to find out if you were ready yet."

"Nearly. Won't be long. I'm just waiting for the coffee for my flask."

"You and your coffee! Shall I fill it for you?"

"You're a sweetie. It looks like Sukie is busy right now. It'll save me time if you would. Thank you."

When Sarah returned to her kitchen, she saw the flask was ready, and she put it in her bag. She kissed the man's cheek.

"All set now, then? I'll tell her you're ready."

"I just have to put on my boots and coat, so the timing will be just right. I'll meet her as arranged."

"Are you sure you're doing the right thing, my dear?"

"Oh yes. Phil and I need some time apart; we've been getting on each other's nerves. I've told the police where I'll be."

"As long as you're sure."

"I'm sure. Thank you."

He left the way he'd come, through the back garden.

Sarah pushed her feet into her grey suede boots and shrugged into her matching grey coat. She tied the belt and wound the pink fluffy scarf around her neck and stood in front of the hall mirror to make sure her grey hat was on straight. Sukie wound herself around Sarah's feet, wagging her tail in anticipation of an outing. Sarah bent down and picked up the little dog.

"Oh Sukcs, I'm so sorry. You can't come with me today. You have to stay in your basket. Daddy will be home soon." As she spoke, she carried the little dog into the kitchen, where she deposited Sukie into her basket with the tartan cushion. Sukie immediately sat up and looked at her mistress. As Sarah walked away, Sukie made to follow.

"No! In the basket!" Sarah pointed and Sukie, head and tail downcast, slunk back to her bed. She lay down with a look of absolute disgust on her face. Sarah quickly left the kitchen and shut the door.

Then, she picked up her handbag and gloves, took the handle of her case and the bag with the food and let herself out the front door, shutting it firmly behind her. She gave a regretful glance towards her beautiful red convertible. 'Oh well,' she shrugged. She'd get herself another one before long. She hastened away from the house, down the drive and headed towards the car, waiting for her by the side of the road. It had picked the perfect spot to stop where trees prevented any of the houses overlooking that small stretch of road. She deposited the case and food bag onto the back seat, made herself comfortable in the front passenger seat, and they were off.

"Like the new look," the driver said. "Did you dye it?"

"Oh no, it's a wig. I have several, you know."

"I'm not sure why you needed a lift. Couldn't you have taken your car?"

"There's something wrong with it. Phil was supposed to be having it fixed for me."

"Ah, I see. Inconvenient time then."

"Exactly. I'll get someone to bring it to me when it's fixed."

They lapsed into silence. Sarah was lost in her thoughts while her driver was concentrating on the roads. It took about an hour to reach Newark.

"Where do you need to go now?"

"If you drop me in the supermarket car park, I can walk from there. It's tricky by road, but there's a shortcut, a pedestrian walk-way. It's best you don't know where I am anyway, in case Philip asks you. I don't want him to know where I am for a while."

"But you will let him know you're alright, won't you?"

"Yes, of course I will. Please keep this to yourself. I don't want all the neighbours knowing."

"Don't worry, we won't say a word. Are you sure you can manage?"

"Yes. I'll take my things to the flat and then I'll come out again later to do some shopping. I've brought some food with me and my flasks, so I'll be okay. In fact, I'll probably eat straight away."

"Good plan. Take care."

Sarah watched as the car drove away, then she made her way along the path towards John Latham's flat. On the way, she hid behind a wall and stamped on her phone, making sure it was in bits, then she threw the pieces away, some in a roadside bin and some in undergrowth.

By the time she'd found the block of flats and climbed the stairs to find the right one, Sarah was exhausted and was thinking longingly of the sandwiches and flask of coffee.

Upon entering the flat, she could see the whole place had been decorated. It was clean and neat, to her relief. The bed was unmade but had clean bedding folded upon it. A small wardrobe stood empty, waiting for her things. She smiled wryly, thinking of her dressing room back at her house in Gladioli Grove.

"Back to where I started," she murmured. Was she right to leave the luxury of her house? Then she thought of the tough Della Downs and knew she'd made the right decision to run. That woman would find evidence of her involvement in Holbeach's death, she was sure of it. She didn't want to give her the chance to bring her in. Going from luxury to a place like this was one thing, but prison was another kettle of fish altogether. She shuddered. Despite wanting revenge for her sister, she should have considered the danger she was putting herself in by helping to dispatch the man responsible for her sister's death. No, she'd done the right thing in running. She'd been helped until now, but there were still people who'd guess where she was. She would not stay here long; this was just a brief breathing-space before she moved on. And when she did so, there'd be no trace for anyone to find.

Right now, though, her stomach told her she needed to eat, and she remembered with pleasure the coffee in the flask. It would be the last of that sort she'd have for a while; it was expensive stuff and didn't come in a jar.

Leaving her case in the bedroom, she returned to the living area. She fetched a no-nonsense mug from the kitchen cabinet - black on the outside, white inside - and took it, along with her food bag, to a comfortable-looking armchair. It was a recliner, worked by a handle at the side. The flat was chilly, so before she made herself comfortable, she switched on the heating. It would take a while, so she fetched the duvet off the bed to tuck around herself. Before she did that, she took off her coat, hat, scarf and the red wig, chucking them on the sofa. She'd put everything away later. Now she was going to enjoy her food and coffee.

She poured out a mugful of coffee, setting mug and flask on a small table by the side of the chair. 'Most convenient', she thought. Her stomach growled, so she picked out a sandwich and began eating. The coffee was still hot, having kept well in the flask. She sipped it carefully and ate another sandwich. The warmth from the duvet was making her feel drowsy, despite the coffee. Her recall of the day was becoming hazy; the satisfied feeling lingered. She'd been clever; she would make sure they never caught up with her. As soon as she could, she'd be out of the country and living somewhere sunny and without a care in the world.

She emptied her mug and poured another. The liquid had cooled as she'd left the top off the flask, and she drank more. Before she knew it, she was asleep, unaware that she still held the mug in her hand, the contents dangerously close to spilling onto the duvet.

Chapter 15

Friday

Della's mind wouldn't let her rest properly and eventually she gave in when she saw it was just after five thirty. Her head ached because of her intermittent sleep. It was hardly fair, she thought, that she should have a hangover without having a night before. Sighing, she extricated herself from the warmth of her duvet and padded to her bathroom, shivering as the chill of the house attacked her. She stepped into the shower and stood under the water, appreciating the warmth being restored to her body. The glow remained when she'd finished as she dried herself and quickly donned her clothes.

She hurried down the stairs and into the kitchen. In order not to put the heating on - no point, as she would soon go out - she turned on two burners on the gas hob. They would soon take the chill from the air in her small kitchen. As her headache gradually receded now she was upright, she drank her first coffee of the day and reflected on her dreams. Amongst the disturbing ones of a cold body in a field, which had mysteriously turned into Ben and, strangely, Amy found him and screamed. Into the mix loomed Tim Masterson, who turned out to be the murderer. Then, it was him lying in the field, his eyes fixed on her, mesmerising her, even though he was dead. She shuddered; she really had to get that man out of her system. If only she could meet someone who could take her mind off him. He was married, and, however inviting his eyes were, there was no way she'd touch him. In any case, if they did anything, it would be the end of her working in Derby, and there's no way she was going to let that happen. He can give her smouldering looks as much as he liked; she wasn't going to succumb. She was not that desperate. She knew relationships were hard for serving officers, especially detectives.

As she ate her porridge, which she'd fancied and had time to make, she reflected on the case. She knew it had to have something to do with Sarah Sutton because of the connection to her sister, but she'd have needed help. Philip Sutton was the obvious person, but for the life of her, Della couldn't imagine him doing it. Although in her job, she knew unlikely people did unimaginable things. Still, all her instincts insisted Philip Sutton wasn't who they were looking for. As yet, apart from the fact no one in the Grove had real alibis, including him, there was absolutely no proof he'd been involved. So, who had helped? After interviewing all the couples from the Grove who had alibied their spouses, Della was almost sure none of them had been involved.

Could it have been someone not from Gladioli Grove? Philip Sutton was bitter about the men his wife had been with; could it be that she'd coerced one or more of those men to help her in her quest? Yes. Today, she'd suggest to Tim that they look into Sarah's extra-marital relationships to see if there had been someone she'd seen more regularly.

She made herself a couple of slices of toast and spread them with Marmite. As she chewed her favourite comfort food, her mind brought John Latham into the fore. The more she thought about him, the more she became convinced he was possibly the key to this entire business. He'd been found guilty of a crime he didn't commit and was incarcerated for it. Wouldn't he want revenge, especially if he knew Darren was the guilty party? They needed to know if he had any visitors and who they were.

She finished her leisurely breakfast with an apple. She knew Ben hated the smell of Marmite, so she cleaned her teeth thoroughly in the hope it would remove hints of Marmite. Well satisfied with her plans for moving forward, she was soon in her car and heading for headquarters. She'd be very early, but she wanted to get started on her ideas.

"Hello there, Della, you're early today," the night desk sergeant, George, greeted her cheerfully.

"Yep, the old cog-wheels are a-turning," she sang back at him as she hurried through reception and keyed in the combination for the interior door. "See ya!"

She heard him chuckle as the door closed behind her. To her surprise, Tim Masterson was already in his office. She knocked and entered at his call.

"Morning, Guv," she said cheerfully.

"Morning, Della. You're looking chirpy this morning, besides being very early."

"Been thinking things through, Guv. Can we find out where John Latham had been residing in Her Majesty's pleasure before Whatton, and if he had any visitors?"

Tim's eyes narrowed slightly. "You think our case is linked to that one, do you?"

"Certainly, it is." She filled him in on all that happened the previous day; he'd gone from the premises early, so was not fully up to date. He listened carefully, nodding as she reported.

"Yes, I think you're right. John Latham is the key. I'll see what I can do regarding him. And you think it may have been someone not living in the Grove who helped Sarah Sutton?"

"Well, it seems she had a variety of men friends; her husband is quite bitter about it. He doesn't seem that upset that she's disappeared, but I also believe he's telling the truth when he said it was a surprise to him. She knows we're onto her and took the chance to do a runner before we came up with any evidence to detain her. I wish I'd arrested her and kept her, but we just couldn't substantiate her guilt at all, so I had no grounds to keep her."

"No, you're right there. As yet we have nothing concrete. I put out the call about her. Actually, I think I might hold a press conference and put her picture out as a person of interest we're seeking to help us with our enquiries. Someone may have seen her. I take it there were no results from the train or bus stations' CCTV footage?"

"None at all. I had the team checking yesterday. Nothing from any taxi firms either; I think she must have had someone meeting her. Maybe they picked her up round the corner or something."

"I think you're right; someone helped her. She'd know we'd be able to track her if she used taxis and a bus or a train. It'll be why she left her car, too.

"I wonder where she'd go? Perhaps I'll get the guys looking into where she has family she might go to."

"Good idea. Thank you for all you've done so far. All those interviews must have been a marathon effort."

'They were, and you could have helped,' she thought. Out loud, she said, "They were rather, but we got through."

There must have been something in her voice that she never meant to betray, for he looked at her sharply and continued to look. She carefully neutralised her expression and eventually, he looked away and nodded. "Carry on then. Keep me updated."

"Yes, Guv." Della left his office, making sure she closed the door, very, very gently, then paced away, being well aware he watched her through the internal window. Blast the man! However he got to be an Inspector, she didn't know, but she was well aware she was the reason he had such an excellent track record since he'd arrived in Derby. Maybe once this case was over, she'd consider applying for a transfer. The trouble was, she enjoyed working with Ben and she was happy living in Chaddesden. Did she really want to uproot herself just to get away from Tim Masterson? She could go from the frying-pan into the fire and end up with a much worse boss than him. Sometimes it was better the devil you know.

Chapter 16

Della wasn't ecstatic about having to go in a car with Tim Masterson, but needs must. At least the drive to Whatton wouldn't take too long, but it would be plenty of time for her to experience the jitters at being so close to him. She hoped he would not catch on to her nervousness. She kept her head turned away from him, looking out of the side window as she practised her deep breathing exercise, which helped her heart rate slow down and calm her frazzled nerves until she could gaze through the front window instead. She concentrated on the road as they crossed the Clifton bridge and headed along the A52 towards Holme Pierrepoint and then on to Rushcliffe. The road became an ordinary road, no longer a dual carriageway. After the big roundabout, the intersection between the roads to Leicester one way and Lincoln the other, they headed towards Grantham. HMP Whatton was on this road and it wasn't long before they had drawn up outside the wired fence that surrounded the prison and were waiting to be allowed to drive into the grounds.

To give Masterson his due, he had behaved impeccably on the journey, concentrating on his driving. He was a skilful driver, Della had to admit silently, and if it hadn't been January, the trip would have been very pleasant. She was thankful the intense cold had lifted, and the roads were clear of ice. She'd not really taken in the scenery; once she'd got rid of her nervousness, she cast her mind forward to the impending visit. She wondered what

John Latham would be like. Would she get any sense of his guilt or innocence? And would they glean any clues from him?

She couldn't help the shiver that rose from her when she walked into the prison after being searched and signed in. These places always made her feel like that and occasionally she felt bad that she did a job that would make sure some people were sent to spend their lives in such places. But she would then shake herself and remember these were people who shouldn't be allowed to remain with the public. They were shown into a room where a man already sat at a table, and a prison officer stood in the room with him. When they sat down at the table, the officer nodded at them and left the room.

"John Latham?" Tim Masterson said. "I am DI Masterson and this is DS Della Downs. We're from Derbyshire Police. Thank you for agreeing to see us."

The man at the table nodded solemnly. He was clean shaven and had a pleasant face. He obviously kept himself fit because he was slim, but his bare arms showed muscle. It seemed to Della that, despite looking physically fit, there was an air about him she couldn't quite put her finger on.

"What can I help you with?"

"Do you know a woman called Sarah Sutton? She was Sarah Smith."

"Can't say as I do," replied John, then he hesitated. "Although my Cindy had a sister called Sarah, much younger. I only saw her a couple of times when I visited their house. She was still a child then."

Masterson showed him a photograph. "Would you recognise her in this picture?"

John studied the photo. "Wow, she's a stunner, isn't she? I can see the young Sarah in her, though. She's very like my Cindy. She was beautiful too, but she was much softer, I think. She had a gentle nature." His brown eyes filled with tears. "I can't believe they think I'm to blame for - for what happened to her."

Masterson kept his face neutral and Della followed suit, but she was sympathetic; the guy seemed to love Cindy.

"Well, the evidence pointed to you."

"That scum, Holbeach, framed me. I know it. He always had his eye on her because she was beautiful. He always boasted he could get any girl he wanted, and he wanted her, but she loved me and wouldn't have anything to do with him. He didn't like that."

"No, I'm sure he didn't. Now, can you tell us anything you know about Sarah Sutton? Has she visited you or has she corresponded with you?"

"No." John shook his head emphatically. "No, not at all. I didn't even know she'd got married."

"Do you get any visitors at all?"

"My mum comes when she can and sometimes my sister."

"No one else?"

"No."

"Well, Mr Latham, thank you for your time." He nodded to Della to knock on the door. When it opened, he stood. "Oh, by the way, you may like to know that Darren Holbeach is dead."

John looked up swiftly. "Really? How?"

"Well, it seemed someone hated him as much as you do, Mr Latham. Our Darren met a - shall we say - a chilly end."

A puzzled look creased John's face.

"Yes, it seems someone else thought he might have committed the crime you're here for and meted out the punishment. But we can't have the public acting as judge, jury and executioner, Mr Latham."

"But I had nothing to do with it!" protested Latham.

"I hope for your sake you didn't. Thank you for seeing us. If you think of anything that might help us, please ask your governor to let us know."

Before they left the prison, Masterson asked for details of Latham's next of kin. "We can find out through our own methods, but it would be easier and quicker if you can let us have the information."

The prison governor gave his permission, and they thankfully left.

Once in the car again and on the road, Masterson asked, "Well, Della, what did you think?"

"I would have great difficulty in believing he had anything to do with Holbeach's murder, guv. He certainly appeared surprised when you told him the man was dead. He could be a great actor, but I'd have a hard time believing that was acting. And it was obvious he didn't know Sarah Sutton."

"No." Masterson sighed. "I agree. Especially as the prison has already told me who visits him and it backs up what he said."

"You never told me you already asked that." Della couldn't help the sharpness in her voice. She was further riled when Masterson grinned at her.

"Sometimes, I get one step ahead of you. I have some credentials, you know. I didn't have you as my sergeant when I passed my DI exams."

Della subsided instantly, and turned to gaze through the front windscreen, her face like stone. A moment later, she faced him again, when he patted her hand, which she snatched away.

"Oh, come now, don't be angry with me. How about we stop somewhere for a coffee before we return to the office, eh? There'll be somewhere in Long Eaton, I'm sure, if you'll come?"

In spite of her annoyance, and the chill running down her limbs causing goose-bumps at the thought of being in a cafe with Tim Masterson, she asked herself, why not?

As if he read her thoughts, he said, "Come on, Dell. I'm sure we could both do with a coffee or something and we'll be in a public place, so you needn't worry about - anything." He kept his face forward, seeming to concentrate on his driving while he waited for her reply. She was silent, and so the drive continued. But she noticed he drove towards Beeston after crossing the Clifton Bridge again, instead of continuing on the A52 past the hospital and then Wollaton Park. The car headed towards Chilwell and Toton and she sighed; she knew he was hoping she would agree to that stop-off. Oh well, in for a penny...

"Okay, seeing as we're here, we may as well," she grouched.

He grinned and turned at the ASDA roundabout and parked the car in the car park.

"The police station is just across the road there," he nodded towards it, "But I thought it would be better to keep away from any questioning eyes, just in case."

Della couldn't think of anything to say to that, so she kept silent, although a worried frown creased her brow. They hastened across the road and came to a Wimpy Bar.

They found a table away from the window. It seemed somewhat intimate for Della's comfort, but the place was pretty busy and so she couldn't object. They ordered coffee. While they waited, he was busy on his phone and she took in the surroundings.

Once the coffee was served by a friendly young man, they settled to talking about the case in low voices. Della was thankful he was being business-like rather than trying to 'get around' her.

"So," he said, "What do you see as the next step, as obviously, or it seems obvious, that Latham hasn't been the instigator of the murder?"

"Well...I think I'd like to see his mother, guv. I'd also like to talk with whoever dealt with the Cindy Smith case if they're still around."

Tim nodded slowly. "Yes, we can find out who it was and if they're still in Newark. The address for Latham's mother is in Mansfield Woodhouse, I believe."

"Oh, that's not too far. Ben and I can do that this afternoon. We don't have contact for the sister, do we?"

"Sadly not, although presumably you may get it from the mother. I'm thinking that we may get information from the team in Newark without having to go over there. Do you have anything in mind to ask them?"

"Yes, I would like to know what happened to the jacket and necklace that were used as evidence against Latham. Are they still in evidence storage?"

"Ah, I'm guessing you feel we might yet find forensic evidence from them."

"Exactly. If Holbeach wore that jacket, his DNA will be on it. It could make all the difference to Latham if it only raises doubts about his guilt."

"You liked the man, didn't you?"

"I did, guv. I know most prisoners protest their innocence, but I actually believe he's innocent."

Masterson grunted. "I'm inclined to agree. And we know if DNA testing had been around ten years ago, they would have acquitted him, most likely."

"It certainly might have cast doubt. But now, we have Holbeach's DNA, so if we find a match on those items, it will be proof enough. But we still have to find out who killed *him*."

"It's a plan. Have you finished your coffee? Do you want anything else?"

"No, I'm fine, thanks."

Masterson signalled for the bill and presented his card. Della reached for her card. He put up his hand. "No, this is on me. I think I can stretch to a cup of coffee." He grinned at her and she flushed.

"Thank you, guv."

"Enjoy the rest of your day." The waiter included them both in his smile and they left.

Although she'd enjoyed the coffee, Della was relieved when it was time to head back. She couldn't wait to remove herself from his presence and hoped he wouldn't make things awkward in the car.

Chapter 17

To Della's great relief, Masterson said very little as he drove from Long Eaton to headquarters in Derby. However, when he finally parked the car and she went to open the door, he said quietly, "It was very pleasant being with you today, Della." Then he alighted from the car and came round to her side. She was already climbing out and experienced an embarrassing almost-nose-to-nose meeting moment as she straightened up. She felt her face redden, and he grinned and shut the car door gently as she walked away.

Although she'd had a coffee in Long Eaton, Della felt in need of something. Chocolate! That was it. She needed chocolate. She headed to the canteen and bought herself another coffee and a Mars bar. She spotted Ben at a table and sat opposite.

"Hello there, Della. How did your morning go with the charming Tim?" he grinned at her and she had to suppress the urge to punch that grin off his face.

She growled at him and tore the paper off the chocolate bar, took a bite, and another, then sat back with a look of bliss on her face.

"That bad, was it?" Ben's voice brought her back. The grin was gone and a look of concern was in its place.

She took another bite, chewed, and swallowed. "Not really. He was a perfect gentleman. But for some reason, I feel like a fly getting closer to the centre of a spider's web. I didn't want to be in a car with him at all, but I've survived it. And the chocolate has helped. No doubt I'll regret it later

- there's so many calories in one of those bars - but it's helped to calm me down. Being in a car with him is one thing, even being bought a coffee is one thing, but it better not give him any ideas!" She gulped down the coffee, finished the chocolate, screwed up the paper ready to bin it, and looked at him. "Are you done with whatever you were having?"

"Yes. Are we off somewhere?"

"We're going to visit John Latham's mother. She lives in Sutton in Ashfield. I have the address in my phone. Let's go."

It took a shade less than forty minutes to reach Sutton in Ashfield and a further ten to find the house they were seeking. It turned out to be a neat little bungalow on a corner. Nora Latham opened the door to their knock. Small and neat like her home, she appeared younger than the age given in the details about her. Although surprised to see them, she invited them in and offered them a drink.

The bungalow was warm and comfortable. They were shown into a small lounge that was bright and cheerful. Della sat on a small sofa, and Ben selected a padded upright chair for himself. A coal-look gas fire danced in the fireplace and next to it was an armchair in which was a curled up black and white cat who barely twitched a whisker to show it was aware of their presence. Next to the chair was a bulging bag with knitting needles sticking out of it.

Nora soon bustled into the room, carrying a tray with mugs of tea and a plate of custard cream biscuits, which she set on the top of a nest of tables. She drew out a smaller table and set it between the two detectives, popped a couple of coasters on it and handed them each a mug. She took the third mug and settled herself on the other side of the sofa. She glanced at the cat in the chair and smiled.

"Lance is a naughty boy. He knows that's my chair! I suppose I indulge him too much, really, but he's my companion."

"Lance?" asked Della.

"Short for Lancelot. My daughter named him. He's her cat, really. But you know what it's like; she couldn't take him with her as she wasn't allowed pets in the flat she had, and now, well, I suppose he's mine by default. She's got her hands full with her two little girls, and Lance doesn't really like children."

"Does your daughter live anywhere near you?"

"Oh yes, she lives in Sutton in Ashfield too, only on the other side of town. I see her often, and my lovely granddaughters. Anyway, what did you want to see me about, officers?"

"For reasons we can't explain just now, we're looking into the rape and manslaughter your son John was convicted of, Mrs Latham."

"Oh, my!" A hand went to the woman's chest, and she hastily set her mug down on the tray. "My poor son, convicted of a crime he didn't commit! It's truly dreadful, dreadful. I can't believe they did that to my boy. He's such a gentle lad, and he loved that girl so much, you know. I don't believe he would ever have hurt her."

"Did you know her?"

"Yes, of course. She was my Jillian's best friend. Their mother was a friend of mine too, until she sadly died of cancer. I knew both girls, both Cindy and young Sarah. Sarah was much younger than her sister, you know. But she used to tag around with the older girls sometimes."

"Do you visit John?"

"Yes, when I can. But it's difficult from here. I usually wait until Jill can take me in the car. Which means we can't go that often because she has to get someone to look after the girls."

"I see. What do you talk about when you see John?"

"Well, there's not that much to talk about, is there? We tell him about Jillian's girls, and I tell him about little things I do."

"Does he ever talk to you about what he thinks really happened to Cindy?"

"Oh yes, it's no secret that he thinks Darren Holbeach did it! I met him once; I admit I didn't care much for him. He turned on the charm, especially when he saw Jillian, but there was something about his eyes."

"Do you know if Sarah ever visits John?"

"Sarah?" The woman's eyes widened in surprise. "No, I've never heard him say. I don't even know where she is now. I believe she got married, but I don't know where they live."

"Why did John live in Newark?"

"Well, you know what young people are like. They want their own lives. He had a job in Newark, so he went to live there. Cindy followed him. She wanted to be near him. My husband, my late husband, John senior, bought a flat for John because it seemed likely he and Cindy would get married and it would give him a step onto the property ladder. I wish he hadn't let that Darren share with him. But I suppose I can understand it. It helped with expenses."

"We'd like to talk with your daughter. Would you give us her address, please?"

"Of course." She told them the address and phone number. Ben scribbled it down quickly in his notebook.

"Thank you for seeing us, Mrs Latham. For what it's worth, I don't think John did it either and I'll do everything I can to prove it. He's already served a substantial number of years in prison and that's tough if he really is innocent."

"Oh, I do hope so." Della had often read in books the expression 'she wrung her hands' and now she was actually seeing it.

They left the bungalow after bidding goodbye to the neat little woman and returned to the car. It took a further fifteen minutes to reach the daughter's address.

Jillian's family lived in a largish detached house. The front garden was small but, going by the hedging, it seemed there could be a sizeable garden at the back. A woman who closely resembled John opened the door to their knock. Peering around at them from behind her mother was a little girl of about three.

Della and Ben both held out their IDs. "Are you Mrs Jillian Edgware?"

"Yes. Are you the two detectives who just saw my mum?"

"We are. I'm Detective Sergeant Downs, and this is Detective Constable Curran. May we come in a talk with you, please?"

"Of course. Please excuse the mess, though. Would you like a drink or something?"

"No, we're fine, thank you. We just had tea and biscuits at your mum's."

"Of course you would have. Mum gives everyone tea."

They followed her into a sizeable lounge. It was comfortably furnished with the addition of toys on the floor. They sat together on the sofa, and Jillian sat in an armchair.

The little girl climbed onto her mother's lap and sat watching the two strangers, her thumb in her mouth.

"Mum said you were looking into our John's case," Jillian said.

"That's right. We have reason to believe there is doubt about his guilt."

"Well, thank goodness! It's about time someone doubted. May I ask what has brought it to your attention?"

"I'm afraid I can't say at the moment, but it may be connected to another investigation that we're a part of."

"I see. I don't see how I can help you really, although obviously, if there is anything..."

"Your mother told us you visit John sometimes. Do you ever visit him without your mother?"

"Not really, no. I wish I could go more often, but it's hard with this one."

Della nodded understandingly. "We're not here to criticise how many visits you make to him, Mrs Edgeware. I know it's tricky when you have a family. I'd just like to ask if John has told you who he thinks killed Cindy?"

"Oh yes, he makes no secret that he's convinced it was Darren. Nasty piece, he is. He's all charm, but I always got a bad vibe from him. He set his sights on Cindy, though. She was beautiful and delicate looking. John couldn't believe his luck when she chose to be with him."

"Do you know Cindy's sister, Sarah?"

"I did, years ago. She got married about six years ago and they invited me to the wedding, but when the time came, I couldn't go because I was actually in labour with my eldest daughter. I haven't been in touch for quite a while. They moved and I don't have their address."

"I see. So, you haven't seen Sarah recently, then?"

"Not since before her wedding, no. What's all this about, Sergeant? Why the interest in Sarah? She was only quite young when her sister died."

"Sarah is missing. We are concerned about her welfare. You have no idea where she may have gone?"

Jillian shook her head slowly. "No, I've no idea. Sorry."

Della rose. "Well, if you have any thoughts that might help us, either with regard to Sarah or John's case, please, will you call me? Here's my card. Thank you for your time."

"You don't think Cindy's killer was someone else and now they've got Sarah, do you?" Jillian wore a worried frown as she set the child on her feet and moved to take the card.

"No, I don't think so, but we're keeping an open mind for now."

After she'd opened the door for them, Jillian said, "I don't want to sound catty or anything, but I didn't really like who Sarah became once she grew. She was always precocious as a child, but she was okay, really. But when she became an adult, she was always so full of herself, full of the way she looked and she'd look down her nose at other women, even me. And I'll be honest, I'm surprised her marriage has lasted this long, because I can't imagine Sarah being faithful to one man; she was always a man-eater, would flirt with anything in trousers." She glanced at the trousers Della wore. "Male, I mean."

"Yes, we understand that from what's been said."

"It was one of the reasons why I didn't keep in touch with her. She even tried it on with my husband - and right in front of me too! Made me cross, especially when he told me she had a go in private too! But my Glen loves me and won't look at another woman, especially one like her."

Della smiled. "I'm glad. A man like that is worth his weight. Goodbye for now, and don't forget, if you think of anything..."

"I'll be in touch."

"Did you believe her, Del?"

"I did, yes. Did you?"

"Yes."

Della sighed; it felt as if they'd wasted their afternoon. "Let's get back, mate."

As Ben started the car, Della snapped her fingers. "Damn! I forgot! Just hold on a minute, will you?"

She hastened out of the car and ran to knock at Jillian's door. The young woman opened it, her eyebrows lifting to see Della there.

"I'm terribly sorry. I forgot to ask. Do you know if the police ever handed over any of John's things to your mother or you, specifically the evidence that comprised his jacket and a leather thong with a pendant on it?"

"I believe they are still in police evidence storage."

"That's good news. I'm going to ask my Inspector to instigate a further forensic search on the evidence in store. Hopefully, they will have other things to tell us, now they can use DNA."

"Gosh, do you think so? I don't really understand what DNA is, but if it'll help get our John out of prison, it would be great. He's suffered enough being in prison all this time, not to mention the fact he's lost the girl he loved and wanted to marry."

"Exactly. I, for one, am in the force to right wrongs, and it seems to me this is an instance of that. I'm sure the police did what they could and believed to be right, but a fresh look at the evidence wouldn't hurt, I'm sure."

"I hope you're right."

"That makes four of us, then. Would you let your mum know for us?"

"Of course. Thank you for your time, officers."

Della sat in the passenger seat and turned to Ben. "Well, my merry man, perhaps some wrongs will be righted after all."

"Right on, Robin. Now, let's get back to the forest."

Chapter 18

At headquarters, Della immediately searched out Tim to persuade him to ask for further DNA analysis on the evidence the police had in store. Once she explained, he readily agreed.

"I'll see to it, Della. It will be interesting to see if Holbeach's DNA is on the things. In the meantime, I've had the toxicology report on him. It has confirmed he had a quantity of red wine in his system, along with the paralysing drugs. Interestingly, they also found chlorine on his skin."

"Chlorine? Had he been swimming that day?" Della frowned.

"We didn't really ask what his movements had been that day," replied Ben.

"Remiss, aren't we? I think we need to see Amy. Let's go, and hope she's in."

It was dusk by the time they reached number ten, Gladioli Grove. Amy was in.

"Hello, Della, Ben. Do you have any news for me?" she asked, as they stepped inside.

"Not exactly, no. But we'd like to ask you if you can tell us what Darren did during that last day."

"I'll see if I can remember. Would you like a drink?"

"No, we're fine, thanks. We won't keep you long if you can remember."

Amy screwed up her face as she thought. "Well, he didn't do much at all, really; just lounged around the house until it was time to get ready to go out."

"So, he didn't go swimming?"

"Swimming?" Amy looked at Della in surprise. "Why would you think he'd gone swimming?"

"Do you have a hot tub?" suddenly asked Ben. Della hid her surprise.

"No, we don't. Some of the others do though."

"Do the Suttons have one?"

"Yes, they do."

Della rose swiftly. "Thank you, Amy. Did Darren have a shower before he went out?"

"Oh yes, he always did before he went out. He always looked smart when he left here."

"Right. Sorry, we have to rush out on you. We have a line to follow up. See you again."

As they hurried down the road to number five, Della gasped, "Ben, you're a genius! Why didn't I think of a hot tub?"

"Perhaps because you're not a genius?" grinned Ben and she slapped him lightly on the arm.

Philip Sutton looked tired and bemused when he opened the door in answer to their knock.

"Sorry to bother you again, Mr Sutton, but some fresh evidence has come up and we need to ask you if you have a hot tub?"

His eyebrows shot up. "A hot tub? Yes, we do. Why?"

"Could we see it, please?"

"Just let me put my shoes and coat on and I'll take you round. Easier than going through the house."

Della and Ben looked at each other and Della sensed they'd hit on something. Philip rejoined them moments later, wearing slip-on shoes and shrugging into a padded jacket.

"This way," he said, as he zipped up the jacket and they followed him round the side of the house, through a gate at the side, and into the back garden. They saw a small wooden building near a blank section of the house wall, and next to it a covered hot tub. He switched on some lights; the power coming from the small building. It gave the patio area a soft and romantic feel. "We use the cabin to put our clothes in when we use the hot tub. The tub will be empty just now."

"Do you put chlorine in the tub when you use it?"

"Yes, just a touch, although we don't really like it, but you have to use something. I'll just show you..." As he was talking, Philip pulled the cover off the hot tub. "It will be empty now. Oh."

The 'oh' was because the tub wasn't empty at all; it had water in it. Stone cold, of course. Della took one look and stepped back. "Don't touch it anymore, Philip!"

Philip jumped back as if it stung him. Della was already on her phone. "I need forensics here at once. Five, Gladioli Gardens. I'll meet you."

"Can we get into the house from here?"

"Yes, through these patio doors; it should be unlocked. Yes, there we go."

They entered the house through the lounge, each bending to remove their shoes. Philip shut the doors behind them.

"Any chance of a coffee, Mr Sutton?" Della asked. He nodded and went off to the kitchen.

Della paced the lounge, berating herself.

"Stupid! I'm so stupid; this should have been noticed when we searched before. I was so busy imagining Sarah bringing Holbeach into the house, but she didn't, did she? She took him around the way we just went to the hot tub, where she had prepared the wine with the drugs in. She would have convinced him to go in naked - more fun that way - and he would have willingly stripped off to go into the tub. We'll have compromised the scene by walking the way they did, but hopefully, the tub and the cabin may find his DNA."

"Don't beat yourself up, Della. If it hadn't been for the chlorine, I wouldn't have thought of it either. I believed what she said about the costume and so on and imagined she'd somehow avoided leaving evidence of him in the house, although I didn't know how she would have managed it, knowing how the team can pick up on the tiniest bit of evidence."

Della nodded. "There was probably never a 'costume' at all; there was never any need to worry about contamination because he would never get near her clothes at all; it would be a straightforward thing to keep them completely separate."

"Do you think they did anything together?"

"Who knows? I'd never put it past her. Being the man-hungry woman she was, she would have enjoyed playing with him. Knowing what was going to happen to him later may well have added shine to it all for her, an extra bit of excitement - and under water, how is there going to be any evidence? That's another area I failed - I should have insisted on having her internally swabbed, but we all assumed she hadn't seen him. Therefore, the question never arose. Now, we have lost our chance anyway, because even if we find her, any evidence there might have been will be lost. But if there is forensic evidence on or around the hot tub, it will prove Sarah had something to do with Holbeach's death. Ah, Philip, thank you."

Philip had arrived bearing three mugs of coffee. He sank into an armchair with a sigh. "Will this thing never end?"

"I'm sorry, but we have to do this. You were surprised there was water in the hot tub. Don't you use it in winter?"

"We haven't used it this winter, no."

"Why do you think she didn't empty it?"

"Well, it's a bit of a palaver emptying it; she usually leaves it to me."

"I see. You've had no news from her since she left? No call or anything?"

"Not a thing, no."

They lapsed into silence, each lost in their own thoughts as they sipped their coffee. Della was just finishing hers when the team arrived. She hastened to don her shoes and went out to see them. She gave them instructions and left them to it.

Inside again, Ben had put his shoes on and was ready when she returned.

"Sorry about this intrusion again, Mr Sutton. The team's work is all outside, so no need to worry about them. You're looking tired; get some rest. That's what we're going to do now. It's been a long day."

Philip nodded and was obviously glad to see them go.

Della hugged herself as they walked back to the car, which was still parked on the road outside Amy's house.

"We've done all we can for today. Let's go home."

Chapter 19

It had been an eventful day, and Della was tired. But she was still wound up, so she decided to go for a run. She didn't care for running on the roads, so she usually ran around Chaddesdon Park. However, the park gates were locked after sundown, so she had to run around the pavements. She hardly noticed where she was running and there were few people out and about; mainly the usual intrepid dog walkers. It was certainly chilly, but she worked up some body heat as she ran. Her mind ran over the happenings of the day and all the things they'd discovered. Della was in no doubt at all now that Sarah had been involved in the murder. She hoped the team would find evidence of Darren's presence around the hot tub. But if Sarah had given Darren the drug while in the hot tub, how would she have managed to get him out? She was far too small to have been able to haul a man of that size, and a dead weight at that, out of the tub. They'd already long decided Sarah had help, but from whom? Who was there in that road who had anything to do with Holbeach or Cindy Smith's death?

Information on all the families in the Grove was being investigated by the team and the civilian assistants. Absolutely nothing had come up that could be related to the Latham/Smith case. Were they barking up the wrong tree? Could Holbeach have been involved in something else that someone wanted to punish him for? But Jess was so sure Holbeach had been positioned exactly like Cindy Smith lay when she'd been found, and the red paint in his groin area and his broken wrist mirrored Cindy's injuries. It *had* to be about Cindy.

Della finished her run and stripped off for a shower. She stood under the water, trying to shake away the thoughts that continually ran round and round in her head. As she soaped herself, other thoughts came unbidden to her mind; for a moment imagining Tim in there with her. She hastily shook that away too, abruptly turning off the water and stepping out to dry herself briskly with the towel. Not long later, she was downstairs again wearing her pyjamas and fleecy dressing gown, her hair wrapped in another towel. The house was cosy and warm and she felt much better for her run and shower.

Just as she was about to go to the kitchen to decide what to eat, a ring came at the doorbell. She glanced down at her cosy night-attire and grimaced. Who could it be?

"Who is it?" she called, standing behind the door.

"Only me," came back Annie's answer. Della hurried to open the door.

"I come bearing gifts," Annie held up a bag as she came in. "Oh, look at you, all ready for bed!"

"Yes, and if it hadn't been you, I wouldn't have been opening the door!"

"Even if it was our Tim?" Annie teased, her eyes twinkling.

"*Especially* if it was Tim!" Della glowered.

"Glad to hear it. The office has been making bets on how long it will take him to get you into bed."

"No! Please, no, tell me it isn't true!" Della gasped.

"I was kidding! No one knows - they're a load of blokes, aren't they? They don't notice stuff like that."

"Ben does."

"Oh well, Ben's pretty special, isn't he? And he's very protective of you."

"He is! I sometimes feel as if he's my father," Della giggled. "He sees it as his role in life to keep me safe from our slimy Inspector."

"Good. But I heard you had to have a trip with Mr Slimeball today. How did it go?"

"Tell you later. What's in the bag? I'm starving."

Anna stayed over that night. It was something she did on the occasions when they'd shared too much food and wine. She kept some night things in the small spare room and happily went off to sleep there when they finally called it a night.

The company and evening of food and laughter meant Della dropped into bed and sunk into a deep sleep.

Saturday

Her sleep was a bit too deep, Della thought, as she gazed through a fog behind her eyes at herself in the bathroom mirror. However, she was grateful for it; she'd soon feel right after her morning cup of tea and breakfast. Anna was already up and about, preparing breakfast while still wearing her night attire.

"Hello girl! Tea in the pot," she announced as Della walked in.

"Lifesaver," grinned Della and headed towards the worktop where her favourite mug sat waiting, the teapot and milk carton standing to attention beside it. "We have to stop doing wine on work evenings," she groaned as she poured the tea. She sipped it carefully, closing her eyes for a moment in appreciation. "Mm, just what I needed. Anyway, it helped my mind to stop circling around the case and somehow in my dreams I've reached a conclusion."

Anna raised her eyebrows in a questioning glance. "Oh?"

"It's got to have been the Newtons and Morecrofts. I've interviewed the others extensively and I don't believe any of them were involved. I have a nose for people not telling the truth. And there was something about the Morecrofts in particular that I felt but couldn't put my finger on; I just didn't see how they could be involved. I'm going to get onto that today and maybe go out to see them again."

"That sounds like a plan. There has to be a connection somewhere, either with the dead girl or with John Latham," Anna agreed.

The young women ate their breakfast of toast and fruit - they agreed they couldn't face anything else - then prepared to wash and dress to face their day.

"Shall I give you a lift in?" asked Anna. "I have to go to headquarters, anyway."

"That would be good. Ben can bring me home."

In the car, Della asked, "How are you getting on with Amy? Is she okay?"

"Yes, she's great. Obviously much happier. I don't need to be with her so much lately, although I've promised to keep her up to date with the investigation. I usually pop in at some point during the day, just to see how she is. She's returned to her painting and is producing some superb stuff, I have to say."

"That's excellent. Pity someone didn't bump him off for her before!" The two laughed merrily at the thought as they pulled into the car park at headquarters.

Della heard a shout and turned to see Ben heading towards her. "Ooh - looks like he means business! See you later, Anna. Thanks for the lift."

"No probs. Hi Ben!" Anna called as she went towards the door of the police station.

Della watched as Ben panted up to her.

"Whatever is the matter? You need to be careful or you'll have a heart attack," she said as he reached her.

"I've been thinking," he gasped, holding his chest.

"Oh no, not again," she teased. "Get your breath. Now, take your time."

"It has to have been the Newtons," he said. "How else would they have got the body into the field without having to carry it up the road?"

"That's quite a thought, Ben, you're right. They had to have gone through their garden; there's a gate into the field in their back hedge. I concluded they had to be involved and maybe the Morecrofts too. I'd planned to look into it today. But you're right, and I want a search team at the Newtons' house. Let's go!"

They hurried towards the entrance to headquarters and Della hastened to Tim's office to get permission for the team. On the way, she spotted Jess. "Hey Jess, can you do a search on Angela and Peter Moorcroft for me, please? I want to know if they come into this scenario. Is there a connection between them and Cindy Smith or John Latham?"

"Will do, Sarge." Jess saluted. Della smiled and nodded as she went to have a word with her boss.

Chapter 20

It was obvious they were not welcome visitors to the Newton household. Louise Newton, clad in green lycra, which showed off her good figure, stood in the doorway, clutching the door as if it were a weapon poised to be closed in Della's face

"My husband isn't at home, officers."

"Where is he?"

"He's gone for a day out with a mate somewhere. Not sure where, sorry. Can you come back when he's in?"

"I'm sorry, but we can't, Mrs Newton. This is a murder enquiry, you know."

"I'm aware of that!" snapped Louise. "But I'm in the middle of something important right now. I don't have the time."

"Well, you soon will have! Plenty of time to sit in a cell and think of how you obstructed me in my duties. Now, are you going to let us in, or do I have to arrest you?"

Scowling, Louise stepped back to allow them to enter the house. Then she spotted the van and two figures in putting on white jumpsuits.

"What are they here for? I'm not having them messing up my house!"

"At the moment, they're not coming into the house. Ben, show them, will you?"

Ben stepped outside again and Della watched him go towards the two white-suited people.

"What are they doing? Where are they going?"

"Now, Mrs Newton, don't worry. We think the killers of Darren Holbeach may have carried him through your garden. They're going to do a search out there. Perhaps you'd like to make some tea or something?"

Muttering under her breath, Louise headed towards the kitchen, and Della followed her. A young man came into the hallway from another room.

"Hey, Lou, what's going on? Aintcha coming back? Oh, halloo, who's this?"

"Just go back in, there's a dear. I won't be long; this officer wants a cup of tea. Can I get you anything?" In contrast to the way she'd spoken to Della, Louise now sounded as if butter wouldn't melt in her mouth as she addressed the young man.

"An officer, eh?" he slowly eyed Della down and up and she felt as though he could see right through her clothes. "Mm, nice. You can arrest me anytime, babe."

"Eric!" Louise's voice was sharp. "Go away!"

Della had to admit he was eye-candy; he was muscular in all the right places, and his grin was cheeky and rather endearing. His blue eyes twinkled beneath a beautiful quiff of brown hair, and when he moved towards Louise, Della noticed he had a very nice butt. He draped an arm around Louise's shoulders. "Oh, don't send me away, Lou. How often do I get to be in a room with two attractive women?"

"Oh, I'm sure you have plenty of attractive women around. Now, please go away and I won't be long. I'm sure the officer has a lot to do elsewhere." Louise unwound his arm and smacked him lightly on his pretty butt. He laughed, winked at Della and left the kitchen, saying, "Don't be too long. I have something special for you today."

Della had a pretty good idea what his 'something special' might be. No wonder Louise was busy; it was a 'cats away' day indeed. She wondered for a moment what sort of cats away day Richard Newton might be having.

"Sweet boy," said Louise conversationally. "He's my personal trainer. Richard can't stand him, but he likes how he helps me keep my figure. He goes out on purpose when he knows Eric will be here. He knows he'll get his reward later." To Della's surprise, Louise winked at her.

"Oh, I see. Seems I need to rethink my lifestyle. Thank you." The last was because she'd been handed a mug of coffee.

"So, why do you think they - whoever 'they' are - brought Darren through my garden? What plausible reason could they have had for doing that? I hope they've not caused any damage. I haven't been out there since that night. Far too cold."

"Just some information we came across. Are you sure you heard nothing that night? Where is your bedroom?"

"At the front. No, never heard a thing. We were up late and when I went to bed, I was rather tired. I slept like the proverbial log." Louise laughed lightly and took a sip out of a bottle of water. "We had much to talk about, you know. We haven't seen the Moorcrofts since they moved out of number ten."

"I see. How come they came now? Why didn't they come in the summer when you could all have met together at one of your famous garden gatherings?"

Louise shrugged. "No idea. They suggested it."

"Okay. Thank you for the coffee. I need to see how the team is getting on. No need to bother with us now; we'll just leave when we're done. Thank you for your time."

Although Louise tried to hide it, the relief was obvious. She stood on the threshold for a moment, a smile fixed on her face while Della made her way to the corner of the house, then she shut the door. Della rounded the corner to see Ben coming towards her. Instead of going further into the garden, she waited.

"Anything?"

"They found a scrap of material caught on the hedging by the gate. Could be from a duvet."

"Really? Wow! If only we can find that cover. But it looks like it may have been destroyed somehow - after all, what self-respecting murderer is going to hang onto evidence? Are they continuing the search?"

"Yes, they will search all the grounds and any sheds and so on."

"We may as well leave them to it. Let's sit in the car. It's too cold out here. Then we can talk properly without our teeth chattering."

Once in the car, it was marginally warmer. Della felt sorry for the forensic team working in the garden in the cold, but she knew they would be diligent. It would be a while before they knew the results of the search.

"It certainly seems that they brought the body through this garden and out through the gate. The big question is, Ben, would the Newtons have known about it? Is it possible someone, or a group of someones, could have come through their garden with a body, in the dead of night, without disturbing the occupiers?"

"We-ell, I suppose it's possible. The gate between the two properties is obviously well used; all the neighbours have those connecting gates. If there are no lights at the back for intruders, no alarms, then they could get through without an alarm being raised, especially if the occupiers sleep in a room at the front."

Della nodded. "Louise said their room is at the front, so it's possible." She laughed. "I must have a character quirk, because I was desperate to arrest Louise Newton! But I couldn't think of a reason to do so - I don't think allowing your personal trainer to give more personal treatment is an arrestable offence! But I sooo wanted to!"

The pair laughed and Della felt better.

"I think the question should not be 'did they know about it' but 'were they involved in it?'. The more I think about it, the more I think that's possible," mused Ben.

Della stared at him. "You could be right there, Benjamin. I don't know why we've been looking at everyone else in the Grove and not at them. But I don't see a motive just now. We have to find something. Let's return to the office. I'm going to get someone to look up information about them.

"Hold on there, Dell. Do we know how it's decided where each man will go on their swap nights?"

Della slapped her leg. "Darn it! We don't! I knew I'd missed something. Who can we ask? I know! We'll see Liz and Bill; they've lived here ages, I'm sure they'll know."

Ben started the car and drove out of the Newtons' drive and onto the road, where he parked near the entrance to the house next door. They hastened up the drive and the door opened before they rang the bell.

"Hello, officers, good to see you again." Elizabeth smiled at them both. "I saw you coming."

"Good morning. We'd like to ask you and Bill something. Can we come in?"

"Of course." Liz opened the door wider, and they stepped inside. "Can I get you anything?"

"No, we're fine. Won't keep you long."

"Bill's in here," said Liz, opening the door to the lounge. Bill was reading a book, comfortably ensconced in a recliner chair with his feet up. He looked up and smiled, pressed a button on the chair and put his book on a side table next to him as his feet went down.

"Hello there, Della and Ben. Come in, sit down." Bill waved a hand vaguely at the furniture.

"How can we help you?" Asked Liz as she perched herself on the arm of the sofa. Ben sat on the sofa while Della went for the chair that matched Bill's.

"We'd like to know how it's decided where the men will go on your swap nights/"

"Ah. Well, these days it's done by computer. I don't understand it really, as I'm not computer savvy, but apparently, the computer randomly selects who goes where, and then a message is sent to each man's mobile phone. We all have one, although I don't get on well with my blinking thing," answered Bill. "It's programmed to send each of us to each woman only once during the ten months we do it."

"I see. So, whose computer does this?" Della's thoughts immediately flew to Philip.

Liz and Bill looked at each other. "You'll have to tell them," said Liz. Colour seeped up Bill's neck and into his face. It was obvious he was reluctant to say anything.

"Oh, very well. It's Richard. He's clever at computer programming and a few years ago he devised the programme. Before that, it was done manually, but the computer programme has made things a lot easier."

Della stood. "Right. Thank you for your help. We'll be off now. Please contact neither of the Newtons or you'll be arrested for obstructing."

As she spoke, she noticed a look of - relief? - in Bill's face, hastily turned to neutral. Now, what was that about? Della mentally shrugged; she'd think about it later.

A few moments later, Della and Ben were retracing their steps down the drive. Liz had already shut the door behind them.

"Back to the Newtons' is it?"

"I need to call the guv. Let's get in the car; too cold to hang around out here."

After she'd closed the call, she said. "Right. The Guv is sending someone to observe. When Mr Newton comes home, they'll notify us and we'll return. Let's get something to eat. I'm starving and I need to get warm. The heater in this car is crap."

"Back to the office, or would you prefer somewhere else?"

"Let's go to Morrison's. I can't take any more of that coffee in our canteen."

It was busy in Morrison's but they found a table. They both plumped for sausage and chips.

"I'm inclined to think that, if the Newtons' are involved, or at least, if Richard Newton is involved, then the Moorcrofts probably are, too. I've always felt it was a strange time for them to pay a visit to the Grove. Why not go in the summer, where they could see everyone? What was so special about now?" Della forked a piece of sausage and chewed thoughtfully.

"Well, for one thing, it happened to be the coldest night of the year. If you were going to murder someone by hypothermia, you'd make sure it was as cold as you could make it, wouldn't you?"

"Of course! So, say the Moorcrofts want to kill Darren Holbeach, so they invite themselves here for an evening, knowing it was likely, due to the weather forecast, it was going to be freezing. Their story about not being able to go home that night seemed reasonable, but we know now the pile-up happened much earlier in the evening and was well cleared by the time they would have left the Newtons'. So, why did they stay?"

"Could have drunk too much? But it's more likely they knew they were going to commit a murder."

"Yep. That's what I think. The swap nights also gave the perfect situation to get Holbeach in a vulnerable situation. When we return to the office, Jess will hopefully have to find a motive; something to connect the Moorcrofts with the Latham/Smith case."

Satisfied with the plan of action, the pair paid more attention to the matter in hand - their food.

Chapter 21

The moment Della arrived in the incident room, Jess had obviously been waiting for her, for she hastened towards her and Ben.

"I've found it!" she gasped. "I didn't want to tell anyone else before you, but apparently, Peter Moorcroft is Sarah and Cindy Smith's uncle! His sister was their mother. And they even had the girls living with them after their mother died."

"Well, that puts a whole different light on things." Della's expression was grim. "Strange that Philip Sutton didn't appear to know his wife's aunt and uncle were living in the same street as them."

"Maybe he knew and didn't think it was relevant?" Ben queried, with a lift of an eyebrow.

"If he knew, wouldn't he have expected to be invited next door for the evening, with her relatives coming over for a visit?"

"Perhaps they'd had a falling out, maybe?"

Della shrugged. "Who knows? We should know better than most about the strange things people do. Right, I have to see the Guv. Get us some coffee, will you, Ben? Won't be long."

*****

Louise's eyes opened wide when she clapped eyes on the young, handsome man standing beside DS Della Downs on her doorstep.

"Change of partner, eh? Lucky lady," she drawled. "But why are you here again?"

"This is Detective Constable Smith. May we come inside, please? I understand your husband is at home now."

"He is. Richard! You're wanted!" she called. "Richard? Where are you?"

"What is it? Oh, hello."

Della looked towards the magnificent staircase to see Richard Newton descending.

"Ah, Mr Newton. We'd like to talk with you further. We'd like you and your wife to come to the station with us, please."

Richard reached the bottom of the stairs and walked towards them, frowning. "May I ask why?"

"To help with our enquiries into the murder of Darren Holbeach."

"But we had nothing to do with that!" protested Louise. "Tell them, Richard!"

"She's right. We didn't."

"Nevertheless, we'd still like you to help us at the station."

"Voluntary?"

"Yes."

"And if we refuse?"

"Then I'll have to charge you with murder, sir."

"No!" Louise cried. "You can't arrest us for murder; we didn't do it!"

"Hush now, Louise, it'll be okay. We'll come with you, officers. Get your coat, darling."

*****

"Tell us about this system you use to decide who goes where on your fun nights." Della put her hands together and leaned forward slightly towards Richard Newton, who was sitting on the other side of the table. Ben sat beside her and she knew Tim Masterson was listening in.

"Fun night?"

"Come on, Mr Newton, don't play with me. I'm not in the mood for it. You wouldn't like me when I get moody, would he, Ben?"

"No, Sarge, he wouldn't like you."

"So, I ask you again. I want to know how it's decided who goes where on your swap nights."

Richard sighed. "I worked out a simple system to make sure each male visited each female only once during the ten months. Every month, I simply look at my list, then send the house numbers to each man by text on the day of the visits."

"I see. But that night, you were going to have visitors, so you made sure you and Clive wouldn't be sent to anyone?"

"Well, I had to make sure none of the others missed out."

"What about Darren Holbeach?"

"What about him?"

"Well, let's see. Obviously, he had to go to the right place to enable the murder to take place."

"What? What are you talking about? Holbeach was killed late in the night, wasn't he?"

"How do you know that?"

"I was told. Or I heard someone talking about it. I'm sure I got the idea from somewhere..."

"From your friend Peter Morecroft, perhaps?"

"What? Peter? No, how could he?"

"You tell me, Richard. Did Peter Morecroft ask you to make sure Darren Holbeach went to Sarah Sutton that night?"

Richard sat back in his chair and crossed his arms, the colour creeping up his neck, belying his outward calm.

"I think I'd like to call my solicitor."

*****

"Now, Louise. We want to know about the night of the murder, or rather, before that night. Whose idea was it for the Morecrofts to come over for a visit?"

Louise frowned. "It was theirs. Angela called me and said could we meet up in Derby and when I was out shopping with her, she hinted that she and Peter would really like to come and spend an evening with us while they were in the area and suggested Saturday. I knew it was our swap night and mentioned it to Angela, but she said Peter would have a word with Richard about making sure we could take that evening off. Then later Rich said Pete had called him and he'd agreed to change the computer programme to get us out of the swap."

"Tell us about that night again."

"Celia and Neville came over and the six of us had a great evening together. We had dinner, which I served, then we played cards for a while. Then we sat around chatting and drinking for a while and I started to feel drowsy. Celia noticed and said it was time they went home. Rich told me to go to bed and said he'd stay up longer with

Pete and Angela. We'd already agreed they were going to stay over because they'd heard there was a pile-up on the motorway. In any case, who'd want to go out at that time of night? And they'd been drinking wine, of course. We thought it would be safer."

"What time did you go to bed?"

"I'm not completely sure. I think it was between ten thirty and eleven."

"And that was it? You never got up again until the morning?"

"No. It was strange how exhausted I was, you know. I can usually hold my drink very well. I felt horrible in the morning, too. I had a real hangover. It took me hours to feel right."

Della and Ben looked at each other. Della nodded to Ben, who told the tape the interview was ending.

"I don't think we need to keep you any longer, Louise. I'll get someone to take you home."

"Oh, right. Thank you. What about Rich?"

"We need to keep him longer. No need to wait. Ben, could you take Mrs Newton down and ask DC Smith if he'll just pop her home, please?"

Della smiled as she watched the pair go down the corridor. DC Smith would brighten Louise's day for a short while.

Tim Masterson touched her on her shoulder. "Della, I want you and Ben to go immediately to the Morecrofts' home. I've secured a warrant to search their premises. A team will follow you."

"Right you are, Guv." Della set off in pursuit of Ben and shortly afterwards they were going out the front door.

Chapter 22

On their way to reception, Della said, "Get another car, for goodness' sake, one that has a working heater."

"We'll take mine," said Ben. "You'll be toasty."

The drive to Chesterfield was, thankfully, straightforward, with no hold-ups on the road.

The door was opened by Peter Morecroft himself, who looked startled to see the two detectives again.

"Back again, officers? What's the trouble?"

"We have a warrant to search your premises."

"What? Look here, you can't do that!"

"I think you'll find we can, Mr Morecroft."

"But, but, why?"

"As you are aware, this is a murder enquiry, and we'll do what we need to do."

"But my wife is out."

"That's fine. We can get on with it."

She stepped inside, and Ben followed. Other officers pulled up and came in.

"Shall we go in here and wait?" Della indicated the lounge and Peter entered the room reluctantly.

They waited in the lounge. While Ben sat rigidly in an upright chair, Della wandered around the room. There were some photos in frames on the sideboard; she was sure some of them weren't there last time they came. She moved in for a closer look and then turned to Peter, holding out a picture.

"Am I mistaken, or am I right in thinking this is a photo of Cindy Smith?"

He set the mugs down on a small table and stepped towards her. He nodded. "Yes, that's our Cindy."

"And the woman and young girl with her are her mother and Sarah, now Sutton?"

The colour in Peter's face grew ashen. "Yes," he whispered. "Sophie was my sister. Angela and I had no children, so when Sophie died, we had the girls come to live with us. That's how Cindy and John Latham met. Angela is good friends with John's mother. We spent a lot of time together. Then John got a job in Newark and Cindy decided she would go too and also found herself a job there so she could be near John. They planned to marry, but you know what happened. Angela and I have never got over it. It was bad enough losing Sophie but losing Cindy too, well, that was even worse, especially the way she died, raped and thrown away like a rag doll and left to die. I'm afraid we indulged young Sarah too much, as she was the only one left. She became completely self-centred. We were glad when she married Philip Sutton; it helped us she would want for nothing, even though for some reason she didn't want to know us anymore. I think she blamed us for her sister's death because Cindy got to meet John through Angela's friendship with his mother."

"I see. How come you lived on the same road as them? Neither of them ever mentioned you, not as if you were relatives, I mean."

"We already lived in Gladioli Grove; we moved there after Sarah took herself off somewhere to live on her own. We weren't sure where. We were surprised, or perhaps not surprised, when Sarah and Philip came to live in the Grove. Surprised, because she knew we lived there, not surprised because she must have seen the houses there and would only have the best and they are wonderful houses. She fell on her feet when she met Philip Sutton. He's well off and was willing to give her anything she wanted. But I'm sure the shine eventually tarnished for him because she was more interested in other men than in him. He definitely became the bottom of the pile. We tried talking to her, to no avail. She ignored us completely. It was pretty much the reason we moved away from the Grove. The other reason was the - erm - lifestyle."

"Ah yes. How did you get around that with you being Sarah's foster father?"

"On the evenings I was supposed to go to Sarah, I'd simply go down the pub. If Philip went to Angela, he was always happy to just watch a film or chat with her or play a game of scrabble or something. We liked him a lot and were worried about him. Despite us bringing up Sarah, we could see Philip was much too good for her."

"And Philip never knew about the relationship? Neither of you ever told him?"

"No, we didn't. I wish we had told him, really; we could have been of support to him. But we felt it was best not to say anything unless Sarah did. The ball was in her court, you might say."

As Della nodded, they heard a door opening and closing and heard a voice call, "Peter? Where are you, love?"

It wasn't long before Angela came hurrying into the room. "What's going on? Why are there police cars outside?"

Della and Ben stood. "Mr and Mrs Morecroft, we'd like you to come with us, please, to assist us further in our enquiries."

Angela's mouth dropped open. "What? Peter, what's going on?"

He went to her and put his arm around her. "They think we had something to do with the murder that happened over in Gladioli Grove, my dear. They're searching the house."

Della watched as the colour bleached from the woman's face and she sat suddenly on the arm of the chair near her. "No," she whispered. Peter helped her up.

"They won't find anything against us. Come on, love, let's get this over with."

"But what about our house?"

"We'll make sure it's secured when we've finished. I'd like you to go with these two officers."

Ros and Mike had appeared in the hallway and they nodded at Della. They led the Morecrofts out of the house.

Della watched as they helped the pair into a police car, and it drove away.

"Right. Let's get down to business. Ben, organise a couple of the guys to search outside, will you?"

"Will do."

Della left him to it and went out the front. She saw a woman in the garden next door and walked towards her. Holding out her ID, she said, "Good day, ma'am. Could I just ask you please if they have collected the refuse since 12th?"

"Not yet. It's only collected once a fortnight now. Recycling one week, black bins the alternate weeks."

"Thank you." Della turned to go.

"But – " Della stopped.

"Yes?"

"I – I don't want to tell tales, and I do like Peter and Angela, get on well with them. They're good neighbours, you know?"

"Yes. But if you know anything, you need to tell me."

"Well, I don't *know* anything exactly, but I saw Peter going out in his car very early Monday morning – and I mean *very* early. It was about four in the morning. I don't sleep well and I happened to glance out of my bedroom window and I saw the car pulling out of his drive. I looked at my clock because I thought it was a strange time for him to be going out."

Della frowned. "I don't suppose you saw him return?"

"I did. Yes, at least, I heard the car because I was downstairs making a drink. I do that in the hope it will help me get off to sleep again, see? When I went upstairs, I looked out my window, and the car was back on their drive."

"How long would you say it was gone?"

"Hard to be exact, but around twenty minutes."

"Thank you. Can I get your name, please?"

"It's Hardy. Eileen Hardy."

"Thank you, Eileen, you've been very helpful. Would you mind popping into your local police station and giving them a statement, please? I'll let them know."

"Yes, I'll do it this afternoon."

"Excellent. Please call me if you think of anything else that might help us." Della handed the woman a card and returned to the house.

An hour later, the search officers agreed there was nothing in the house to help them.

"Okay, we need to widen our search. I've had information that Peter Morecroft went out in the wee small hours of Sunday night in his car. Where did he go? Could he have dumped the evidence somewhere? I'm going to contact the local office and ask for their help. You all return to headquarters and leave us to deal with it. Ben, let's go."

A couple of hours later, Della and Ben had returned to headquarters. Their counterparts in Chesterfield had taken upon themselves to do the searches, having worked out how far Peter Morecroft could have driven in about ten minutes from his home, based on the evidence given by the neighbour. They promised to be in touch right away if they found anything.

Chapter 23

Time was now of an essence. Although they had arrested the Morecrofts, they had yet to bring proof. As soon as they had reached headquarters, Peter Morecroft had insisted on calling a solicitor so they could not begin interviewing the couple until the solicitor showed up.

Masterson had arrested Richard Newton for murder and he'd been interviewed in the presence of his solicitor, a sharp-suited man by the name of Nathaniel Aldridge. He had insisted his client say 'no comment' to every question asked, except his name and address. Masterson had had a frustrating session with them, gleaning little from the experience.

When the solicitor for the Morecrofts finally arrived, Masterson and Della interviewed Peter first. The detectives and the solicitor, Daniel Hamilton, gave their names to the tape and Della gave the date and time. Masterson looked at his notes.

"You are Peter Morecroft of 73, Ash Lane, Chesterfield?"

"Yes."

"And you formerly lived at number 10 Gladioli Grove, Derby?"

"That's right."

"And you spent the evening of the 12th January visiting with Louise and Richard Newton, who live at 7, Gladioli Grove, Derby?"

"Yes."

"And you also spent the night staying at the said address?"

"Yes."

"Why did you visit that particular night?"

"We were in Derby visiting other relatives and friends. My wife had met up with Louise during the day before and she invited us to come on the Saturday evening. She said she would invite our other friends, Celia and Neil, from number eight to join us for dinner."

"Wasn't it a strange time to be visiting, in the middle of a month of freezing weather?"

Pete shrugged. Della said, "For the benefit of the tape, Mr Morecroft shrugged."

"Didn't the residents of Gladioli Grove have lots of garden parties during the summer months? Why not visit then?"

"How do you know we didn't?" Pete responded.

"We ask the questions, you answer them," Masterson shot back. Pete smirked. "We know you didn't visit. We have a statement from Louise Newton which says, and I quote, 'We hadn't seen them since they left the Grove.'"

"No comment."

"So, I ask you again, why did you want to visit in the coldest month of the year?"

"No law against it, is there?"

"Not at all, no. But Chesterfield is hardly on the other side of the country! You could pop down at any time. Why pick a time when travelling can be treacherous, to say the least? Could it be because you knew it was going to be well below freezing and you had murder on your mind?"

"Why would I have murder on my mind?"

Masterson sorted through his papers. "Apparently, you have connections, Mr Morecroft. First, you are Sarah Sutton's uncle and foster father, are you not?"

"Yes. So what?" Pete folded his arms and stared at the DI.

"Isn't it rather strange to visit some old friends living in the same street as your niece and yet she wasn't invited to the gathering?"

"I explained that to your minion there," Pete insolently nodded his head towards Della. He seemed as if he'd had a complete character change since their conversation at his house.

Masterson gave no sign of aggravation but continued calmly, "Tell us again."

"We fell out with her and haven't had contact with her since before she was married to Philip, poor sod."

"Why call him that?"

"All out for herself, isn't she? Only thinks of money, posh clothes, nice things, and an easy standard of living. She doesn't love him; it was only because he's well off and can give her all she wants."

"I see. So, although you lived on the same road as your niece, you had nothing to do with her?"

"No."

"What did you do on the wife-swapping nights when you were scheduled to go to her?"

Della was amused to see the solicitor's eyebrows shoot up.

"As I told her," Pete nodded again towards Della, "I used to go to the pub."

"I see. Let's return to the night in question. We believe you needed to be in the Grove that night, because you had planned to kill Darren Holbeach."

"No."

"We also believe you were not estranged from your niece at all because you needed her help to commit the murder."

"No."

"We believe you roped in Richard Newton because you needed to be sure Holbeach would go to Sarah's house that night and there you captured him, carried him to the field, stripped naked and left him to die in the cold."

"No. Why would I do that?"

"Why indeed? Because we know about the murder of Cindy Smith, your other niece. We also know your wife was best friends with her murderer's mother. John Latham has always maintained he was innocent, and Darren Holbeach was the one who raped her and left her to die. Revenge is sweet, is it not?"

"No comment."

"So, I put it to you that you and Angela, together with Sarah, plotted to kill Darren Holbeach and you put your plan into action on the coldest night of the year, to make sure he would die."

"No comment."

"I believe that although you and Sarah may have been estranged, but you had reconciled. When did that happen? When you sold your house to Amy Holbeach, knowing her husband was the person you all think killed Cindy Smith?"

"No comment."

"We think Richard Newton helped you by making sure Holbeach went to Sarah's that evening."

"No comment."

"Did Richard help you with moving Holbeach?"

"No comment."

"Here is a picture of Holbeach after his death." Masterson moved a photo towards Morecroft. "Not a pretty sight. Strange that his position and injury to his arm exactly match Cindy's position and broken arm, although she did still have some clothes, albeit torn to shreds."

Morecroft barely glanced at the photo. "No comment."

Masterson ended the interview there. They took Morecroft back to his cell, and they moved to the next interview room, where Angela Morecroft waited with a PC in attendance.

The same solicitor was in attendance at the interview. Although obviously upset, Angela was just as uncooperative as her husband and apart from saying her name and address and admitting she'd been Sarah and Cindy's mother's friend and took in Sarah, she would not respond to anything else, following her solicitor's advice to respond 'no comment.'

As the interview seemed to come to a natural end, someone knocked on the door and asked for Masterson. Della hastily stopped the interview and switched off the tape. She exited the room, leaving Angela and the solicitor together to talk.

Following Masterson to the incident room, she saw him putting down the phone. Seeing her, he strode towards her.

"That was Chesterfield. They've found some things fly-tipped which they think could be the things we're looking for. They found a duvet in a black bag, and some men's clothes in another one. They're sending them over in a squad car and they can go for testing."

"That's brilliant, Guv."

"Forensics will do their stuff and we'll see if they can provide the evidence we need."

Chapter 24

Milly Allen awoke and stretched her legs carefully, one by one, in her bed. She hoped the day would be warmer; she was thoroughly fed up with the cold. January and February always seemed so long and dreary. She hated going out when it was slippery underfoot and she'd avoided it for days. But she knew she'd have to make herself go out because her supplies were getting low. Her daughter, Daphne, was always telling her she'd get her shopping for her, or else she could order it by phone. She had her house phone with the big buttons. Not that she used it much. There weren't many people she would call.

That was another thing she hated about the cold - her arthritis was always worse when it was cold and damp. Daphne had often spoken with her about the possibility of going into sheltered accommodation.

"You'd have a much nicer flat than this one, and there would be a common room where you could meet up with the other residents. They would probably cook dinner if you wanted and you wouldn't have to worry about cooking. I've been to see a lovely place in Sherwood. You'd love it, Mum, I'm sure you would, and you'd have friends to chat to."

Reluctant to leave her cosy bed, Milly lay and recalled Daphne's words. Certainly, a day of being alone stretched before her yet again. She loved this flat. She'd lived here for many years. But she had to admit to herself it wasn't the same as it used to be. When there was someone living in the one next to hers, it felt as though she wasn't alone. She remembered that nice young man who'd owned the flat a few years ago. He'd always been kind to her and even often brought things for her to save her from going out in the cold. She shook her head; even now, she could hardly believe he'd done what they said. It just goes to show. You can never tell. He'd raped and beaten his young lady and left her outside to die all alone. He had to be mentally unstable to do a thing like that. Despite the warmth of her cosy cocoon, she shivered. He might even have done it to her if they hadn't taken him away! Milly recalled the sweet face of that poor girl. She'd seen her often going to and from his flat and she always smiled and said 'hello'. So awful to have her life snuffed out like that, at such a young age. But then she remembered the other one, the one who'd been staying with John. Although he never gave her any cause, Milly hadn't liked him. There was something about him she didn't trust. Now, if it had been him who'd brutalised the girl, she would have understood. But the police insisted it had been her boyfriend. Apparently, there was evidence.

Thankfully, the other young man hadn't stayed at the flat once his friend had been arrested. Since then, there had been various tenants. None of them seemed to stay that long. Some were friendly, some were not. Recently, though, decorators had been in there; obviously freshening the place for new tenants, or perhaps new owners? She didn't know, and they didn't offer any explanations. Of course they wouldn't. She kept herself to herself and never asked questions.

She recalled the young woman who had come to the flat a few days ago. Milly had hoped she was getting a new neighbour, but she hadn't seen the woman since then. There had been no sound from the flat at all, so she assumed the woman had not stayed.

Sighing, Milly reluctantly put a foot out of bed and slid it into a fur-lined slipper and then drew the other foot out to slot into the other one. She drew her old-fashioned quilted dressing-gown around her and hobbled to the small bathroom, where she performed her ablutions as quickly as her crooked hands would allow, then headed back to her bedroom. Once dressed in her warmest clothes, she made her way carefully into the living area and the small kitchenette to make her first cup of tea of the day. She flapped at a large fly, making sure it wasn't going to land in her drink, and took her mug into the living room to sit with it in her favourite chair. As she waited for her tea to cool sufficiently to drink, she frowned at the fly which had followed her from the kitchen. A fly, this time of year? Strange.

She picked up a magazine and used it to wave at the fly when it came near her. She became aware there was another one in the room, too. Where were they coming from?

When she finished her drink, she carried the mug back to the kitchen and set it in the sink, just in time to see another fly come up from the plug hole. She hurriedly put the plug in to make sure no other flies could enter her domain that way. Slowly, she went to the bathroom and did the same there. She didn't want flies coming up through her pipework.

Returning to the kitchen, she popped a couple of slices of bread into the toaster. While she waited, she selected a pear from a bowl and cut it up carefully. She had long since given up eating apples; they were much too hard for her dentures to manage, but pears were fine. This one was lovely, so soft and juicy, just right. As she wiped her hands on a paper towel, her toast popped up and she buttered it liberally (well, who cared at her age about too much butter?) and spread marmalade on it. She carried her plate through to her lounge and switched on the television. She always watched while she breakfasted. Today, she'd need to keep an eye on those dratted flies and make sure they didn't get to put their mucky feet in her marmalade.

There was another appeal for that young woman who had gone missing. Such an attractive woman. There was something about her that reminded Milly of the young woman she'd seen going in next door. However, the one on the television had beautiful long, blonde hair, whereas the one she'd seen had deep red locks. Could it have been the same woman? Milly wondered.

Milly chewed her toast and thought about it. Surely she was mistaken? Should she tell someone? If she called the police, they'd think she was just a batty old woman.

She looked out the window and sighed. The skies were grey and threatening. She explored her cupboards in her mind. She still had some bread and cheese. There were some tins of soup, too. Maybe she would make a cake. There was enough to keep her going for today, and maybe tomorrow as well. She settled down to watch Homes Under the Hammer and forgot all about the red-headed girl next door.

Chapter 25

Sunday

Daphne stood outside her mother's flat and turned her nose up. What on earth was that smell? Was there a dead cat lying around somewhere? She looked around but couldn't see anything significant.

She tapped on the door, opened it, and called, "Mum! It's only me."

"Come away in, duck. You're just in time for a cuppa," came back the answer.

Daphne found her mother in the little kitchen.

"There's a horrible smell out there," she remarked as she kissed her mother on her cheek. "Is there something wrong with the drains?"

"I don't know, love, but there could be. I have to keep the plugs in because otherwise flies come out of the plughole."

"That's odd. Has stuff been draining away?"

"Seems to. But I can't open the windows either, not that I want to this cold weather, but if I did, I couldn't. Loads of flies are out there too."

"Hm, strange. I think I should call a plumber or the water board or something. Perhaps the drains need clearing."

"Yes, perhaps you're right. I noticed there seems to be a smell, so perhaps there is something. Will you see to it, please, dear?"

"Of course, Mum, don't you worry. In fact, I'll just do it now and maybe they'll come before I leave."

Daphne went into the living room and searched through the phone book. When she found what she wanted, she made the call. It took quite a while because of the usual 'press one for queries, press two for...' and so on. Eventually, she could make the appointment.

"They said someone will be round tomorrow, Mum. I'll try to be here. Is that tea ready? I'm gasping now after all that. Oh, I've brought you some cakes, those little French Fancies you like so much, and some other bits and bobs, too. But I expect you need me to get you some serious shopping?"

"Oh, yes, please. I've been trying to talk myself into going out, but I don't want to, it's so cold."

"No, you shouldn't go out. You need to stay in the warm. It's easy for me with the car. In any case, it's still slippery in places and I don't want you to be laid up with a broken leg or arm."

"Goodness, neither do I. Now, what have you got to tell me?" Milly helped herself to a French Fancy - she particularly liked the pink ones - and settled down to have a good chinwag with her daughter.

*****

Monday, second week

On the dot of nine, Ralf Long and his assistant, Andy, were on Milly's doorstep. Like Daphne had the previous day, they wrinkled their noses in disgust at the smell. They were well used to pungent smells in their line of work. To Ralf, though, this was different. He had immediately identified it to himself, but not to his young companion. Unlike Daphne, he knew exactly where it was coming from, and it wasn't from the flat they'd come to.

"Go back to the van, lad, and stay there," he ordered.

Andy looked at him in surprise.

"But aren't we going in there?" he nodded at Milly's front door.

"No. Change of plan. I want you to go to the van. I'll join you in a moment."

Andy turned and hurried away. Ralf knocked on the door of Milly's flat.

When she opened the door, he touched his cap and introduced himself.

"Do you mind if I just use your phone, please? I've found a problem and need to make a call."

"Help yourself, young man," said Milly. "There's the phone."

"Thank you." He punched in the numbers. Speaking quickly, he gave the address. Putting the phone down, he called to Milly. "Thank you. I'm going outside now."

She reappeared from the kitchen. "Don't you want a cup of tea?"

"Maybe later, thank you, after we've finished. The problem is outside. Keep your door shut."

"Don't worry, young man, I will."

A few minutes later, he joined Andy in the van.

"Wassup, man?" Andy said. "What are we doing?"

"Waiting for the police," Ralf replied grimly.

"What? Why?"

"Because I know that smell. I have every reason to believe there may be a dead person in the flat next to the one we were called to."

Andy looked aghast. "You're kidding me!"

"Wish I was, lad. I'm hoping I'm wrong. We have to wait here until they come. Let's have some of our coffee while we wait, shall we? I need something."

Normally, Ralf was a stickler for them not drinking their coffee until elevenses. It showed Andy that his partner was deadly serious. Without another word, he dug the flask out of the bag and poured out two cups of the steaming liquid.

The two men sipped their drinks and watched the road. As they did so, a car pulled up and a woman climbed out, carrying some shopping bags. They saw her laboriously carry the bags to the entrance of the flats and not long later, she appeared on the upper terrace and stopped at the very door they'd been called to. Ralf and Andy looked at each other, and Ralf put his cup into his partner's hand and once again exited the van. He hurried into the block of flats, knocked on the door where they'd stood not long before and waited. Moments later, the door was opened by the same woman, still wearing her coat.

"Oh hello," she said. "You must be the man from the Waterboard. I'm glad I arrived in time. My mother is elderly," she added.

"I'd like to speak with you, please. Outside, if you don't mind. It's rather, erm, delicate."

A puzzled look crossed the woman's face, but she stepped outside, closing the door behind her.

"It's like this, Mrs - erm -"

"Foster. And my mother is Mrs Allen."

"Mrs Foster. I have called the police because I have every reason to believe there may be a dead person in the flat next door."

Her hand went to her mouth with a gasp. "Really?"

"Yes. I recognised the smell. I'm hoping I'm wrong. But I don't have the authority to break into a property, so I've called them. Will the old lady be alright?"

"Don't worry, I'll look after her. Oh! It looks like they've come. I'll go in, so I'm out of the way."

"Indeed. They may want to talk with you and your mother."

She nodded. "Yes, of course. That's fine. I'll stay here with her."

When she'd gone in, he looked over the balustrade to see Andy talking to the two police people, pointing towards him. He waved as they looked up, and then they started towards the entrance. It wasn't long before they'd joined him outside the flat next door to Milly's. Ralf rapidly explained why he'd called them.

"Do we know who the owner of the flat is?" asked one constable.

His partner, an older man, grimaced. "If I remember correctly, this flat used to belong to someone who is a guest of Her Majesty. I'll have to call in to see if they can find out who owns it now."

He called in for instructions, then paced up and down the terrace while awaiting a reply. When his phone sounded again, he answered and listened. "Right. Will co." He looked at the others. "I've been instructed to break in as the owner is still inside and they don't know who is overseeing it now. Right. Let's do this."

He tried the door first, finding it locked.

"I've got some tools in the van," said Ralf. "Might come in useful."

"I think I can do this." The sergeant took out a credit card and inserted it into the crack of the door. He carefully manoeuvred it and they heard the lock click open.

"You didn't see me do that, Brent," he said to his companion.

"Of course not. But it's better than kicking the door in."

"Exactly. Now, brace yourself, lad. Mr Long, you stay out here, please."

The burly police officer opened the door and the smell immediately became four times worse. The young constable staggered back, almost gagging. He put his hand across his mouth and nose.

"Yep. No doubt about it. We have a death. Everyone out."

Neither Brent nor Ralf were going to argue with that; they each were eager to put as much space as possible between them and that smell.

Sergeant Ball drew the door to and was again speaking into his phone. "From what I could see, a young female sitting in a chair in the lounge, wrapped in a duvet. Dead for some time, by the looks. Yes, sir."

Closing the call, he turned to Brent. "Right. Crime scene tape. The team will be here soon; let's be ready." Turning to Ralf, he said, "If you give your contact details to Brent here, I don't think you need to hang around. Someone will contact you in due course. Thanks for your alert."

"No problem. Oh, by the way, the lady who lives next door is elderly but her daughter is with her at the moment. You may want to let the detective who comes to know that so they can speak with the old lady while her daughter is still here."

"Yes. Good thought. I'll pass the message on. Brent, you just stay here and guard this door while I fetch the tape."

Ralf and Sergeant Ball left together. On the pavement, they parted, the Sergeant to his car to collect the tape and Ralf to join Andy as he sat in the van listening to music on the radio.

"Well? Was it?" Andy asked.

"It was indeed, lad. Horrible. We don't need to be at our next job yet. Let's go find something to eat; I need a pick-me-up."

Chapter 26

DI Jimmy Hart arrived at the scene an hour later, having driven from Nottingham. There were several vehicles parked in front of the flats, an ambulance among them. A handful of people, obviously curious onlookers, stood around, being kept from getting too close by the uniformed officers. On showing his ID to a young constable, he made his way towards the entrance, where he was met by Sergeant Ball.

"What have we, Sergeant?" he asked, as the other man showed him the way.

"A young female, sir. Cause of death is not obvious as yet. The doc is with her now."

"Ah, good."

Jim donned protective clothing and entered the flat. He'd put a little vapour-rub under his nose in preparation and so could stand the smell without it turning his stomach over.

"Detective Inspector Hart," he said to the man now standing by the chair on which reposed the body. "Are you the doc?"

"Indeed, I am. Harry Edwards at your service, Detective."

"Can you tell me anything?"

"Not much at this point. A young woman, in her late twenties, I'd say. No evidence of attack; I suspect she's been poisoned. Probably in her flask."

"Could it be suicide?"

The doctor pulled at his beard. "Well, yes, it could be. There is the remnant of a packed meal on the small table beside her. She could have wrapped herself up to be as comfortable as possible to die."

"Can you give me any idea...?"

"How long she's been dead? You detectives want everything immediately! I can't say for sure until I get her on the table and it's very hot in here because the heating is on, but I'd say she's been dead for around three days."

Jim nodded. "Thanks, Doc. I'll let you get on."

"Yes, we're ready to move her now."

He stood by while they moved the woman onto a stretcher and zipped into a bag. Without wishing to touch anything, he glanced around, noting the coat, hat, gloves, scarf and wig on the sofa. A member of the forensic team put each item into polythene bags. He exited the flat to find the sergeant out on the walkway.

"Poor young woman," the police officer remarked. "Too young to die."

"Quite," Jim replied. "Neighbours?"

"There's an elderly lady next door, sir. Her daughter is with her right now, I believe. Do you wish to talk with them?"

"I do. Ah, I'm glad to see you, Dave." Jim spotted his partner coming to join us.

"Sorry, Guv, got stuck in traffic," the newcomer, DS Dave Taylor, said, as he joined his boss. "What do we have?"

"Did have. They've taken her away. Young woman, dead a few days, apparently. Could be suicide; we have to wait for the doc's report. We'll go to the local nick and set up there, but first I want to talk with the neighbour. I was just going to do that as you arrived. Then we need to do our own search of the flat."

Leaving the forensic team to do their thing, Jimmy knocked on the door of the flat next door. It opened so quickly it was almost as if the woman had been standing there behind the door waiting for the knock. He judged she was around fiftyish with a pleasant face, her dark hair streaked with grey, tied back in a sort of bun that was trying to escape. She looked harassed, but invited them in on seeing their IDs.

"Come in. Would you like a drink? I've just put the kettle on for tea, or perhaps you'd prefer coffee?"

"Coffee would be great, thank you," replied Jimmy. "Dave will have coffee too, won't you?"

The other man nodded, and the woman acknowledged it. "I'll take you through to see my mother. She's the one who lives here."

"Thank you."

They followed her into a small lounge, where sat an elderly lady with her feet on an old-fashioned pouffe, a crocheted blanket on her lap.

"Mum, these are detectives and they'd like a chat with you."

The old lady's eyes sparkled. "What fun! Do sit down, detectives. Excuse me not getting up, but my arthritis is really giving me some jip. It's the cold, you know."

"Don't you worry, Mrs erm?"

"Allen. But do call me Milly, dear."

"Milly. Thank you for seeing us. I'm Jim Hart and this is my colleague, Dave Taylor," Jimmy said, as he pulled up a wooden chair in order to be near her. "Have you lived here a long time?"

"Oh yes, I have. Daphne and I moved here when my husband died. Couldn't afford the upkeep of our house after he'd gone. Took too early, he was."

"I'm sorry."

"Don't you worry, duck. It was a long time ago now. We managed, didn't we, Daphne?"

Daphne had just entered the room carrying a tray with four mugs. "What's that, Mum?"

"I was saying we managed here after your dad died."

"Oh! Yes, we did." Daphne handed the mugs to Jimmy and Dave. She put a mug on a small table near her mother. "Be careful with that, Mum. It's very hot."

"Thank you, dear. Now, what did you want to talk with me about?" Milly asked Jimmy.

"Did you see the young woman next door at all?"

"I saw her arrive, at least I think it must have been then. I saw her go past my window." Milly nodded with her head and Jimmy turned to see there was a window behind him; the small lounge had a large window behind the old lady's chair looking over the back of the property and a small window facing the front opposite.

"I sit here in this chair most of the time, so I can see anyone going by that window, which I like, because I prefer to see who might knock on my door."

Jimmy smiled. "I can see you're safety conscious and that's a good thing. Can you tell me what day that was, please?

"Hmm, let me see, what day is it today? Monday? It would be Thursday then. Yes, Thursday, around lunch-time or a bit later. Yes, it was nearer one-thirty, I think. I couldn't help noticing her and her lovely red hair. I remember thinking how nice it would be to have a neighbour again and I've been disappointed not to see her again. In fact, after I heard her door close, I heard nothing else, not a whisper. But she must have put her heating on because it's been warmer in here the past few days and that only happens when next door is heated too. I'm not objecting, mind, every little helps. Oh dear, I'm rambling, aren't I? Sorry."

Jimmy smiled indulgently. She reminded him of his gran. He made a mental note to visit her as his earliest opportunity. He hadn't been in a while.

"So, you saw her on Thursday and nothing since?"

"Not a thing, no. I hope she's alright?"

Jimmy's eyebrows raised. Hadn't the daughter told her? He made eye contact with Daphne and she shook her head slightly. Inwardly, he sighed.

"I'm very sorry to tell you, Milly, but your young neighbour is dead."

"Dead?" She sat up straight. "How? When? Who is she?"

"I'm afraid I don't have any answers yet, Milly."

"That's so sad. I think that flat is jinxed after what happened ten years ago."

"What happened ten years ago?"

"The young chap who lived there killed his girlfriend. Raped and left her to die in open ground. He's in prison."

Jimmy and Dave looked at each other. "Is that so? Interesting. Do you know who owns the flat now, Milly?"

"No idea. It has had tenants sometimes, but none of them have stayed very long. But it's been decorated recently, so maybe it was sold? Although a 'For Sale' notice never went up."

"We'll look into it. Thank you very much, Milly. You've been very helpful."

"Have I?"

"Oh yes. We now know when she arrived, and it helps to build up our picture."

"When you find out who she is, would it be in order for you to let me know?"

"I don't see why not." Jimmy stood, and Dave followed suit. "Well, thank you for seeing us, Milly." He clasped her hand gently and smiled.

"And thank you for the drink, Mrs Foster. We both needed that after our drive from Nottingham."

"You're welcome. I'll see you out."

*****

Daphne returned after seeing the two detectives out and sank into the other armchair to drink her cooling tea.

"What a very nice man," commented Milly. "But that poor girl. I do hope they find out who she is and what happened to her."

"Indeed. Whoever owns that flat is going to have problems getting tenants if it becomes known that girl died there."

The two women sat in silence for a few minutes, each thinking their own thoughts.

"You know, Daphne, I don't think I want to live here any longer."

Daphne looked up in surprise. She'd been trying to get her mother to move out for ages and she wouldn't budge.

"Really?"

"Yes. I don't enjoy being here without a neighbour and the steps are getting too much for me now. I'm thinking it would be nice to be in a sheltered place and have some company."

"You could come and live with me and Jack, you know. We have the room." Daphne knew Jack wouldn't be best pleased. She mentally crossed her fingers.

"Oh no, I wouldn't encroach upon you two. I've been thinking about it a lot lately and it would be nice to have some company my age. Will you look into it for me, duckie?"

Daphne heaved an inward sigh of relief. If she was living alone, she'd have had her mum with her, no doubt about that. But with Jack, it was better not.

"Yes, of course. And you'll need to get the flat valued. I can see to that too. Are you sure about this?"

"Yes, I'm sure."

When Daphne left the flat later, she reflected that life was full of surprises. It was sad about the death of the unknown young woman, but it seems it had been the key to making her mum want to move. As she climbed into her car, she grinned. It was a good thing the handsome detective would never need to know about *that* particular motive!

Chapter 27

"Right. I want to know who owns that flat, or what agent deals with the lettings. We know the girl arrived on Thursday, so we'll put out a description and appeal for anyone who might have seen her in Newark on that day."

DI Jimmy Hart was in the Newark offices, giving instructions to the willing uniformed officers. They had made a photofit of the dead girl up with red hair for them to take out onto the streets of the town. Dave was to trace the information about the flat.

"Until we get the report back from the doctor, we don't know if we're dealing with a suicide or murder, or who the dead girl is. So, until we get some of that information, we'll just have to work with what we can. It's going to be difficult; most people's memories are short and if they only had a glimpse of her, they'll probably not remember, anyway. But we have to try. There's a supermarket across a footway from the flats, so could someone go there and ask if they have any CCTV footage of the day in question, please? It's possible she parked her car there; see if there's been any vehicles impounded from there or is still there for a few days if they don't impound, or any car left for a few days in the area. I know we don't have much to go on, but do your best, please."

"Dave, can you do a search to see if any young women have been reported missing recently, please?"

"Sure thing, boss. I'll do that right now." Dave's fingers were already tapping the keys of the computer.

Jimmy envied his partner's skill; he was a two-fingered typist, and he wasn't that happy working with computers. He had to admit they were making police-life easier though, and he had no doubt the systems would be refined and get better and better over the years. He knew he needed to get up to speed. He'd do it, he would...

Coffee was what they needed. He headed towards the machine and got two coffees, one for himself and one for Dave, and took them back to where his partner was busy.

"Jimmy! I think I know who she is!" Dave was excitedly looking at his screen. "Derby police put out an APB on her. Their girl has long blond hair and our girl's hair is short, but still blond. The description fits otherwise."

"Good work! I hadn't seen it, having only just returned from leave. Well, that's amazing results. I didn't think we'd identify her so quickly. We need to inform Derby. Find out who is the SIO on that, would you, please?"

"Of course, be a mo. Ah, it's DCI Alan Smethwick, with DI Tim Masterson's team."

"Oh, the Masterson slimeball," Jimmy sighed.

"You know him, boss?"

"Yes, I know him. I suppose he's alright really, but he can't help himself around women; he thinks he's God's gift."

"Oh, that sort. I hope, if he has any women in his team that they're strong."

"Indeed. I'm going to call him now, tell him the news. Oh, can you get onto the pathologist and let them know we think we've identified their latest cadaver?"

"I'll do that." Dave picked up his phone.

Jimmy took himself into another room to make his call.

*****

Della's phone rang.

"DS Downs."

"Della, we have a call from a DI Hart, of Nottingham police. He wanted to speak with DI Masterson, but he doesn't appear to be in his office. Will you take the call?"

"Of course. Hello, this is DS Downs. I'm afraid the Inspector is out of the office at the moment. Can I help?"

"This is DI Hart, of Nottingham. I'm currently working in Newark, having been called here for a suspicious death. It has come to light that she may be the woman you took an APB out on, Sarah Sutton?"

Della gasped. "Really? Can you tell me more? Where was she? How did she die?"

"She was in a flat in Newark. We're not sure yet how she died, but the pathologist says she's been dead a few days."

"A few days! Goodness. I think we may have to come over to see you."

"Actually, the postmortem is being done at Queen's. Perhaps we could meet there and the pathologist can talk with us both together. I don't hold out with gleaning much information here and my partner and I both live near the city, so it would be easy for us too. The police station in Newark is only open during the day and doesn't have an investigative team, which is why my partner and I were sent over. We would have brought in our team, but I don't think that's going to be necessary now. I'm sure we can work together on it as this is really more your case than ours. We can compare notes."

Della smiled; she liked the sound of this man, so different to Masterson. "Sounds good. Obviously, I'll have to inform my guv."

"Of course. I'll call the pathologist and arrange a time to see him. I'll call you back shortly, or my partner will."

"Thank you."

As soon as she put the receiver down, she stood. "Gather round, everyone. I have news."

They all came and stood around her, or perched on the edges of desks.

"What's up, Della?" Ben eyed her questioningly.

"I've just had a phone call from a DI in Nottingham police. It seems Sarah Sutton has been found. Unfortunately, she's dead."

There were a few gasps in the room. Ben asked what they were all thinking. "How? Where? Was she involved in an accident?"

"I can't tell you the 'how' at the moment, but apparently, she was in a flat in Newark and has been dead for a few days."

The buzz of murmuring arose and fell. She held up her hand. "To date, we don't know that many details and it has yet to be confirmed it is her. As her DNA is on the database, the pathology lab will confirm it easily enough, although we can take Philip Sutton over to see her. He'll possibly want to see her, anyway. Oh crap, we have to tell him. We should get over there now. Anyone know where the Inspector is?"

"He left early. Said he had to take his wife somewhere," Mike said. "I saw him on the way out when I was coming in. Asked me to tell you."

Della scowled. "Okay. Thanks, Mike. Ben, we should see Philip Sutton. Mike, if DI Hart calls or his partner, jot down the time I'm supposed to be meeting them at the morgue, please."

"Will do."

"Come on then, Ben. Let's get this over with. Actually, the rest of you may as well go home. There's not much more we can do tonight. Mike, when you've got my appointment for tomorrow, you can go too. If it's an earlyish appointment, call me at home, would you? If it's for later in the day, don't worry. I'll pick it up when I come in."

"Right." Mike nodded his head.

Chapter 28

When Philip Sutton opened his door to their knock, Della thought he looked even worse than he had before. He was obviously not sleeping; the dark shadows round his eyes behind his specs told their own story. He scooped up the little dog that suddenly appeared at his feet.

"Have you found Sarah?" he asked.

"May we come in, please, Mr Sutton?"

His face creased into a frown, but he opened the door further and stepped back to allow them entry. He led them into the lounge. It was pristine and felt as though no one lived there, although it was warm.

"Would you like a drink, detectives?"

"No, thank you, we're fine. Please come and sit down. We've come to tell you we've had news of Sarah."

Philip perched on the tip of an armchair, having put the dog down, while Della sat on the white sofa. Ben remained standing to one side.

"Have you? Where is she? Have you arrested her again?"

"I'm sorry to have to tell you, Philip, we think Sarah is dead."

"Dead?"

Della could tell he was genuinely shocked.

"How? Did she have an accident or something? And where did it happen? And you *think* she is dead?"

"We are pretty sure it's Sarah, although we need to be positive. Are you up to coming with us to confirm her identify?"

"Oh! Erm, yes. Now?"

"Yes, please, if you would."

"Where...?"

"At Nottingham's Queen's hospital. We'll take you and bring you back."

"Right. Erm, I'll get my coat." He stood and then sat again. "Sorry. I'm in shock, I suppose. Everything that's gone on lately has been too much, and now this. Although she was difficult and selfish, she was my wife and she was still so young. Please, before we go, tell me how it happened and where was she?"

"She was in a flat in Newark, apparently – "

"Newark? Whatever was she doing there? And – and, did she die in the flat? But how?"

"She died in the flat, yes. As yet, we don't know how, there'll have to be a postmortem. It's thought she'd been dead a few days."

"A few days? But – she's only been gone a few days..." Philip looked even more confused.

"We still have a lot of questions to find answers for. Believe me, we'll do our very best to find those answers, Philip. But right now, we need to make sure we haven't told you that your wife is dead if it isn't her. But we want you to be prepared. Are you feeling up to it now?"

He nodded and stood. They followed him out of the room and waited while he took his coat from a cupboard and put it on.

"I'd better just put the dog in the kitchen." He picked up the dog and carried it down the hallway. Della heard him say, 'Basket', the sound of a door being closed and Philip reappeared. They left the house, waited while Philip locked the door, got into the car and set off.

Philip never said a word throughout the drive. Unfortunately, it took longer than it usually would because it was the rush period and the A52 was very busy. Once they left Derby behind, the traffic moved smoothly until they neared the Wollaton area leading up to the Queens Medical Centre, known locally as 'Queens' or QMC. They eventually got through onto the slip road leading to the hospital and Ben found a place to park near to the entrance nearest to the morgue. Ben put the 'Police on Duty' sign on the car and they entered the hospital.

A man who introduced himself as Doctor Harry Edwards, Pathologist met them. He led them to an area where a figure covered by a sheet was lying on a metal table.

Doctor Edwards lifted the sheet and folded it to reveal the face of the victim. Philip looked and his hand went to his mouth and his eyes filled with tears. He raised his eyes to look at Della. "It's Sarah," he croaked. "I can't believe it."

"I'm sorry for your loss, Mr Sutton," said Dr Edwards. "Would you like to stay with her for a few minutes?"

"No. No, I don't think so, thank you, doctor."

The doctor covered Sarah's face again and Philip turned away. Della thanked Dr Edwards while Ben led Philip away.

"I'll be attending the post mortem tomorrow, doctor," she whispered.

"See you then, Detective."

It was a quiet drive back to Derby. Della took a few discreet glances at Philip in her mirror, to see him remove his glasses and dab at his eyes with a handkerchief. By the time they reached his home, he had composed himself and replaced his spectacles.

As they pulled into Gladioli Grove, Della said, "Are you going to be alright alone, Philip? Is there anyone we can call to be with you?"

"No, thank you. Actually, perhaps you could drop me off at number nine, please? I think I'd like to be with Liz and Bill. They're like second parents to me."

"Of course. We'll be happy to do that."

They pulled onto the drive of number nine and Philip climbed out, thanked them and rang the doorbell. Liz. Della watched as a moment later, the older woman's arms went around Philip. She lifted a hand towards their car and drew the younger man inside and the door shut.

Ben started the car and drove slowly down the drive. "Home?"

"Yes. Home. Thanks Ben."

Della felt unaccountably weary. Just as they thought the case was drawing to a close with all the ends sewn up, she now had more ends to deal with. But they could wait until tomorrow.

Chapter 29

Tuesday, second week

Della was not happy. Once Tim Masterson had been told about the proposed meeting at Queens, he insisted on accompanying her rather than Ben.

As last time, they travelled in Tim's car. Della was thankful they weren't going as far as they'd had to go before when they visited the prison. As it was, she felt vaguely uncomfortable at first, but he put on Classic FM on the radio and she allowed herself to relax, well, almost.

"This case seems to be more complicated, don't you think, Della?"

"Yes, sir. We have the right suspects, I'm sure, for Darren Holbeach. I'm just puzzled about the death of Sarah Sutton."

"Hopefully, we may get some answers soon, perhaps even this morning. When the forensics comes back to us with their report on the things found in Chesterfield, we'll know where we are. I just hope they do so before we have to release our suspects."

There seemed no answer to that, so Della just nodded slightly, and resumed her watch out the window. Tim allowed the silence between them to continue as he tapped his finger on the steering wheel in time to the music playing on the radio.

It took less than half an hour to arrive at QMC and around to an entrance in West block, where the mortuary was. Tim parked the car, with a notice 'Police on Duty', and they went inside. On reaching their destination, they found the pathologist in conversation with two men. As they came closer, the other three spotted them. One of them came forward, hand outstretched, towards the DI.

"Tim, good to see you. This is my colleague, DS Dave Taylor."

"Well, Jimmy Hart! How are you, old boy?" Tim shook the other's hand and then turned to shake Dave's hand and then the doctor's. "This is DS Downs."

Jimmy immediately turned to Della. "Ah, it was you I spoke to on the phone yesterday. Nice to meet you." As they shook hands, Della couldn't help comparing his open, friendly face to Tim's. He wasn't classically handsome like Tim, but she liked the way his eyes crinkled when he smiled, and he seemed to make the rather cold area feel warmer somehow. She judged him to be around Tim's age, perhaps slightly younger. She had no doubt this man had a wife he was happy with. Dave was younger, around her own age, she thought. He seemed friendly too.

Once the introductions were over, attention returned to the doctor. Della was highly relieved when he told them he'd already done the autopsy in the presence of the other two detectives.

They followed him into a room with plastic chairs along two walls and a drinks machine on another wall. Apart from those things, the room was somewhat austere.

"This is the room where people wait for death certificates or to see a dead relative. Normally, we'd go into my office, but it's rather small for five people," the doctor said apologetically. "The post mortem revealed the young woman was in good health. The cause of death was definitely something she'd ingested. Hopefully, the toxicology report won't take too long. Until the results of those tests come through, I can't tell you what the substance was, I'm afraid. Except that it was in the coffee. The other flask was full of drinking chocolate and hadn't been opened. There were no drugs in that flask. Whatever the substance was, the cup still held some coffee, so that will be tested too. But I think we can be fairly sure whatever killed her was in the flask of coffee."

Della and Tim looked at each other. "That means she must have brought it from home." She turned to the doctor. "Could it have been suicide?"

Dr Edwards shrugged. "It could be. Hard to know, really. Unless there was someone in her house who could have slipped the drugs into her flask, or someone could do it along the way somehow. Or, there was someone waiting for her in the flat."

Dang! Could Philip have done it after all? Della was certain he was shocked by her death, but could it have been an act? She'd always prided herself on being an excellent judge of character and she was sure Philip Sutton wouldn't dream of doing something like killing someone, even that money-grabbing, man-eating wife of his...

"Della?"

"What?" Della was brought out of her deep thoughts by the sound of her boss speaking her name. "Sorry, I was trying to work something out, sir. What were you saying?"

"It looks to me like suicide. She was frightened of going to prison; we know she was involved in the murder of Darren Holbeach."

Della nodded. For now, she was happy to go along with that theory. She looked up, to notice Jim Hart was watching her, one eyebrow raised slightly. She met his gaze and was surprised to see him give a barely noticeable wink, his eyes darting to Tim and back in an instant. She felt a bubble of laughter, which she hastily suppressed. Jim cleared his throat.

"There was no evidence of anyone else in the flat and there were no finger-prints on the flasks, only Sarah's. It looked to me like she'd just arrived there, but she'd hung away the clothes she brought with her and eaten the food she'd packed. There were no other prints on any of that either. Of course, everyone knows to wear gloves these days, so it's no surprise. We found prints not belonging to any of the people there that day, but because of the positions of them, I'd guess they belong to whoever decorated the place. We're looking into who they might have been."

"Well, if you don't mind, I need to get on with my work. I'll leave you to the detecting. I'll get the toxicology report to you as soon as I can," said Dr Edwards.

"Thank you very much, Harry," said Jim.

Dr Edwards nodded to them and left the room. Tim also stood. "I don't think we can do any more here. Good to see you, Jim. Let us know if you discover anything more."

"I will."

"Oh," said Della. "Can you tell me the address of the flat where Sarah was found, please?"

"Flat 2, Acacia Gardens, Lincoln Road."

Della frowned. "Isn't that the flat that's owned by John Latham?"

"You know about him?" asked Jim.

"Oh yes, indeed. The case we're working on is tightly connected with what happened there a few years ago. We know the flat is still owned by John." Della frowned. "I wonder how Sarah had access to it?"

"We've tried to find an agent for the flat, haven't we, Dave?"

"Yes boss. We've found nothing. We don't have any idea who holds the keys for the place."

Della looked at Tim. "I think I need to contact John Latham's mother. Perhaps she has them, or she'll know who does."

"Would you let me know what you find out, please?"

"Of course. We'll keep you fully informed. We need to go now, Della. I have another appointment."

"Could we have a contact number for you, please?" Della had turned to Jim.

His eyes crinkled, and he fished a card from his pocket. Della took it and they smiled at each other for just a moment.

"Della!" Was Tim Masterson actually tapping his foot? As soon as he saw she was coming, he turned abruptly and left the room. Della followed him but risked a glance behind her, just in time to see Dave make a rude gesture towards Tim's retreating back. She grinned and hurried to catch up with her boss.

"I'd better have that card," Tim said as they settled back in his car. "I'm the one who'll have to liaise with him."

Della handed it over without a word. He took it, put it in his pocket, started the car, and pulled away.

"You know him then?"

"Yes, I know him."

Della waited for him to continue, but he didn't. He looked pointedly through the windscreen and gave every impression of concentrating on his driving. A side glance Della risked, revealed his jaw muscles flexing as if he was gritting his teeth. She looked away hurriedly and put her efforts into appearing interested in the passing scenery, but her mind was working ten to the dozen. What was that all about? After a while, she forgot about Masterson as her mind returned to the question of Philip Sutton. Had he put something in Sarah's drink? If he hadn't, who did? Della couldn't bring herself to believe Philip Sutton had done it. No more than she believed Sarah Sutton had killed herself.

Chapter 30

Masterson drew up outside headquarters. He hastened out to hold the door for Della while she alighted. As she stood, her eyes came into line with his for a moment. He still looked grim, and she frowned.

"Are you okay, guv?"

"Why wouldn't I be? Anyway, I've got a meeting in town. Be back around two." Masterson shut the passenger door and Della heard the car pulling away as she climbed the steps to the entrance.

As she entered the incident room, the team looked at her. She nodded to them. Ben wasn't in the room, but a few moments later, he entered, carrying a cup of coffee in one hand and a Mars Bar in the other.

"Saw you coming, Del. Figured you'd need these." He set the drink and chocolate on her desk.

"Ben, you're a star! If your wife ever leaves you, I'll marry you." Della broke open the Mars Bar and took a bite, her eyes closed, savouring the moment. "We'll have a chat, guys, as soon as I've finished my caffeine fix. Give me five." She saw a variety of thumbs-up around her and continued to eat her chocolate.

A few minutes later, having been revived by the chocolate and taken some cautious sips of the coffee, which was still hot, she stood in front of the incident board.

"Gather round, people." She waited until she knew she had everyone's attention.

"The DI not coming?" Someone asked, and there were some quiet sniggers.

"He's gone to a meeting in the city, apparently, so we'll carry on without him. Sarah Sutton was killed by a substance in her flask. Since she took the flask with her, our boss has decided she killed herself because she didn't want to face prison. But my instincts tell me otherwise. If that was the case, why not do it at home? DI Hart told us she was carrying about a thousand pounds with her. Philip said she had a phone, but it wasn't found. Why carry that amount of money with her if she was going to top herself? It doesn't make sense. Also, she was found in the flat belonging to John Latham."

A few quiet gasps came from around her as the team realised the significance. Della nodded. "Quite. Philip Sutton identified the body late yesterday afternoon. He is a suspect, of course, but he seemed genuinely surprised and puzzled when we told him she was dead and was upset when he saw her body. He could have been acting, but..." She let her sentence hang with a shrug.

"Are you going to bring him in?"

"I'm reluctant, but I suppose we'll have to. Actually, I'd like to know first who holds the keys to John Latham's flat. Carol, would you call his mother and ask her, please? Jess will have the number."

"Sure will."

"Have we had any reports from forensics yet?"

There was a general shaking of heads. "Oh well, let's make use of the time to finish our paperwork and look at some of our other cases."

A few general groans were heard as the team returned to work at their desks.

"So, how did it go this morning?" asked Ben, quietly. "How was the boss?"

"He was okay going, but coming back he was grim."

Ben raised his eyebrows. "Grim? How?"

"On the way there, he put on music. He didn't talk much but seemed relaxed. Coming home, he looked like he was clenching his jaw and never said anything until we arrived here and said he had a meeting in the city. That's all."

"Strange. What was the other DI like? Hart, was his name?"

"He seemed nice. Completely different to his lordship. No airs and graces, no feeling of upmanship or superiority. It seems they knew each other."

"Who? Hart and Masterson?"

"Yes. Oh, and that was another thing. DI Hart gave me his card, but Masterson asked me for it when we were in the car."

Before Ben could respond, Della's phone rang. "DS Downs. Oh, yes, that's right. I gave the card to DI Masterson. Yes, that would be very helpful, thank you." She wrote a number on her pad. "Yes, thank you very much. This is my number, if you wouldn't mind passing it on for me?"

When the call was over, she put the receiver down. "That was DS Dave Taylor, DI Hart's partner. He's given me the number where I can reach Hart. Apparently, he wanted to be sure I had it and for me to keep him updated on the business with the flat."

"Hmm. I get the feeling DI Hart knows our DI better than we thought. Either that, or he's got the second sight."

The pair grinned at each other, then turned as DC Carol Morris came to them. "I've spoken to Mrs Latham,

Della. She says Pete Moorcroft holds the keys to John's flat because he manages it for her while John is in prison, and he's recently had it redecorated."

"That's interesting. Thank you, Carol. Ben, we need to have a little chat with Mr Moorcroft."

*****

Pete Moorcroft sat in the same chair in the same interview room they'd been in with him before. He had his arms folded in front of his chest and was trying to look unconcerned.

"Don't I need to have my solicitor here?" He asked as soon as Della and Ben walked in.

"I don't think that's necessary, Mr Moorcroft. I wanted to have a chat with you about John Latham's flat."

The man's face creased into a puzzled frown. "John's flat? In Newark? Why?"

"Before I answer that question, can you tell me if Sarah Sutton has a key to the flat?"

Pete's arms unfolded, and he ran his right hand down one cheek. "I'm not sure. I have an idea Angela may have given her one, although I'm hazy as to the reason." He put his hand on the table and looked up. "It was recently redecorated, which I oversaw. I was going to put it in an agent's hands in Newark, but I hadn't got around to it. Tell you the truth, I'd forgotten about it, what with one thing and another."

"I can see planning a murder would take your mind off other things," remarked Della. For that, she received a mutinous stare from Moorcroft. He refolded his arms and leaned back in his chair.

"Why the interest in the flat?" he asked.

Della looked at him for a moment, trying to figure out whether he already knew what she was about to tell him. "They found Sarah Sutton in John Latham's flat yesterday. She was dead."

"Dead!?" Moorcroft sat up suddenly, a shocked look on his face. "How can she be dead? How did she die?"

"Apparently, she took something."

"Took something? What's that supposed to mean?"

"She had a flask of coffee, and whatever it was, was in the flask."

Moorcroft leaned forward, placing his elbows on the table, his head in his hands. "No!"

Della and Ben exchanged looks. More gently, Della said, "My DI thinks she took her own life."

His head shot up again, an angry look on his face. "Your DI is a fool! There's no way Sarah would kill herself. She loved life too much!"

"She might not if she'd gone to prison for murder."

Calmer, he nodded. "That's true. But I still can't believe she'd do that. Someone must have put the drugs or poison or whatever it was in her flask. That husband of hers, most likely. Have you told Angie yet?"

"Not yet, no."

"It's gonna kill her."

*****

Angela eyed Della warily as they brought her into the interview room.

"Just want to ask you a couple of questions, Angela. Do you know if Sarah had a key to John Latham's flat in Newark? Pete thinks you gave her a key, is that right?"

Angela cast her eyes down and nodded.

"May I ask when you gave her the key?"

"After the – after what happened."

"Did she say why she wanted it?"

"She planned to leave Philip and wanted somewhere to stay for a few days." Angela looked at Della defiantly. "She wasn't happy with him and she knew you'd eventually work out what happened and wanted to get away."

"So, you helped her by giving her a key to the flat."

Angela nodded again. "I know it was wrong, but I had to help her. She's like my own daughter," she whispered. "Has she been captured?"

"I'm sorry to have to tell you, but Sarah was found dead in the flat."

"No! No, she can't be dead! She was only going to be there a few days and then was going up north. She had it all worked out! She's not dead. I don't believe you!"

Angela broke down and sobbed. Great howls of anguish sounded from her. Ben handed her a wad of tissues and then left the room. Della watched the woman cry out her pain; she couldn't help feeling sympathy for this woman who had now lost both her foster daughters, whom she had brought up and loved. What a tragedy! All because these people thought it was okay to take the law into their own hands.

Ben returned with a cup of tea, which he placed on the table near Angela. Her sobs gradually became quieter, and she wiped her face with more tissues given to her by Ben.

"I'm sorry for your loss, Angela. Are you able to answer another question about Sarah?"

Angela sniffed, her shoulders hunched as she tried to stem the sobs, and nodded.

"In your opinion, would Sarah kill herself?"

"Kill herself?" The notion actually made Angela stop and stare at Della. "Why would you think she'd done that? There's no way – like I said, she had plans to get away. How did she...?"

"It appears there was something in her coffee flask. She seemed to have settled down in a chair and died as she slept."

"Oh...," said Angela, faintly. "Oh, my poor girl. Surely Philip wouldn't have done that? He's not the type, he's so gentle. He was too good for her really but we loved her. It must have been him, though, mustn't it?"

Chapter 31

'And that,' thought Della, *'is the ninety-five-million-dollar question* – was it indeed Philip?'

She needed to talk to Masterson. When she returned to the incident room, she called Ben, Mike, Ros, Carol and Shane.

"Right. We're going to arrest Philip Sutton on suspicion of murdering his wife. Mike and Ros, I want you to search the house. We're looking for tablets and medication of any description, plus any empty packets in the bins. Carol and Shane, I want you to take a couple of uniform and go to Philip Sutton's office. I want all bins there and any public council bins near his office to be searched. If they've been emptied, find out where to. Let's go!"

Ben and Della travelled in Ben's car and were followed by Mike and Ros in a marked police car, their lights flashing and sirens sounding.

Philip Sutton opened the door to their knock, still looking like he hadn't slept. Della hardened her heart against the sympathy she felt for him.

She flashed her ID at him. "Philip Sutton, I arrest you under suspicion of murdering Sarah Sutton. You do not have to say anything, but anything you do say will be written down and may be given in evidence."

Philip was obviously dumbfounded and his face turned ashen. He slipped his feet into shoes and put his coat on, as two officers pushed past him to begin their search.

He never offered a word of protest or denial; in fact, Della thought he just looked resigned.

As he was being walked to the car, a figure ran up the drive. It was Amy, and she was breathless.

"I saw the cars. Philip, what's going on?"

"They think I killed Sarah, Amy."

"No! No!" Amy turned to Della. "How can you think that? He wouldn't do something like that! Philip, what can I do?"

"Will you look after the dog, please?"

"Of course." Amy was crying now.

Ben made Philip get in the car.

"No more talking, please." Ben was kindly but firm as he helped Philip into the back of the car, protecting the top of his head with his hand.

Della really hadn't wanted to do this, but Tim had insisted. It was true that Philip was the obvious suspect, and they had to go through the motions. She recalled how Amy and Philip looked at each other; had this second murder been in order to free Philip for Amy? Could Amy also be a suspect? Perhaps they planned it together? Della shook her head slowly; she just didn't buy it. She had great experience and prided herself on being a good judge of character. She couldn't believe it of these two, Amy especially. Della could have sworn Amy was the sort of person who wouldn't even have an affair, never mind kill a woman in order to have her husband, however much she loved him – and it was obvious she was in love with Philip; there was no way she could hide that. But Della also knew that sometimes you just couldn't tell when someone would do something out of character.

*****

Tim Masterson put Philip through a gruelling interview session, with Della the accompanying officer. Philip's solicitor was present, a Mr Dominic Holland. After a couple of hours, in spite of Tim's interviewing technique, they failed to gain a confession from Philip. All four looked and felt exhausted. Tim called the session to a halt, knowing they were getting nowhere.

"All his body language says he's innocent, sir," said Della to Tim after they'd left the interview room.

"I have to agree. However, let's see if forensics comes up with anything. We can hold him a while longer; we have at least another twenty-one hours."

Mike and Ros returned from their search of Philip's house.

"We just found the usual things – a first aid kit with a box of cold remedy tablets, a box of sore throat lozenges and an almost full box of paracetamol, as you can see here." Mike held up the items in plastic bags. "No empty packets of anything anywhere."

"Right. Thank you."

Not long after, Carol and Shane returned too, also empty-handed.

"The city rubbish bins are emptied regularly, so there was nothing to find. They are taken to the landfill site; it would be like looking for a needle in a haystack and even if we find packets, we won't know if they're what we're looking for or where they've come from," reported Carol. "Do we actually know yet what was in the flask?"

"No, we don't. Toxicology hasn't got back to us yet. I was just hoping to get something in readiness to hasten things along. That's backfired on me. Oh well, thanks for trying."

"No problem, Dell. We all knew it was a long shot, anyway."

Ben came into the room then, looking smug.

"What's up?"

"Tests have turned up trumps on John Latham's jacket. Apparently, it has Holbeach's DNA all over it, as does the medallion. Semen samples taken from the body at the time have also been retested and have proven to match his DNA. Overwhelming evidence he was Cindy Smith's killer, or at least enough to cast doubt on the guilty verdict for Latham. They are going to take it to appeal."

"Oh, well, that *is* good news. Let's hope the wheels turn quickly to get John Latham out of prison."

"I'm sure they will. His mum is going to be a very happy lady."

"I'm glad. I liked her."

"Me too."

"Shall we go and tell her? There's not a lot we can do here just now."

"Why not?"

The drive to Sutton-in-Ashfield was pleasant, and the visit to John's mother was a pleasure. With tears in her eyes, she thanked them, plied them with tea and cake and thanked them, over and over. She called Jillian, who said she'd come right away. She was as good as her word, for she arrived not long later, just as Della and Ben were leaving.

"I can't thank you enough, DS Downs. What wonderful news to think our John could soon be free!"

"You can thank the development of science, Jill, especially how we can use DNA to help us in our work. It doesn't always help, but in this case, it certainly does. We must go, but we so often have to tell people bad news. It feels good to have some cheerful news to share for a change. Goodbye. 'Bye, little one," said Della, as she smiled at Jill's small daughter.

"Well, that felt good, didn't it, pardner?" said Della after Ben started the car and they'd been waved off by the two women, the little girl standing beside her mum, thumb in mouth.

"It did, Dell. Can't help wondering how long it will take for Latham to complain about being unjustly imprisoned."

"Ever the cynic," she teased. But inside, she deeply sympathised with the young man who had spent nearly ten years in prison for a crime he most likely didn't commit, and she hoped she'd never cause anyone to suffer the same fate because of her investigations. Philip Sutton's ashen and drawn face drifted into her mind.

Chapter 32

"There was no evidence of any other finger-prints on the flask, Della. In fact, both flasks only had Sarah Sutton's finger-prints on them," DI Hart's pleasant voice explained to her over the phone. She'd called him to see if they had discovered any evidence they didn't yet know about in her department. "We have followed up the prints and forensic evidence found in the flat, and it's all from the two men who decorated the flat. They were there several weeks ago and did not know who was coming to live in it. They confirmed they'd been hired by Pete Moorcroft and they check out. We spoke again to Milly, the lady next door, and she confirmed there had been no one in the flat since they left and the young woman came. So, we don't have anything to go on from that."

"No toxicology reports?"

"No. That's going to go to you anyway. It's what we arranged with the pathologist. Hopefully, you should have it soon."

"Good. We've arrested the husband, although I'm not convinced it was him. But I'm sure she didn't kill herself; she was not the type. Her foster mother has told me she had plans for getting away and the flat was supposed to be a temporary bolt-hole."

"Hmm. Well, it turned out to be rather more than that. If I get any more information, I'll be in touch."

"Okay, thank you."

When the phone call ended, it surprised Della to find she wished they could have talked for longer. When she asked herself why, she admitted she liked the sound of his voice, and the memory of his open and happy face was forefront in her mind. He was such a refreshing change from Tim's highly sexual broodiness. Then she shrugged her shoulders; no point in thinking about Jimmy Hart. She was sure he'd have a wife and children. She didn't go in for trying to break up marriages; that was the main reason she'd always kept Tim at arm's length – that, and instinct told her that if she gave in to him, he'd use her until he found fresh prey. She knew he used her skills as a detective to make his career look good, and although it galled a bit, she could live with it. But not anything more personal, no way.

The object of her thoughts broke her out of her reverie. Tim Masterson stood before her, holding something out to her. "Toxicology report, Della. Take a look. It's rather odd."

Della frowned. "Odd?"

She scanned the document. "Hmm, a large quantity of paracetamol, Valium, Melatonin – what's that? And a quantity of Tamoxifen? What the heck is that?"

"Apparently, Melatonin is something you can buy to help you sleep; I know that because my wife has it. But I don't know what Tamoxifen is."

"I'll look it up." Della tapped on her computer. "Hmm, that's odd. It's treatment for breast cancer."

Della and Tim looked at each other, frowning. At that moment, Ben joined them. "What's up?"

"We've had the toxicology report for what killed Sarah Sutton." Della gave it to Ben to look at.

"A lethal cocktail alright. But what's Tamoxifen?"

"That's what we were just talking about. It's treatment for breast cancer."

"Really?" Ben frowned. "Well, I'm pretty sure Sarah Sutton didn't have breast cancer. The pathologist would have found it when he did the postmortem."

"That's exactly right. He said she was a healthy young woman – apart from being dead, of course."

"So, the question is, where did this Tamoxifen come from? And what about the Valium? Was she in the habit of using that?"

"Certainly, there were no signs of it either in the house or the flat." Della turned to Tim. "Think we'd better have another word with Philip, Guv."

"Yes, I'll get him brought up to the interview room."

*****

"Do I need to have my solicitor here again?" asked Philip once they were in the interview room.

"Not really, unless you think you need him. We just want to ask you a couple of questions about Sarah," replied Tim.

Della switched on the recorder and did the preliminaries.

"Philip, was your wife in the habit of using Valium?"

A frown creased Philip's face. "No, not at all, as far as I'm aware."

"What about sleeping tablets?"

Philip shook his head. "No, certainly not. Sarah could sleep for England. She never had any problems sleeping."

"Do you know anyone who has breast cancer?"

Philip's eyes flew wide. "What?"

"Breast cancer. Do you know anyone with it?"

"Um…no, I don't think so." The puzzled look deepened. "What's all this about? Why are you asking me about those things? As far as I'm aware, the only tablets we have in the house are cold remedies and for sore throats. And I have paracetamol, because sometimes I get headaches from working on the computer so much."

"Thank you. I think you are free to go. Don't leave town; we haven't yet resolved this issue."

"Oh! Oh, well, thank you."

"We'll get someone to take you home."

*****

Della was glad to be home. The rest of her day had been spent with the never-ending paperwork. She was trying hard to be patient waiting for the forensic report on the things found in Chesterfield that were thought to connect to the Darren Holbeach case; she hoped against hope it would come tomorrow. Everything hung on it; it would make or break their case against the Moorcrofts. In the meantime, she was trying to get her head around the mystery of Sarah Sutton's death. Certainly, someone had put that cocktail of drugs into her flask, but if it hadn't been Philip, who on earth could it have been?

She knew well that, even if she worked out who the culprit was, there was no evidence to prove it. The perfect murder? Seemed like it.

Although she was at home, she was restless. She'd go for a run; maybe it would help her think with better clarity.

By the time she arrived home from her run, Della hadn't solved the problem, but she felt better for the exercise. She stood in her shower, enjoying the warmth of the water. She decided she'd enjoy her evening and let tomorrow take care of itself. If they could just get the Moorcrofts sorted, at least that would be a good stride forward. Then maybe she might find the solution to the mystery of Sarah's untimely death. The young woman had run. It was true she feared spending many years in prison for murder. Della was certain she'd been involved, maybe even the instigator of the crime – and she couldn't blame her for that. Who would want to go to prison? Especially a young and glamorous woman like Sarah. She wasn't a nice person, Della hadn't liked her, but no young life should be snuffed out by someone else.

Chapter 33

Wednesday, second week

To Della's intense relief, the report did indeed arrive the next day. Tim Masterson came into the incident room, waving the paperwork.

"We have the forensics on the duvet and other things found by the police. Darren Holbeach's DNA is all over it, and so is Pete Moorcroft's. They also found a croquet hoop which matches the four holding down the body, and a knife with a thin blade, which was probably used to scratch the word on his chest. Although it has been cleaned, there were still traces of Holbeach's blood caught where the blade joins the handle. There is no doubt Moorcroft was the person who carried the body to the field, with the help of Richard Newton, whose DNA was also on the duvet."

"So, it looks like we have evidence to convict both Moorcroft and Newton but there's nothing to convict Angela Moorcroft unless she confesses, except Louise Newton's witness statement saying it was Angela's suggestion they visit on that Saturday night," observed Della.

"That's right. But at least this proves the case for us. Arrange for the respective solicitors to come in, would you, and we'll get started on the formalities."

By the end of the day, all three of the accused were remanded in custody; Peter Moorcroft of murder, Angela and Richard of accomplices to murder. It was obvious Sarah Sutton had played a major part in the plan and may even have been the person who planned it and carved the word on the victim's chest. Even Tim, with his interview technique, could not glean any kind of confession out of either of the Moorcrofts, but Richard was more forthcoming, having been assured they would 'see what they could do for him' if he told them what he knew.

After having an in-depth discussion with his solicitor, Richard actually told them how the murder was carried out.

"I was asked to make sure Darren Holbeach was scheduled to go to Sarah that night. As I was changing the schedule anyway to put in that Neville and I were supposed to be straight swapping that night, it was easy to put Darren into the slot for Sarah. At that point, I did not know what they had planned for Darren; I think I assumed they wanted to keep him well out of their way or something. I admit I was puzzled, but after I'd done it, I never gave it a thought. Except to envy Holbeach going to Sarah; she's always so much fun." His eyes lit up for a moment, a smile on his face. Then, as he realised where he was and who he was talking to, he cleared his throat. "Sorry."

"So, tell us what happened on that night," prompted Tim. "You had dinner?"

"Yes, we had dinner, and afterwards we played cards and chatted. Celia and Neville left us around ten-thirty-ish. I'm not exactly sure what time it was. Louise had already gone to bed because she seemed exhausted. Pete and Angela asked earlier if they could stay because they'd heard there was an accident blocking the motorway and Louise had made sure the guest room was ready for them before she went to bed. I showed them to their room, and I went to my room. Lou was absolutely dead to the world; when I got into bed, she never moved. That's not really like her and I remembered thinking perhaps she was sickening for something. Anyway, as Lou was so sound asleep, I read for a bit – you know, winding down after entertaining for an evening. After a while, I heard a quiet tap at my door.

When I opened it, there was Angela. She said Pete needed my help next door at Sarah's. She couldn't tell me what it was about, so I got dressed and put my coat, boots and gloves on, because it was freezing out there, and went to see what he wanted.

"I was shocked when I saw that Darren Holbeach was asleep in Sarah's hot tub and Pete and Sarah were struggling to pull him out. But Sarah wasn't tall enough to do it, so that's why they needed me.

'We're going to wrap him in that duvet,' Pete told me. I thought that was okay; it would be hard to dress Darren like that, so I helped haul him out, and we laid him on the duvet and rolled him up in it. Pete told me to get hold of his feet end and I did, expecting to help carry him into Sarah's house, but he started back towards our house. I thought, well, I suppose that's okay, we can lay him on the sofa, but once we were in the garden, he headed towards the gate that led from our garden into the field.

'What are you doing?' I asked. I tried to put my end down, but Pete got cross, so I picked it up again and just followed him, carrying the rolled-up duvet with Darren in it across the field, where we finally stopped and laid the roll on the ground. That's when Pete told me to go away.

'What are you going to do?' I asked.

'You don't need to know. Just go away, Rich, you're not involved in this.'

Sarah pushed me away. 'Go on, Rich, go home, go to bed, and don't think about this. But you don't tell anyone, okay? Not even Louise. Promise?' She looked at me all sexy as only Sarah can and she whispered that she'd give me something special, extra to my usual night." Richard hung his head then, as obviously he was ashamed to admit how she'd persuaded him.

"And did you leave them?"

"Yes. I was afraid to stay; afraid of what I might see. Although I admit I didn't think they'd kill him. I went home, went to bed, but kept waking up on and off all night. And when I slept, I had terrible dreams. I was glad to get up in the morning.

"I was concerned about Louise; it was obvious she wasn't feeling good. I was relieved when the Morecrofts left; I just didn't want to see them. Then, of course, later, we heard about Darren..." His voice faded away. "I can't believe I helped them kill a man," he whispered. And then he was silent.

Tim allowed the silence to continue for a few minutes. "What about Angela Morecroft? Was she outside with you?"

"No, after she called me to help Pete, she stayed in the house. I imagine she went back to their room; I'm not sure, really. I was too upset to wonder where she was, to be honest."

"And when you heard what had happened to Darren Holbeach, how did you feel?"

"I was shocked. And angry that I'd been used by people I'd always thought of as being friends."

"It never occurred to you that you should report it to the police?"

"Of course it did! I often tried to persuade myself to do it. But I was afraid. I realised what I should have done was refuse to help them and call the police right away."

"But you didn't."

"No."

"And a man died that night. You could have saved him. Instead, you went to bed."

"Do you think I haven't thought about that often? How I wished I'd done differently. Then gradually I told myself that at least Amy was now free of the husband that abused her. It made me feel a little better about not helping him."

"I see."

"Do you, can I, I mean, I don't know why they did it. Do you know why they did it?"

"Oh yes, we know why. We also have no doubt that Sarah instigated it. You see, Darren Holbeach murdered her sister."

"Oh. My. Goodness. How dreadful." Richard stared at Tim and then at Della.

It was Della who gave Richard his final shock. "And now, someone has killed Sarah."

Chapter 34

Thursday, second week

"Phone call for you, Dell."

Della had only just arrived at headquarters and had yet to take off her coat.

"Who is it?" She asked Mike.

He put his hand across the mouthpiece of the receiver. "DI Jim Hart."

She took the phone. "Hello, Della Downs speaking."

"Hello, Della, this is Jim Hart. I have some information for you regarding the investigation into our murder victim."

"Oh, yes?" Della struggled to get her coat off, and when a pair of hands took the weight of the garment, enabling her to lift her arms from the sleeves, one at a time, swapping hands on the phone, she shot a grateful nod of thanks to Mike, who popped it over the back of her chair.

"Yes. We had witnesses come forward in answer to an appeal we put out. It was a couple, a Mr and Mrs Bennet, who were in the car park of the supermarket, near to the flat. They're sure they saw a red-haired woman get out of a car. They noticed it because they were actually following the car round the car park, looking for a place to park. The car stopped near the store and the woman got out. She was carrying a suitcase and a bag, but didn't go into the store, but headed towards the pedestrian path leading from the premises. They pulled past the car as it had stopped, but when they reached a space, they noticed the same car following them, but it went out of the car park. They did their shopping and forgot about it until they saw the appeal on our local news."

"So, someone gave her a lift. Are these people certain the woman was Sarah?"

"It was Thursday, and the time-frame of around lunch-time fits. We'd shown a photo of Sarah but with a red wig superimposed on the screen. Mr Bennet noticed her because she was very attractive and his wife was cross with him. But she agreed the woman was attractive and their estimate of her height and description of the coat and hat she was wearing also fits in with Sarah and what we found in the flat. I'd say it was definitely her."

"What about the car?"

"It was, in the words of Mrs Bennet, 'a posh silver car'. Mr Bennet thought it was a Rover."

"Mm."

"Oh, and Mrs Bennet was almost sure the driver was a woman."

"A woman? That surprises me."

"Really? Why?"

"Only because of what we know about our victim, that's all. Just shows how wrong conjecture can sometimes be."

"Right. Anyway, I shall send their witness statements so you can read for yourself."

"Thank you. So, we're looking for a woman who has a posh silver car, possibly a Rover. That's more than we had to go on yesterday. Thank you, that's a great help."

"I hope you'll keep me in the picture if you discover anything?"

"You can be sure I will. Thank you so much, Detective Inspector."

"Do call me Jim. Please?"

Unbidden, Della felt a little jump in her chest at his request; she needed to find out more about him!

"Jim it is. Thank you."

"Goodbye for now, Della."

After bidding Jim goodbye, Stella beckoned to Ben, who came over.

"Is the Guv in yet, do you know?"

"Don't think so."

"That was DI Jim Hart on the phone. Apparently, he has witnesses who saw Sarah Sutton being dropped off in the supermarket car park on the day she left here. She was in a silver car, possibly a Rover, driven by a woman. Not completely sure the driver was a female, but our witnesses were fairly sure."

"So, I'm guessing we need to find a silver car, possibly a Rover? Needle in a haystack job, methinks."

"Possibly. But we must think about who Sarah would have known. We assumed it to have been a man-friend who gave her a lift, given her um – wandering nature, which would have made our search harder. However, if the driver was a woman, I think we should narrow the search down to those who we know she knew, beginning with those who live on Gladioli Grove. If we have no luck there, we'll ask Philip and others if they have any suggestions."

"Good thinking. Do you think it could have been Angela Morecroft?"

Della thought for a moment. "Going by her reaction when I interviewed her, I seriously doubt it. However, there's no harm in checking what cars the Morecrofts own."

"I'll get Jess onto that, and we'll start checking up on the cars in the Grove."

Della picked up her phone. "Hi, Judy, is the Guv in? Ah, right. Can you ask if I can pop up to see him, please? Thanks."

She looked at her companions. "Guys, I have to pop up to the Guv to put him in the picture. I'll won't be long."

"I'll have a coffee ready for when you come down, Del," said Ben, grinning. "Good luck."

"Ta." With a sigh, Della set off to beard the lion in his den.

Tim listened carefully to the information and what they were now investigating.

"So, if someone gave her a lift, could that person have had time to slip something into the flask?"

"That's the big question, isn't it? We could do with something to substantiate the time between when she left home and when they arrived at the car park in Newark. But I don't know how we'd get it."

"If we can find a registration, perhaps there might be a camera somewhere that might have picked it up on that Tuesday morning. I'm sure there's one on the Pentagon and there may be one on the Clifton Bridge."

"That's true. I don't think the one on the Pentagon would have got anything though, unless there's one on each slip road."

"Get someone to check."

"Right. Is that all, sir?"

"Who did you speak to from Nottingham?"

"DI Jim Hart, sir."

Tim frowned.

"Is there a problem, guv?"

"Just a brief word of warning. Don't have too much to do with DI Hart, Della."

"Oh? May I ask why, sir?"

"He's trouble. Well, he may not be now, but reputations die hard, don't they? Best not to deal with him too much. In future, try to have conversations with his sergeant instead."

Della left her boss's room, exceedingly puzzled. What was so bad about Jim Hart? She hadn't got any bad vibes from him at all. In fact, she'd felt comfortable around him, which she absolutely couldn't say about her own DI.

Chapter 35

Ben was waiting for her when she returned to the incident room. A cup of coffee and a KitKat were waiting for her on her desk.

"You look a little, well, confused? Bemused? Not sure which, Dell. What's up?"

Della shook herself slightly. "I'll tell you later. Not to do with the case. Thanks for the KitKat, just what I need." She unwrapped the biscuit and broke off a finger. "Why is it I always seem to crave chocolate after being with the Guv?"

"I'm surprised you only need chocolate, Dell. Some women would need a Valium."

Della popped the last bit of the first finger into her mouth. "Valium. The more I think about that cocktail that killed Sarah, the more I wonder. Any luck with the car yet?"

"Della!" Jess hurried towards her, waving a piece of paper.

"What's up, Jess? Slow down, there's no fire!"

"I think I may have found the car! It's a silver Rover 200 and belongs to a Mrs Elizabeth Harrington-Smythe!"

"Liz!" Della and Ben looked at each other. "Great work, Jess, thanks so much!"

"No problem, Della." Jess returned to her end of the office in a more sedate manner.

Della knocked back her coffee and put the remains of her KitKat in her drawer. "Let's go, Ben. See what the lady has to say."

Grabbing coats, the pair hastened towards the door. When she reached the door, she stopped and turned. "Mike, can you please call DI Hart or DS Taylor and let them know we think we may have identified the car, give them the licence number and ask them if there's any possibility of it having been caught on a camera somewhere near Queens Medical/Clifton Bridge area, please."

"Will do, Della," Mike answered, and turned to his phone. He was dialling the number as Della and Ben left the office.

*****

"And there's the car," muttered Ben as they pulled into the drive of number ten, Gladioli Grove. The door of the house opened before they'd had a chance to knock, and there was Elizabeth, bundled up in a coat, scarf and hat.

"Oh!" she gasped. "You gave me a fright! And how strange, because I was just about to call on you."

Della held up her warrant. "Mrs Elizabeth Harrington-Smythe, I'm arresting you on suspicion of murder and attempting to pervert the ways of justice in helping a person under suspicion of murder to leave the area."

Elizabeth's eyes opened wide, and she staggered back a little. "Bill!" She called.

Bill appeared from the lounge, his eyes lighting up when he saw Della and Ben. "Hello there! The wife was now coming to see you. You must have felt the vibes. Come in and make yourselves comfortable..." He trailed off, obviously realising something was amiss. "What's going on?"

"I'm sorry, Bill, but we have to take Elizabeth in," said Della.

"But – why?"

"I've arrested her for perverting the laws of justice."

"Call our solicitor, my darling. Don't worry, it'll soon be sorted."

Della sat in the back of the car with Liz while Ben drove. It only took a short time to reach the police headquarters, where Liz was processed and led to a cell, having been told she'd be interviewed when her solicitor arrived.

"I wonder if our friendly neighbours in Nottingham have found anything helpful for us."

Della dialled the number for DI Hart. As she did so, she felt a twinge of guilt, remembering Tim's orders. However, it was Dave Taylor who answered.

"Can't tell you anything as yet, DS Downs. The footage is still being looked through."

"Do call me Della."

"Della it is. The boss wanted me to let him know if you called. Can you hang on a minute?"

"Oh, well, erm..." Della was flustered.

Before she could give a proper answer, Jim Hart's warm voice spoke. "Hello, Della?"

"Yes."

"I was wondering if we could meet up – to discuss the case, of course."

"Oh, erm." *'Get a grip, Della,'* she told herself sternly. *'Stop acting like you've forgotten how to speak.'*

"Look, can I take you out for something to eat this evening?"

Della's heart did an uncomfortable leap. "Yes, I suppose so."

"Good. Would it be best if we met somewhere?"

"Yes. That would probably be best."

"Do you know the Blue Ball in Risley?"

"I do, yes."

"I'll book a table for eight. Is that alright?"

"Yes, that's fine."

"Good. I'll see you then. Oh, wait a minute. Something has come in. It's a witness statement from a man who was on the road workings gang on the A 52 on that Thursday. He saw a silver car with two women held up by the roadworks. He particularly noticed the 'attractive redhead' and actually watched them as they inched forward. He said the lights were only letting a few cars go through at a time because the road was busy. He said he could see them clearly and the driver just looked ahead all the time. He watched the young woman refresh her lipstick and then she smiled at him; she knew she was being admired."

"Did he give a time to when he had this show?"

"He said it was between 11.30 and 11.45, because he was having a coffee break."

"Right. That would tie in with the witnesses who saw Sarah being dropped off."

"Indeed. The witness said he was sure he saw the same car returning, around an hour later, minus the redhead. He recognised the number of the car and the driver; he described her as a 'silver-haired lady, very smart-looking.'"

"Indeed. That sounds like Elizabeth."

"Have you arrested her?"

"Yes. We haven't interviewed her yet, though; we're waiting for her solicitor."

"Right. Yes. Well, good luck with it. You can tell me about it later. By the way, do you have a home phone?

You can never tell when something comes up and I have to cancel. You know what it can be like."

"I do indeed." She told him her home phone number and wrote it down when he told her his. "Because it could happen with either of us."

When she put the phone down, it was to see Ben looking at her, one eyebrow raised. "What?" She put on her most innocent expression.

"Better be careful a certain person doesn't find out."

"Are you clairvoyant, Mr Curran?"

"You'd better believe it."

Chapter 36

It turned out that Dominic Holland, Philip's solicitor, was also Liz's. They brought her up to an interview room and allowed time to talk with him before Tim and Della joined them for a formal interview.

After telling the tape the necessary details, the interview began.

"You are Mrs Elizabeth Harrington-Smythe of nine, Gladioli Gardens?"

"I am."

"Do you understand the charges?"

"Yes."

"Let's deal with the first issue. Did you take Sarah Sutton in your car to Newark on Tuesday, the twenty-second of January?"

"I did, yes."

"So, you admit to that?"

"Yes. I was coming to tell you about it when the detectives arrived at my house this morning. I know I should have come forward before, but I was afraid. My husband said I should tell you, though, so that's what I was coming to do."

"I see. Why did you do it? I thought you weren't particular friends with her?"

"I'm not, or rather, I wasn't. Neither of us were. But we love Philip."

Liz carried on, "When Sarah asked me if I'd give her a lift somewhere, she said she needed to get away from

Philip for a while because the atmosphere between them was bad. I wasn't keen, but we thought Philip would be happier without her in the house for a while. She said it was only temporary, and she also assured me she'd given you the address of where she was going – I asked her specifically, knowing she was under suspicion. She said she'd cleared it with you. I admit it somewhat surprised me to be asked to go to Newark. I thought she'd go to stay with Pete and Angela."

"Did you know about the relationship between her and the Morecrofts, then?"

"Oh yes, of course. I think the only person who didn't know was Philip, poor lad."

"And why didn't Philip know?"

"Sarah didn't want him to know. And what Sarah wants, Sarah gets," said Liz, bitterly. "I have since discovered that Sarah had previously asked Chris at number two, but she'd refused. It is what I should have done, of course. I know that now. They say you get wiser as you get older, but I'm not sure that's true." She gave a small dry laugh with no humour involved.

"Okay, so run me through the events of that day. What time did you pick her up?"

"I think it was getting on for eleven."

"Where did you meet her?"

"On the road by her house."

"Why didn't she take her own car? Did you ask her?"

"I asked her, yes. She said it was because there was something wrong with it and Philip was going to get it fixed for her."

"Okay. So, you met her out on the road. Did you go into the house at all?"

"No, I waited for her in the car."

"What did she have with her?"

"She had a small suitcase, a handbag and another bag, which she said had food and flasks in."

"Were those things put in your boot?"

"No. She put the food bag and the suitcase on the back seat and she kept the handbag with her."

"Did you stop on the way at all?"

"Not to rest, no, although we were held up at roadworks on the A52, not far from Belvoir. Normally, it would take just under an hour to get to Newark, but that day it took us a bit longer. I think it was around twelve-fifteen when I dropped her off."

"Where did you drop her?"

"Tesco's car park. She said she would walk from there. She didn't want me to know exactly where she was going."

"Do you know what Tamoxifen is?"

Liz frowned in confusion. "Pardon?"

"Tamoxifen. Do you know what it is?"

"Not a clue. What is it?"

"Apparently, it's a treatment for breast cancer. Have you ever been on Valium?"

"Not ever, although I think I could probably do with one now," Liz gave a strangled laugh. "Why are you asking me about Valium and Tam – whatever it is?"

"What about sleeping tablets?"

"Well, I have used them from time to time, yes. But not for ages. Why?"

"Mrs Harrington-Smythe, did you handle the flasks at all?"

"No, not at all."

"Are you sure? You didn't have a drink when you stopped at the roadworks, for instance?"

"No, of course not. There wasn't time. In any case, I had to keep an eye on how the traffic was moving. Sarah never touched them either. She told me she was saving them for where she was going because there wouldn't be anything in her lodgings. The journey only took us not much over an hour, for goodness' sake!"

"And you never went into her house before you set off?"

"No. I told you I didn't. What's all this about?"

"Those three things were in the cocktail of drugs that killed Sarah. They were in the flask of coffee she had."

"Oh..." Liz swallowed hard. "And you think I'm the one who put the stuff in the flask? Well, I didn't. I might have done wrong in giving Sarah a lift, but I didn't put any drugs into her drink. I didn't kill her."

*****

Elizabeth was allowed out on bail. Because there was no proof, they had dropped the charge of murder. She was exhausted when she was brought home by Mike Smith.

Bill opened the door, and she fell into his arms. He helped her into the lounge and made her put her feet up.

"Stay right there. I'll bring you a cup of tea."

When he returned with the tea, she was fast asleep, so he fetched a blanket and tucked it around her. He drank the tea himself as he settled to read a book. However, he was unsettled and let his mind wander. In repose, with her eyes closed, Bill could see the young Liz that he'd fallen in love with. He recalled all the years they'd been together. If there was anything he deeply regretted, it was the 'swinger' lifestyle they'd lived for far too many years. Why did they do that? He wondered. She had always been enough for him, and yet she hadn't been ready to settle for just him. She'd needed the excitement of sex with other men, but insisted it was only because it 'kept their marriage alive'. Their daughter had hated it when she had found out, and so had the other children who grew up in the Grove. They generally couldn't wait to leave.

He sighed; that was the 'swinging sixties' for you, he thought. It made you think it was okay to have extra-marital sex and far too many other couples coming to live on their road had been only too willing to take part. He knew that he'd been attractive and he'd had quite a few offers from other women over time, not only those in the Grove, but apart from the 'swap nights', he'd never strayed from Liz. In his eyes, no one could ever match her. She was beautiful, intelligent, fun, adventurous, but also loving and caring. If he had to be entirely honest, he had to admit some of the women in the Grove had been enticing and there had been those he'd looked forward to having his one night a year with them and they had opened his eyes to some things which he'd no doubt had benefitted his and Liz's personal relationship. But he hadn't loved any of them. And the time came when he definitely didn't want to partake any longer and he knew Liz didn't either.

It was, perhaps, inevitable that love would eventually come into things, and it came in the form of Amy. The love Bill had for Amy had nothing to do with swap nights or sex; it had everything to do with the fact he wanted to protect her, to watch over her, and above all, give her what she wanted.

She was the sweetest thing he'd met since his beloved Liz. She was caring and kind, but was also abused and suffering. Bill knew too, that once her abusive husband had gone – and wasn't that amazing, that others had done what Bill himself had seriously thought of doing- Amy was still suffering. Although he would have killed Darren some other way, he was glad he hadn't had to do it, because he would have been discovered for sure and then he couldn't have done what he did about Sarah. It was likely Sarah would have gone to prison for murdering Darren Holbeach, but Bill knew Philip well enough to know he would feel obliged to stand by her. That was another thing; Bill knew Liz loved Philip like a son. She wanted him to be happy. Bill and Liz both knew that Philip loved Amy, and Amy loved Philip. To them both, Philip and Amy were right together.

So that was why Sarah had to go altogether. To completely cut off any chance she would keep Philip tied to her. By giving Phil and Amy the chance to be together with no complications, Bill was also, hopefully, making his Liz happy too.

Bill had gathered a load of tablets; everything he could find, and crushed them up in a bag. He didn't know when he might get the chance to administer them. So, when Sarah had called Liz to ask for a lift, he felt fate was on his side. He couldn't believe his luck when he got to Sarah's to see if she was ready, to find he had easy access to her coffee flask. Already wearing thin rubber gloves under his leather gloves, he could pour the tablet mix into the flask and the coffee on top, wearing only the rubber gloves to keep his prints off the flask, and screw the top on, and as Sarah returned to the kitchen, he had just put his leather gloves back on. He knew it was hit and miss; after all, she may not actually drink the coffee, but he also knew she was more likely to drink that than the hot chocolate. With the incriminating bag in his pocket, he told Sarah he'd tell Liz she was ready, and headed home. While Liz was out, he burned all the boxes, the gloves and bag in the Aga. It seemed his plan worked; Sarah was gone.

He was so deep in thought; he didn't notice when Liz opened her eyes. He came to abruptly when he realised she was moving.

"Oh, my darling. How are you feeling now? Are you ready for that tea now?"

"I think I'd like something a little stronger. Do we have any of that red we had last night?"

"I'll get it." Heaving himself from the chair he went to the kitchen. He returned a few moments later with a bottle. He took two glasses from the sideboard cabinet and poured the drinks.

She took a sip and closed her eyes a moment in appreciation. After she'd drunk half the glass, she looked at Bill. "So, how did you do it? And were you never going to tell me?"

"I thought it best you didn't know. How did you?"

"I twigged the moment I heard Tamoxifen mentioned and remembered your mother used to take it. Whatever possessed you to put that in?"

"Didn't know what it was. I just gathered a load of stuff which I knew was still in her bag of medications, which we've never got around to getting rid of. I put it all in, along with a load of paracetamol. I hoped it would do the job, but couldn't be sure. I needed to try. She had to go, Liz."

"I agree."

"Do you really?"

"Of course I do. She'd always stand between Philip and Amy, even if she was in prison or away somewhere.

Being him, he wouldn't say no to her; he'd do anything for a quiet life. He'd believe it was his duty to help her, even if he was with Amy. I felt bad about taking her that day and if I could have done something without being found out, I would. Except I couldn't think of anything. I couldn't believe it when I heard she was dead."

"I know. I could hardly believe I'd succeeded. Mind you, the thought I've killed someone in cold blood troubles me at night."

"The thing is, that detective sergeant is convinced I did it. Are you sure you have got rid of all the evidence?"

"I have."

"The other thing that worries me more is, do you think Amy will always be suspicious that Philip was the one who killed Sarah and refuse to be with him? If that happens, what shall we do?"

"If that happens, we'll have to tell her. But let's hope it never comes to that."

Chapter 37

That evening, Della arrived home feeling like nothing on earth. The last thing she wanted to do was get dressed up and drive to Risley. However, the thought of spending a couple of hours with Jimmy Hart motivated her to draw on her reserves. She showered and tried on several outfits before deciding on a pair of black trousers and matching jacket over a green, high-necked jumper. She didn't want to appear as if she thought it was a date; it was a business dinner after all. The green complimented her auburn hair, and she knew she looked good. She knew nothing about Jimmy Hart, not even if he had a wife, but she still wanted to make an impression! A gold pendant finished the outfit and Della was satisfied. She applied her makeup carefully to achieve a natural look and made sure her short bob was smooth. Then she was in the car.

It only took just over ten minutes on that quiet evening to reach the Blue Ball. Thankful the place had a car park, she went into the main entrance, wondering if Jimmy would be there. She hoped he would be; in her mind, there was little worse than having to sit alone at a restaurant table, waiting for someone who didn't come.

Her fears were unfounded; she spotted him as soon as she walked into the room. He stood up to greet her and sank down again as the waiter held her chair. She thanked the waiter, who handed them each a menu and left. Suddenly shy, she looked at Jim. He wore a dark suit with a white shirt and a blue tie with a diamond pattern. He wasn't handsome in the classic sense like Tim, but he had a pleasant face; the kind of face that made you know he was a good bloke and someone to trust. To her, he looked good.

"Thank you for coming; I wasn't sure you would," he said. "You look – amazing."

She felt heat rise to her face. "Thank you. Why would you think I wouldn't come?"

"Well, not sure really."

"If it makes you feel better, I wasn't sure you'd be here."

They laughed then and Della felt the atmosphere lighten.

"Let's order, shall we? Then we can talk."

Afterwards, Della couldn't believe how swiftly the evening had passed. They had discussed the case and agreed there was no evidence to convict Liz or anyone for the death of Sarah Sutton.

"She was definite that she hadn't tampered with the flasks at all, and there are no fingerprints or her DNA on the flask, or even on the bag they were in. She hadn't touched them at all. So, unless she confesses, and she was adamant she was innocent, there's nothing we can do."

"But why would she want Sarah dead?"

"The only reason I can think of is so that Philip would be free. She has no personal reason for wanting her dead."

"What does your boss think?"

"He's convinced it was suicide."

"I see. But you're not?"

"No. Although there's no evidence and she's not admitting to it, somehow, I think she may have had something to do with it. But I think our hands are tied; there's absolutely nothing we can do about it."

"You win some, you lose some," said Jim, philosophically.

Della sighed. "Certainly seems like it. I must confess I don't really want to see her in prison; she's so darned *nice.* Anyway, the guv seems happy because we have lots of evidence to prove the guilt of our suspects who murdered the first victim. In his mind, it's enough."

"Will you pursue it?"

"I don't know. It will be going against the guv if I do."

"Want Tim wants, Tim gets," murmured Jimmy.

Della looked at him sharply. He raised his palm towards her as if warding her off. "Sorry. Out of line. Forget it."

"No, you're right. You obviously know him well."

"Did. I prefer not to know him now. If I'd realised he was in Derby, I may not have taken the post in Nottingham. Still, I don't suppose we'll cross lines often."

At that point, he looked at his watch. "Sorry, Della. I think it's time to leave. The waiters are looking at us pointedly. I have to be in early tomorrow. Have you finished with your drink?"

Della nodded. "Yes, thank you."

He called for the bill. Della held some money out to him. "For my share of the meal."

"Absolutely not. I invited you. It's on me."

She withdrew the money reluctantly and watched while he paid.

They walked together to her car.

"I enjoyed this evening. Thank you so much, Della."

"Don't thank me; you're the one who suggested it."

"Ah, but you came." He grinned at her; she could see him clearly in the lighting in the car park.

She grinned back. "I did, didn't I?"

She unlocked her car and climbed into the driver's seat. Jimmy closed the door gently. He raised his hand in farewell as she drew away from the spot. She looked in her rear-view mirror as she pulled out onto the road to see he was still watching.

As she drove home, feeling warm and fuzzy, she realised that, although she'd just spent an evening with Jim Hart, she knew no more about him than she had before she came.

She really hoped there would be other times, although he'd not mentioned another date. Had it been a date? She really wasn't sure exactly what it had been; she only knew she liked him.

Later, just after she'd settled into bed, her phone rang. She groaned – surely, she wasn't going to be called out again?

"Hello?"

"Oh, erm, sorry, were you asleep?"

Her eyes widened at the sound of Jimmy's voice. "No, I just got into bed. Is there a problem?"

"Yes."

Her heart thumped uncomfortably. What was he going to tell her? "What's up? What problem?"

"Two problems, actually. I hope you'll understand."

'This is where he tells me he's happily married,' she thought.

"I think you'd better tell me, quickly."

"Well, the first problem is, I didn't ask if I could see you again and I'd like to."

Almost dizzy with relief, she smiled. "And the other?"

"I wanted to kiss you goodnight, and I didn't."

She chuckled. "Well, Detective Inspector Hart, you should know how to ask correct questions."

The sound of his answering chuckle down the line lightened her heart.

"I should, shouldn't I?"

"So, ask the correct question and maybe we can find solutions to your problems."

Not long later, Della put out her bedside lamp and settled back on her pillows, a dreamy smile playing about her lips. Life was about to get interesting; she couldn't wait.

Thank you for reading. Please consider posting a review on Amazon and/or Goodreads. Stars are good, but not helpful, either for any potential readers or for the author. They're really important because they help us sell our books. They don't have to be long, just a few lines saying why you liked it/didn't like it. And please tell your friends!

I hope you enjoyed meeting Della, Ben and Jimmy. I hope there will be more stories about them to come. I had to set this story in the 1990s because of the nature of the Latham story; it had to pre-date routine DNA testing.

One thing to note; the pub/restaurant called the Blue Ball in Risley is now called The Risley Park. Other pubs/clubs are imaginary.

I'd like to thank my beta readers, Sue Hayworth, Robert Southworth and fellow author Liz Martinson, who all thought this story worth publishing. And to my proofreaders with the eagle eyes, thank you.

Thanks yet again to my brilliant cover designer, Dave Slaney. I absolutely love this cover. I'm so proud of it!

Thanks also to all the wonderful people who support me in my efforts and whose encouragements keep me writing, even when I feel like giving up. My beta readers are three of you, but there are others, too many to name, but I want you all to know how much I appreciate every one of you.

It seemed this book would never get published. It, or I, have been dogged with one set-back after another – the first thing – and the most dreadful, was the sudden death of David Monaghan-Jones, who was a wonderful help and mentor for this work.

A couple of weeks before Christmas, we had a burst pipe in our roof space and had water cascading down into our hallway, kitchen and bathroom. Ever since then, we've been living in various stages of disarray, and things are still not sorted over six months later. Mould and wet plaster have contributed to my 'not wellbeing' and greatly disturbed my ability to concentrate on my writing. The delays have been caused by further ill health – covid, the coughing virus and other things I won't mention!

Nevertheless, I count my blessings. Parts of the inside of our house might be a mess, but we have a beautiful garden which gives us joy and I've been grateful to have a home to be poorly in, knowing there are many out there who are not so fortunate. I'm blessed with wonderful people who do what they can to help me. Although I've already mentioned Liz Martinson, I must mention her again, because what she does for me to help me with my books is outstanding and I'm so indebted to her.

I'm also grateful to my husband, Tony, who has to put up with me sitting (and lately, sleeping) in front of my computer for long hours on some days and into the evenings. And for all he does, cooking meals and many other things. My very caring children, who check up on us regularly, should get a mention too – Joanne, Michael, Sam, Tim and Rachel, including Sam's lovely wife, Helene. They all mean so much to me, plus, of course, all our grandchildren and great grandchildren.

Obviously, the people in my life are all important, but my books are a bit like my children, I'm proud of each one, and because, like my children, they're all different, I'm proud of them in different ways. I know readers will like some more than others, but that's the prerogative of us as individuals. I never imagined, when I wrote The Sixpenny Tiger, that I'd ever be able to write any more books, but here we are with number seventeen!

If you enjoyed 'Cold Murder', here's a list of my other books you might like to take a look at.

Other books by Jeanette Taylor Ford:

The River View Series: (Cosy Crime)
Aunt Bea's Legacy – Introducing Lucy, her beautiful house, River View, and the village of Sutton-on-Wye. Under the strange conditions of Aunt Bea's will, Lucy comes to live at River View. But ghostly footsteps and other weird happenings disturb the peaceful atmosphere. Is the house haunted, or is something else behind them?
By the Gate – D.I. Cooke and D.S. Grant investigate a seventy-year-old murder when human remains are found in one of Lucy's fields.
Fear Has Long Fingers – a new family comes to Sutton-on-Wye which brings great danger for another resident of the village. Can our two detectives find the kidnapped teenagers and save the woman snatched by a ruthless underworld criminal and his gang?
Jealousy is Murder – a young woman is found dead in a camper van and her young son is missing. But what has her death to do with residents of Sutton-on-Wye?
Behind the Mask – Daisy Roper runs from her abusive husband to the safety of River View and a job working with Lucy. But Gary Roper is determined to find her.

Cruel Deception – DI Dan Cooke is in Sutton Court having respite care after his near-fatal injury. Strange things begin to happen at the nursing home and Dan can't help getting involved, in spite of him being on sick leave.

Rosa, a ghostly psychological thriller. Elizabeth (Izzy) has to run from an all-consuming affair and comes to manage her grandfather's estate in Norfolk. But all is not well at Longdene Hall, and Izzy soon finds herself in a terrifying situation. Who can she trust?

Bell of Warning, a haunting historical novella. Jeanie loves her hometown of Cromer. She also has the 'Gift' and begins to 'see' the mysterious Kendra, who once lived in the village of Shipden, now sunk into the sea off Cromer's coast and to hear the legendary warning bell of Shipden's church, which rings out when there is danger. Can Jeanie find out what it all means and can she save her neighbours from impending doom?

The Sixpenny Tiger, a touching story of a boy in a children's home and the young woman he runs to when things get too much. Together they discover the true meaning and power of forgiveness and love.

The Ghosts of Roseby Hall, a romantic ghost story. Inspired by a ruined mansion in Derbyshire, this 'little bit of nonsense', as I call it, tells how Beth is confused by the two men in her life, but she's also in danger.

The Castle Glas Trilogy. Now also as a box set on kindle:

The Hiraeth – how Shelly, abandoned as a baby, finds her family, aided by two modern-day witches, a ghost and a wonderful Welsh castle.

Bronwen's Revenge – continuing the story of Shelly and her family's fight against her Aunt Bronwen, now a vengeful ghost

Yr Aberth, (The Sacrifice) More adventures with Shelly, including the final banishment of Bronwen.

For Children:

Robin's Ring – Robin finds a magic ring, but can he and his cousin Oliver find the other Items of Power?

Robin's Dragon – further adventures with Robin and Oliver. The wicked Bowen the Black has kidnapped Edric's daughter. Can the boys, with an exciting helper, find the Princess Adriana and bring her home safely?

Robin…Who? Robin, Oliver and Marian go in search of a magic bowl and encounters the legendary Robin Hood.

I love to hear from my readers. I can be contacted on Facebook:

(5) Jeanette Taylor Ford, 'My Words, My Way' | Facebook

Twitter: (20) Jeanette Taylor Ford (@jeanetteford51) / Twitter

If you'd like signed copies of my books, they can be ordered through my website:

Jeanette Taylor Ford (samonafiction.com)